DEAD
REFLECTIONS

By
Carol Weekes

JournalStone
San Francisco

JournalStone books may be ordered through booksellers or by contacting:

JournalStone
www.journalstone.com
www.journal-store.com

ISBN: 978-1-936564-70-5   (sc)
ISBN: 978-1-936564-71-2   (ebook)

Library of Congress Control Number: 2012953063

Printed in the United States of America
JournalStone rev. date: February 8, 2013

Cover Design: Denis Daniel
Cover Art: M. Wayne Miller

Edited By: Norman L. Rubenstein

ACKNOWLEDGEMENT

I'd like to acknowledge the help and expertise of Norman L. Rubenstein in proofing and polishing the final manuscript, and thanks as well to publisher Chris Payne for making this book a reality. Thanks also to artist M. Wayne Miller for his talent in bringing together a superb cover, the talents and insights of all of these people bringing about the final products you hold in your hands.

TABLE OF CONTENTS

DEAD REFLECTIONS

By
Carol Weekes

Old Superstitious Belief

It is thought when a death occurs within a house, that all mirrors must be covered, lest they capture the souls of the living. To look into such a mirror is to become as one with the dead.

CHAPTER
1

His boys were with his parents. He'd told them he was going out to talk to his real estate agent, promising them that he wouldn't go back to the house. Sometimes promises needed to be broken. They'd look after the boys if anything should happen to him. He needed answers; he wanted to find his wife.

Robbie Parker stood on the front porch of the house he and Tanya just bought, now for sale barely a week later. He let himself inside, unsure of what he would do once he got to the room in question. He had to see the mirror and look into it. He wanted only to find her. Then he'd deal with the house.

CHAPTER
2

It is ubiquitous. It walks naked through sunlight and dances through the nocturne. It sings quiet tunes that fade in and out with the melancholy discord of broken chimes. It keeps rooms and it takes in guests on a regular basis. Some chambers are darker than others, temporal scorpions hiding within the folds of time and space. Death is a dark flower, its perfume heady and dangerous as it pulls you into its bosom. It maintains many levels within the bloom of its existence, some of them pockets of toxic waste.

The house had waited for its new owners with the patient tenacity of something that knows it has time on its side – it had eternity. A house is a layer of skin over its guts; two-by-fours, plaster, copper wiring, PVC piping, carpeting, lamps, furniture, décor, all part of the elaborate costume that covers a monster hiding within. Monsters do live in closets, beneath beds, within the tenuous web of shadows. They lurk inside refrigerators, behind innocent, shining, clean coffee mugs, in a handful of sea salts you're about to drop into your bath. That bottle of Aspirin in the medicine cabinet can become lethal, when you open it and stick your unsuspecting finger inside that smooth, plastic vial, feeling for something that's supposed to help you…until you sense something *in* there move back; so can the hand-held blender, or the plastic disposable razor. Anything in a house like this poses a risk. Even your kid's favorite teddy-bear. The monster will be wherever it wants or needs to be in order to sustain itself.

Like the bathroom mirror.

Call it what you will – ghoul, entity, demon, spirit, bogey, phantom, ghost.

The entity of darkness knew it had them from the moment they pulled up beside its 'House For Sale' sign to take that first, tentative look. Its 'Sucker' sign.

Their worries with an old place had been structural, such as the condition of the foundation, insulation, roof trusses, wiring, and plumbing. They'd checked out other houses in their area of interest, a small rural town outside of Massena, New York and close to the Canadian border. The town was Amberstead and the bulk of its homes were turn-of-the-century fare. Some were simple frame farmhouses made of red brick, field stone, or wooden siding. Others closer to the core of the town, which boasted a healthy population of almost eight thousand, were of the more elaborate Victorian design complete with wraparound porches, turret rooms, and gingerbread work. What homebuyers would call 'nice digs.'

They'd taken a look at half a dozen in the downtown core, as he'd had a preference to be located closer to amenities, but each of the homes had presented their own unique problems. One needed a proper slab foundation as its basement consisted of nothing more than dirt and standing water; another had no insulation other than thin plaster walls against brick – not something that would provide much comfort during typical northern winters. Some others were filled with the delights of formaldehyde insulation.

They were about to give up and he'd suggested that they purchase one of the nice, single story dwellings in a new sub-development when Tanya had noticed the sign in front of an old place near the edge of Amberstead. They'd turned up this road by accident in an attempt to find their way out of the district. Fate happens like that. It is not chance or coincidence. It plots.

CHAPTER
3

The house stood off from the road, a quarter-mile long dirt drive leading to its entrance and bordered on all sides by excessive foliage, as well as decades-old maples and centurion oaks. It was three stories high, the top floor encompassing a full walk-around attic. It had a small red barn behind it and enough land that it may have qualified as a hobby farm.

"Robbie, look!" Tanya tugged his arm as they approached the sign. He slowed the car and they peered at the massive structure. Its exterior was grey fieldstone. It had a wrap-around porch; one of those sides enclosed in glass for all-season living, and two upper verandahs with railings and gingerbread work. It looked to be in good shape, but was far larger than what he'd wanted to consider, even if they *did* have two teenagers and a pre-teen who would be moving in with them.

"It's huge," he said. "It must have at least fifteen or more rooms. What would we do with it all?"

She laughed. "We could do all the things we've talked about for years. The kids would each have their own room and a shared study area. You and I could have our offices. We could do up a den, a library, a formal living room..."

He smiled a little. "It's probably way beyond our budget." He noted the realtor company and sighed.

"It doesn't hurt to look it up and see how much it is." She looked at him, hopeful.

"I suppose not." He stared at the place. It was early spring, the ground damp from the last of the winter snow melts, and tiny buds had already formed a verdant haze on the surrounding trees.

He saw one vehicle parked near the house at the end of that long driveway (his mind had already begun to calculate that he'd need to attach a plough shovel to the front of his truck in order to clear the thing from snow); the vehicle was a fairly new SUV, a bright shiny red. Expensive enough.

"Don't get your hopes up," he told her. "I think it'll be beyond our means, but we can keep looking for an older place if you really want one."

"I *really* want one," she said.

"Okay. Well, try contacting the agent. Price will decide for us right away."

They parked while Tanya made the call. He glanced around the area. The end of the road led to a cul-de-sac that terminated in field grass, then thick woods. The vicinity had an isolated feel to it. This was one of the first developed areas a century ago as wealthy farmers and industrialists created towns along the St. Lawrence River with its shipping bounty.

"Yes, hello," Tanya said, pulling her hair out from inside her coat collar so that she could better hold the cell phone to her ear. "My name is Tanya Parker. My husband and I have been looking for older homes in the Amberstead area and we just noticed a sign in front of a place on Ash Street." She strained to see the address number on the mailbox at the end of the drive. "23175 Ash Street. It's a big Victorian."

He heard a man's voice say 'ah, yes' on the other end of the phone.

"Could you tell me the price? That'll determine our ability to say 'yes or no.'"

He waited for what he thought would be a response in the $275,000 to $350,000 range, given the vast amount of property that came with the house.

"Really?" Tanya's face lit up. Robbie stared at her, curious. "Yes – we'd love to arrange for a showing. By all means." She nodded while he raised his eyebrows at her. "Tomorrow at ten? That sounds wonderful. Thank you so much. We'll be here." She hung up.

He gripped the steering wheel and looked at her before laughing out loud. "So what's the shocking news? It's falling apart inside and they're letting it go for a dime?"

She shrugged her shoulders. "He says it's going for $175,000; that the family is eager to move – the husband has taken a job over an hour away, and they're selling for what they bought it for a year ago. They just want to break even. Apparently, it's beautiful inside."

"That sucks for them, but if it's as nice as he says it is, it might be okay for us. Strange that they'd let it go that cheap, though."

"I'll live with their price," she said. "Smaller places are going for more."

"I wonder how they heat it." He bent to peer closer and saw several wood stove and brick chimneys sprouting from various parts of the roof. "I suppose wood stoves, but lumber's gotten expensive too."

"Well, let's not jump to conclusions before we even see it," Tanya countered.

"I suppose," he said. "I always get this feeling that something might be wrong when you hear 'cheap price'; hidden black mold or urethaformaldehyde inside walls. Something they won't admit to because they want to get rid of the place, but that they found out about after *they* moved in and began to come down with illnesses."

"You're a pessimist," she said, feigning irritation.

"I'm a realist," he sent back. "This is our investment and where we want to stay for years, maybe for the rest of our lives."

"I'm sure it'll be fine," she said with a pleased sigh as she regarded the place. "Look at the land around it. I could even buy a horse."

"No horses. No, that's too much of an expense. A dog, sure. A cat, yes. No horses, no cattle. You can trot up the road and pat the farm animals over there if you want to socialize with agricultural beasties."

He stared at its rows of dark, paned windows. It had a deep green tin roof that looked to be in good condition.

"It's going to need a lot of yard maintenance," he tried one last time, knowing he was already defeated. He wondered why he wanted to dissuade her, other than the sheer size of the house seemed formidable. One or two good wood stoves could adequately heat even a large house, although he hoped at least one would be wood pellet instead of hardwood.

"We'll look but we won't jump to a decision with the agent around," he told her. "We'll discuss it and then contact him. Okay?"

"Okay," she said.

CHAPTER
4

Robbie drove away, feeling defeated, knowing that Tanya had already fallen for a house whose insides she hadn't seen. He watched it grow smaller in the rearview mirror. He shivered a little and attributed it to the cool weather and damp ground. He turned the car's heater on and allowed the soothing heat to flow over him.

"What is it about old houses that draw you so much?" he asked Tanya just before they reached home. They had two months to find a house before their agreed-upon closing date. He'd always grown up in new places, his father having been military and moving his family about every three years, so Robbie held no special affinity for these turn-of-the-century places. Tanya was stubbornly enamored with them.

"I don't know," she shrugged, smiling. "Their beautiful architecture; their high ceilings, and maybe this sense of tradition and pride, like you're carrying on something special and these houses love you for it."

"It's just a structure," he said. They pulled into their driveway and he cut the engine. "It's brick and stone and plaster and wood. It's not like the building knows or feels anything."

"I don't know about that." She looked at him before they disembarked.

"What do you mean?"

"Oh," she shrugged. "I've been in a lot of old places and they're like quiet, polite guests at a party; they sit in the background and observe what's going on around them. They don't make themselves conspicuous, but they're there, just the same."

"That's weird," he said.

She just laughed.

* * *

10:00 A.M.: The Next Morning

They waited in the car. The agent, a fellow named Desmond Hawkins, had agreed to meet them in front of the place. At 10:02 they saw a car pull over a hill and up behind them. A stout, middle-aged man with short, dark hair, wearing a red ski jacket and black chinos, walked towards them. He held a clipboard with papers.

Tanya and Robbie got out and they shook hands with the man.

"Des Hawkins. Pleased to meet you."

"I'm Robbie Parker and this is my wife, Tanya. Thanks for agreeing to show us the place."

Hawkins laughed. "Hey, my pleasure and my job. It's quite the house inside."

They strolled up the long drive.

"I have a truck," Robbie said. "If it's what we think we want, I guess I'll need to get a shovel attachment."

Des Hawkins grinned. "There are a few guys in town who'll plough for a reasonable fee, but sure, a shovel would save you money. The place comes with a lot of charms that will override things like long driveways. Wait until you see it."

"Full wraparound porch," Hawkins continued, "with a partially enclosed, winterized section that contains blown-in hot air from gas furnace vents. You'll be able to sit out there in the middle of January to enjoy the morning sun and read your newspaper."

"Sounds wonderful," Tanya said.

"Oh, it's quite the show place." Hawkins brought them up to the front door, knocked first, and when he got no reply, used the passkey to let them into an expansive foyer of stained glass, polished oak floors, and a carved oaken staircase that bent around to reach the second story landing. Tanya pulled in her breath. Even Robbie had to admit he was taken by this first impression.

"It's in beautiful condition," he said. "But I have to ask...why are they letting it go at a break-even price, even if the fellow took another job? Sometimes a spouse will stay behind a few extra months in order to get a good price."

Hawkins glanced at him, then down at his information sheet. "Here's a copy of the real estate info on the place. From what the husband told me, and I've only met the couple twice, he has taken a job in Montreal. He travels a lot with his work. The wife doesn't work outside the home and doesn't want to be left here alone for several weeks at a time. She finds the house too big. They're willing to forfeit profit in order to meet their required closing date."

"Which is when?" he asked, curious.

Hawkins looked at him. "As soon as possible. They've already put in a conditional bid on a condo in the city."

"Ah." It made a little more sense to him now. They could lose their desired abode if this one didn't sell quickly enough, and not everyone wanted a house the size of a small castle. The wife sounded a bit needy and nervous too. Tanya wouldn't have a problem being on her own, but that was just Tanya, Robbie reasoned.

Hawkins brought them through the main floor with its sweeping kitchen, its formal dining room, its library, its den, its parlor, and a spare bedroom, all with expansive ten-foot high ceilings done in elaborate plaster molding and exquisite paneling and woodwork, each room with inlaid stained glass windows above long dormers. A powder room with a separate bath waited off the main kitchen. Cupboards and cubbyholes abounded everywhere. The place contained a feel that combined rural comfort with exquisite accessories. It had a dumb waiter in which to hurl laundry down to the basement apart from the main stairwell. They peeked into the dumb waiter.

"We'll have to keep Cory away from that," Robbie said. "He'd try to use it as a hidey tunnel."

"Kids," Tanya laughed.

"You have access from all ends of the house with an extra stairwell," Hawkins commented. "Not only does it provide an interesting architectural design, but for safety reasons alone, having more than one access out is a positive consideration."

Robbie nodded, thinking in terms of a house fire. He'd have never attributed it to anything else at that moment.

The second story via the main stairwell branched out in two directions and around the top of the main stairs, leading to six well-sized bedrooms, a main bathroom, a guest bathroom, and a built-in tub and shower in the master bedroom.

"Oh Robbie, it's amazing," Tanya grabbed his arm.

He had to admit that, for the money, it was a lot of house and, from what he saw so far, in exceptional condition.

Hawkins took them into each of the bedrooms, opening closets to display depth, shelving, storage nooks and crannies. They walked into the room dubbed the guest bedroom. The current family had done their best to decorate the house, but it had become clear to Robbie that it had been more house than they'd been able to adequately furnish. He had to say the same for themselves, but reconciled the fact that, one day, Tanya and he would have grandchildren from their three sons and that the extra bedrooms and living space would be better accommodated in the future.

The guest bathroom was small, but efficient with white tile throughout, a crisp old-fashioned claw foot tub, wrap around shower curtain, but modern showerhead. An antique barn-board cabinet held a small, oval porcelain sink above which sat a huge antique mirror framed in gold guild, its glass marred in spots with age and the silver lining behind it having broken down in spots. He regarded the mirror, thinking that, antique or not, he might want something clearer and more modern in here. Hawkins motioned for Tanya and Robbie to follow him into the corridor again.

A fly buzzed in the bathroom window; thick, furry bluebottle insect, intent on trying to get out. Another couple of flies just like it lay dead on the windowsill. It was spring, cow country; flies might be an issue. And then, out of nowhere, Robbie saw the fly spiral like a small jet shot down, buzzing, to the sill. He cocked his head in confusion. Insects didn't tend to die like that. They'd gradually slow and become lethargic. The fly convulsed and thrashed, as if sprayed with some kind of neurotoxin, and yet nothing had touched it. Within seconds, it went still like the others. He felt fascinated observing it.

"Strange," he murmured.

He went to follow Hawkins and found himself facing the mirror.

It wasn't his reflection that looked back at him.

It was his clothes, his build, his haircut; the features were his, but the eyes were not. Something dark and foreign regarded him from the depths of his corneas. Horror burned like acid. He saw a shadow move across the wall behind him, and then, as quickly as the fly had expired, the impression and sensation passed. Robbie took a step back and felt himself hit the wall. He almost screamed. Tanya and Hawkins were in the next room, discussing something about floor stains. He stared at the mirror. Morning sunlight hadn't penetrated this room yet; it remained in soft shadow. He leaned toward the mirror, examining himself. He saw the details that were familiar to his face – his freshly shaven cheeks and chin that promised a shadow of whisker by the evening; the small pimple that had popped out at the base of his chin a few days ago; the tiny capillaries beside each nostril. The dark blue eyes looking back at him were his this time. His expression was one of shock. He regarded the mirror from different angles. It must have been a play of light.

He left the bathroom, then on impulse, walked back into it again and quickly glanced in the mirror. He saw only himself and three dead flies lying on their backs along the sill, lined up like small trophies.

"Robbie?"

"Yeah!" he called. "Just taking a last minute look at the tub in here." He caught up with them in the master bedroom, a magnificent room with polished, inlaid maple flooring, a massive stone fireplace mantel, and walk-in closets the size of a small bedroom he'd once had as a child. His heart pounded, but he forced himself to take a deep breath. A high molded ceiling in ornate plaster provided a gothic appearance to the room. The family had furnished in earthy, simple furniture and tones. Off of it, another bathroom, this one large with a fully sunken tub and expensive accessories. A wall-length mirror, modern, adorned one wall. He scanned it and saw nothing out of place; just his, Tanya's, and Hawkins' reflections, their expressions benign.

"Isn't it beautiful?" Tanya gushed. "Robbie, I love the place. If they want to get rid of it this cheap, that's our gain."

He wanted to agree with her because what he'd seen of the house so far had been wonderful. Hawkins brought them through the remaining rooms, up to the third story which consisted of four distinct sections of fully finished attic: a recreation style room, a small office, a play room, and a storage space where someone had built in a closet and intricate cedar shelving. The windows, although antique, were in sound shape. They finished on the main floor and basement, the basement a clean and solid concrete floor with a brand new natural gas furnace and recent plumbing. Electrical was up to code. Robbie couldn't find a reason to fault the house, especially not for the price.

"Wouldn't a place like this net them a lot more?" he wanted to know.

Hawkins shrugged. "Not everyone wants such a big house. It's had a few showings prior to yours. Either they don't want the maintenance of the grounds, or they don't want to heat the place. It's your gain if you don't mind a big house, especially since you'll be the folks who could turn around and sell it for a profit at any time, especially if you maintain it or add to it and you have the time to let it sit on the market for a while."

"It's a solid investment," Tanya said.

"Yes," Hawkins nodded. "A pretty good one, given today's economic situation. The stock markets aren't turning any real profit. Real estate usually turns over well."

"But we won't want to sell it," she added. "This is my dream home."

"What's their closing date again?"

Hawkins face took on the expression of someone who knows he's snagged a deal. "Exactly a month from now – May 12th; it doesn't give you much time to secure a mover, but I'm sure I could pull a few strings. Then there's the usual paperwork, but given you sold your last place for just under the price of this one...you'll owe peanuts on a mortgage; less than most people's car payments for a couple of years."

"I can't believe it." Tanya beamed. "The kids are going to love it. Don't you love it, Robbie?"

He glanced around the main foyer again. They walked outside and took a look at the general grounds. The house came with ten acres of property.

"Yeah," he said finally. "It's quite the deal."

They had the papers signed and everything approved by eight o'clock that evening and the house was theirs. He thought of the mirror in the guest bathroom, but cast it from his mind. He'd not grown up in an old house, had never lived in one, and scratched the impression up to that of someone who felt a little spooked by a house so large. It had been a trick of shadow and light, he reasoned. Nothing else.

* * *

Their youngest son, Cory, who was nine, had the most questions about the house. They'd brought all three kids, Chris, eighteen; Cole, fifteen; and Cory, wedged between his brothers in the back seat, to see the outside of the place a week before the move. They'd all (especially the older two) been both curious and insistent upon knowing where they were about to live.

Chris, who was about to begin college the coming autumn, peered at the house through the car's side window.

"It looks like the house in *'Salem's Lot*," he commented, wrinkling his nose. "I don't know if I like it."

"How can you not like it?" Tanya asked him. "The rooms are huge. You'll each have oodles of living space."

He shrugged. "It just doesn't look like a home."

"You're too used to the modern bungalow," Tanya continued. "Once you become accustomed to a house like this, you'll never go back to the other."

Cole just said "Cool," and asked which bedroom could be his.

"Any one you want," Robbie told him, "other than the master bedroom. There are six rooms on the second floor."

Cory looked enthralled. "Does it have any hidden stairways or secret rooms?"

Robbie laughed. "I don't think so, but you can always make-believe."

"How old is it?"

He squinted as he recalled the realty sheet. "It's almost 140 years old."

"That's old," Cory said. "Is it haunted?"

The question made Robbie swallow hard. He hadn't thought about his impression in the mirror for a few days, but now that feeling of initial unease rushed back at him.

"No," he said. "Why would you think that?"

"Aren't all old houses haunted?"

"I don't believe this one is," he said, "but if there's a ghost, I'm sure it'll be a friendly one."

"Our house was haunted," Tanya said. "We had all sorts of experiences there."

"Oh, don't get him going." Robbie gave Tanya a look that said 'we have to live in this place now; we don't want him crawling into our bed every night with nightmares.'

"We'll just call it Casper if there is one, okay?" Tanya said, good-natured.

Chris rolled his eyes and Cole guffawed. They drove on.

Moving day rolled around faster than they could keep up with their schedule.

CHAPTER
5

The moving truck had backed up the long drive so that the four workers could unload through the big double doors leading into the main foyer. Robbie had Cole and Chris help Tanya while he sorted boxes to various locations, and sent Cory outside to play and explore the grounds.

"But stay within eyeshot of the house, okay? If I call you, you need to hear me," Robbie told him.

"Can I come back inside if I get sick of it out there?"

"Of course you can. But don't get in the way of the movers."

"Yeah, Dad."

"Good boy," he said. "You can go upstairs and take a look at the bedrooms; see which one appeals to you." This excited him. He bounded up the big wrap-around staircase two steps at a time, making Robbie's heart leap, lest he trip and fall. He heard his running-shoed feet hit the top of the landing and grinned to himself. It was the right move, he thought. The place would give the boys room to grow.

Over the next three hours the movers, Tanya, Robbie, and the older boys got every box and item into its respective room. Finally, it was done. Robbie thanked the movers, signed the necessary paperwork, and they were on their way, leaving them in their new-old house. Both Tanya and he had the next week off to get themselves set up here. For tonight, he would concentrate on getting beds arranged with some linens, a few lamps plugged in, and a fire going in the woodstove in their living room so that they could have some heat rise to the upper floors.

Tanya busied herself in the kitchen, opening and unpacking boxes. Robbie walked over to her and hugged her. "Congratulations, Mrs. Parker. Shall we summon the staff in to prepare dinner and set the table?"

"Oh, don't you wish," she giggled. "I think ordering out would be a good idea for this evening. What do you think of Chinese? I crave some chow mein."

"We can do that. The boys might want pizza."

"Well, they can have pizza then. Where's the wine we brought?"

He pondered. "Hmm…I think it's still in the trunk of the car. I'll go get that." He kissed her and strode outside, noting how clouds had begun to push out the sun, throwing the day into a kind of subdued golden sunset. He retrieved a cloth bag containing six bottles of various wines they'd picked up, shut the trunk, and turned back to the house, his gaze perusing the various floors, examining the stones and looking for anything that might require some pointing and plaster work before the winter. When his gaze reached the attic window that jutted out from that quarter of the house, he saw the shape of an adult form, the silhouette dark against the paler backdrop of the window, watching him. The form looked male, stoop-shouldered. He stopped walking, gripping the wine bag, his mouth coming open with surprise. He brought his other hand up and over his eyebrows to cut the glare of the day. The figure stepped back from the window. He ran to the house, hearing the wine slosh, and pushed into the kitchen. Tanya stood by the pantry, stacking canned goods along a shelf. She whirled to face his commotion and saw his face as he placed the wine bag on the floor.

"What's wrong?"

"Were you just upstairs in the attic?"

"No. I've been here the whole time."

"I'll ask the boys," he said, turning towards the main stairwell.

"Why?" she called out. "It's not a big deal if they go up there. It *is* a finished attic. Maybe one of them would like a bedroom up there."

"I'll be back in a few minutes," he said. He ran up the stairs, taking two at a time, thinking about the form he'd seen at the window. It had been a man's form and had looked bigger, taller than any of his sons with their lithe, adolescent frames.

He found Chris and Cole sitting together in the bedroom Chris had chosen. They were setting books up on a built-in bookshelf. They glanced at him as he stepped in the doorway.

He was out of breath. "Were either one of you just upstairs in the attic?"

They regarded him, puzzled.

"No," Chris said. "We've been in here for the past hour, arranging stuff."

"Where's your brother?"

Cole shrugged. "He's been exploring the house. He's around. Maybe he went up there. Is something wrong?" Cole asked. He held a copy of a collection of Sherlock Holmes stories in his hand.

"No," Robbie stammered. "Just wondering where everyone is. I'll go find your brother. You guys want Chinese food or pizza for dinner? We're ordering out."

"Pizza," they said unanimously, without hesitation.

"Thought so." He then went through each of the other bedrooms, looking for Cory. The shape he'd seen in the attic window had not been that of a little boy. Cory had chosen the bedroom across from Tanya's and his, and he saw that Chris and Cole had helped him set his bed up and to put his room in order. A few opened boxes revealed his toys, puzzles, games, and some clothing. But he wasn't in there. The only room on this floor that he hadn't checked was the guest bedroom. He hurried along the corridor, past his other two sons who were engaged in conversation again, and stepped into it. It was the only room on this floor that remained devoid of furniture. They didn't have a guest bed, and none of the boxes had been directed here. They weren't sure what they'd do with this room yet. Tanya had mentioned possibly turning it into a study for the boys. It contained an empty, cavernous feel, his footsteps echoing against bare walls.

"Cory? You in here?"

No answer. More flies hummed in the windows and the closet door sat propped open an inch. The bathroom with the mirror that had bothered him waited at the other end of the room, like a held breath. He didn't realize he'd clenched his palms until he felt his fingernails dig into the skin.

"This is stupid," he said. He strode over to the closet, a tall stained oak door and gripped its handle, hauling it open. A dim maw awaited him, its clothes bar empty other than a few abandoned metal hangers. The door's coat hook was painted the same pale yellow as the plaster walls inside the closet. He listened, although he couldn't have told anyone what he listened for.

"Cory?"

Something dropped in the bathroom behind him; a soft noise, like a matchstick hitting the surface of something solid. He whirled and stared at the bathroom. Its open doorway provided him a partial view of the window. The mirror waited on the opposite wall. A feeling of dread seized him, but also an inner pulling. He felt as if the mirror sensed his proximity and somehow prepared itself. It called to him, with a gentle yet persistent persuasion to come, take a look.

"Cory? I just want to know where you are."

Silence like this felt like a hand whose cold fingers brushed the sides of his face, teasing, tickling.

He hurried into the bathroom. He'd just bought this house for his family and here he was, scared of being in this room, a room just up the corridor from where they'd all sleep, and more scared to look around the corner at a piece of looking glass. He saw the shower and tub, its plain white plastic curtain drawn back. He realized that he stood with his left profile to the mirror. He could see the shimmer of glass from the corner of his eye. *Turn and look at it.*

He whirled, his eyes wide as he stared at himself.

It was just him, looking almost furious. He stepped closer and examined his eyes. They were still just his, and yet he felt mocked, as if someone hid behind something and laughed quietly at him. He stepped back from the glass. No play of light. It was just an undecorated room that looked too stark without any semblance of 'home' in it yet.

Cory was not here. He looked inside the cupboards beneath and beside the bathroom sink. Empty. He walked back into the corridor where he heard Chris and Cole laughing over some shared joke.

"He's got to be upstairs," Robbie mumbled.

"You find him yet, Dad?" Chris called out.

"No. I'll look up in the attic, then outside."

* * *

He stood at the mouth of the attic.

"Cory?" His voice echoed in its vastness. "Where are you, son?" A walk through each of the rooms produced nothing.

He must still be outside playing, Robbie told himself. But when it began to rain heavily, Robbie became concerned.

Tanya was just finishing up making a call to a restaurant.

"I've ordered an extra-large pizza for the boys," she started, then saw his face. "What's wrong? You're running around like something's upset you."

"I haven't seen Cory for the past couple of hours. Cole said he was exploring the house about an hour ago, but I can't find him."

Tanya gripped the telephone receiver. "He must be outside, or maybe exploring the basement. You know how curious he is. I'm sure he's fine, honey. They're going to spend days exploring this place."

"I'd just like to know where he is," he snapped.

"Robbie. He's a *kid*. He's going to go play. One of the reasons we bought this house was so that the boys could have a lot more room."

Robbie turned and went into the basement, searching. He opened the two car garage and peered into its murk. No Cory. He hurried outside, dodging the rain and stepped into the small barn, poking inside the stall, behind leftover hay that he made a mental note to remove soon, and climbed the ladder to the loft.

"Cory!" He yelled. His voice floated away, drowned out by a rumble of thunder. Frantic, he spent the next twenty minutes searching the grounds and edges of the woods around the house. Tanya ran out with an umbrella towards him, her expression mounting in concern.

"No luck?"

"No, and that creek is filling up from this rain." For the first time, fear crossed her features.

"You don't think he'd try walking into town, do you?"

"I'm going to go get the boys and have them help search for him. This storm is increasing and I don't want him outside in it."

They burst in through the front door and he mounted the stairs towards Cole's room where he could still hear his older boys conversing.

"Boys! You need to help Mom and I find your brother."

At the same instant, he heard a thud come from inside the guest bedroom area and felt the hair on the back of his neck lift. He thought he heard something shuffling.

CHAPTER
6

"What the hell is going on?" he said and hurried into the room. The main room was empty, but he sensed something in that damned bathroom again. He ran into it. Cory, looking dazed and sitting on the bathroom floor, stared up at him. His clothes were dusty. Robbie gaped at him.

"There you are! I've been looking for you for almost an hour!"

He looked like a disoriented kid waking up from a heavy sleep, his lids heavy, his gaze unfocused. He had cobwebs in his hair and a scrape along the inside of his right forearm, freshly beaded with blood. Robbie squatted down beside him.

"Son, where have you been? And what happened to your arm?"

He seemed to look through his father. "I don't know. I came to look in this room. I wasn't sure if I wanted this one or the other one. I can't remember."

"Did you fall asleep in a closet somewhere?"

"I don't know."

Robbie helped him stand.

"Did you find some hiding spot in the house?" he persisted. "I won't be angry. I just want to know where you went. I looked through these rooms. Where did you come from?"

Again, Cory just stared at him. Chris and Cole came into the room behind them.

"I don't remember," Cory said. "I came in here and then I just don't remember." Tears formed along the lids of his eyes.

"Okay, okay," Robbie cuddled him. "Don't cry. At least we found you. It doesn't matter."

"Is he all right?" Cole asked.

"Yeah," he said quickly, although his gut told him otherwise. "Did you see him come into this room?"

"No," Chris said. "We've been in our room the whole time and he never walked past us."

"Well, he had to have done it because he's here, right? And he wasn't in here when I searched before."

Tanya reached the top of the stairs now. "Did you find him?"

"Yes," he said above the boys' heads. "He's here. He's scraped his arm somehow, and he seems out of it as if he fell asleep somewhere."

Tanya looked at Cory.

"Honey, where were you? You scared Dad and I. We know you want to explore, but Mom would really like it if you keep tabs with us, okay? Cory?"

He looked past her, at the mirror in the guest bathroom. Robbie saw his reflection and how his eyes looked like deep, dazed orbs. He shivered powerfully. Had he seen something in that glass too? What the hell was it with this mirror? Robbie wanted to ask, but didn't want to upset Cory any further than he already was. He made a note to wait until the right moment.

"I'm thinking that you fell asleep somewhere, like maybe inside a closet or a cupboard and that you've just woken up." Tanya kissed his forehead. "I'm not sure how you scraped your arm, sweetie, but I'll get that fixed up for you. Let's all go downstairs. Food's on the way. Dad will get a nice fire going in the wood stove for us."

A bolt of lightning cut through the sky, followed by a rumble of thunder that seemed to shake the house. Tanya took Cory by the hand and led him downstairs. Chris followed them. Cole waited in the spare room for Robbie as he stood in the bathroom, his face quizzical.

"Go down and join them," Robbie told him. "I'll be there in a minute."

Cole hesitated.

"What?" Robbie said.

"What's bugging you?" Cole asked. "You're acting weird. He's okay. Like Mom said, he probably fell asleep somewhere. Everything's cool."

"I know." He lied to him next. "I just want to clean up these insects first. Go ahead."

Cole shrugged, turned, and Robbie heard his feet banging down the stairs a few seconds later.

* * *

Robbie rested his hands on the counter top and looked into the mirror. He tried to move the frame, but it wouldn't budge. It was adhered to the wall. It was old, smoky glass. He knew that Tanya might want to keep it because it was probably original to the house, but he realized that he wanted it gone. The house had a few other mirrors; one inside their walk-in bedroom closet, a modern one in their bathroom, another mounted in the main entrance hall. A house needs mirrors, he thought. But he certainly didn't like this one.

"What did you do to him?" he asked. He examined every facet of the mirror, using his fingers to follow along its frame and edges, seeking anything that could indicate an entrance point, a lever or switch that might open it and into a crawl space behind a wall...anything that would make sense to him because now he *knew* that the stuff on Cory's clothing *was* plaster dust. He'd been somewhere *between* the walls of the house, some internal crawlspace or area not meant for daily living. He also knew that his two other sons were telling him the truth when they said that Cory hadn't walked by their room to get here. That meant only one thing: he'd been in here all along when Robbie had first looked for him, but he'd been hidden from sight. Where and how?

"Fucking room," he murmured and examined the tub area, behind the door, opening the cupboards and searching for any crawlspace or hole that could lead into the house's walls. He found nothing. He stood up, exasperated, as the doorbell rang.

"Pizza's here, Robbie, if you want some," Tanya called.

"I'll be right down."

"Don't get any funny ideas," he said to the mirror, not sure what or who he thought he addressed. He felt as if he'd just purchased a house with a malignancy in it. To argue to sell it would crush Tanya. She'd think him insane. And what would he tell her? That he wanted to sell because he was afraid of the mirror in the guest bathroom, afraid of the house in general because something about it felt 'funny,' something for which he couldn't put a finger upon? He went down to join his family in the kitchen for dinner, but he'd lost any semblance of an appetite.

CHAPTER
7

After they finished dinner, Robbie got a fire going in the woodstove, given the day had grown cool and damp. They sat on the floor with their food and drinks. Robbie picked at his food. Tanya noted it.

"You not feeling well?"

He shrugged. "I'm tired; long day. Maybe I'll want to eat more later." He pushed the plate away.

Cory, on the other hand, had snapped out of whatever funk he'd been in when Robbie had found him. He looked through some electronic gaming magazines that Chris had found inside a box. Robbie watched him. When his usual smile returned, Robbie relaxed a little, but he'd be keeping an eye on him over the evening and into the next few days to see where he went. A part of him wanted to deny access to that guest bedroom, but that would make it frightening to his family and he couldn't offer a rational explanation for doing so. Who wanted to live in a house with a concealed room that sits like a secret behind plaster and paint?

"I'd say it's time for you to go to bed soon, sleepy head," Tanya told Cory who'd curled up in a nearby chair.

"Can I sleep in your bed tonight?" he asked. Tanya looked surprised. It was not something that Cory had asked to do since he'd been three or four years old.

"But we set up your bed, honey," she said, "and it's all ready to go. Your nice blankets, some of your toys; it's your own space."

"The house is so *big*," he said. Something about his words made Robbie shiver again.

"What if we start you out there and see how it goes?" Robbie asked. "You can't sleep with us every night."

"It *is* really big," he said. "It goes *everywhere*."

"Everywhere," Robbie echoed, wanting to ask him what he meant by that, but Tanya interjected.

"We can leave a soft lamp on in the hallway for the first few nights so that you can find the bathroom, okay?"

He nodded.

"Let's go," she said. "Pajama time."

Robbie reached out and touched her hand as she passed him, and she gave his fingers an affectionate squeeze.

"I'll be back in a few minutes," she told him. He didn't want her to leave Cory alone, not even in their bedroom. He had this overwhelming fear that he'd go to check on him and he'd be gone again. There had to be a rational explanation that he just hadn't discovered.

Chris and Cole got up a few minutes later.

"We're going upstairs to play some backgammon."

"Okay," Robbie said, feeling better that the older boys would be up there. Then another thought struck him: what if something happened to all three of his children? Okay, he thought. Enough. This was not a good way to begin living in their new house.

"Have fun, boys," he said. "Do me a favor and peek in on Cory over the next little while. Make sure he doesn't get up and go wandering again."

"Yeah, okay," Chris said, his tone suggesting that Robbie was being the overly-worried parent yet again. Robbie sat in the parlor and watched the reflection of flames dance across the walls of the room.

Tanya returned and they poured more wine to enjoy in front of the fire.

"You happy?" he asked her. "With the house?"

She gave him the biggest smile. "Sweetheart, it is a dream come true," she said. "I couldn't be happier. I love you."

"I love you, too," he said, and thought that it was a good thing she couldn't see his face because, as happy as he was for her, he couldn't rid himself of a dreadful anticipation of something unknown. He heard the older boys pad along the hallway, a toilet flush, and knew that one of them peeked into his and Tanya's bedroom. Nothing undue occurred. At eleven o'clock Tanya and he went upstairs to bed, the woodstove fire nicely kindled for the evening. Cory was fast asleep in the middle of their bed.

"I'll get him into his bed," Tanya said and went to reach for him.

"No," Robbie said. "Let him stay with us tonight. I don't want him falling down those damn stairs in the dark."

Tanya laughed. "I can leave the light on the bathroom. Robbie, the boys will be fine."

"Just let him have tonight with us," he said. "We'll get all of their rooms fixed up tomorrow."

"Okay," she said. "I'm glad we have a queen-sized bed."

Tanya fell asleep with Cory snuggled against her. Robbie laid awake in the dark and listened to the house go quiet. He heard rain tap along the roof and move along the eaves. He felt the gentle warmth of the heat from the woodstove rise up the stairs to embrace them. Sometime after midnight, he finally fell asleep.

* * *

He wasn't sure what woke him up, but it came as a sound that traveled through his sleep like a gentle but persistent nudge. Robbie's eyes shot open in the dark. He felt a sense of disorientation, then remembered where he was. He saw Tanya's sleeping form, her face pale in soft moonlight. Cory slept with his mouth open. Robbie relaxed, yet listened for something. He heard the toilet in their bathroom trickle water along a pipe. The storm had long passed on, leaving the night sky clear and star-studded.

Something slid over the floor in another room. He propped himself up, listening, wondering if one of the boys was awake. He rose and padded into the corridor, pausing by Chris's room. Chris was asleep. On impulse, he reached into the common bathroom and sought the light switch. He felt a sudden need to yank his hand back, as if something in there might grab onto his fingers. Warm light filled the room and spilled into the hallway. He edged along the corridor, peeking into Cole's room. Cole was also asleep.

Robbie faced the doorway of the guest room. The air near it felt cooler, as if the continuing warmth from the woodstove met some kind of transparent barrier outside its entrance. He put his hand up and felt inside. It was definitely cooler and the air smelled faintly of chalk. He closed Cole's door so as not to wake him, switched off the light in the bathroom, then padded back through darkness to the spare bedroom. He stepped inside, triggered the light switch, and shut the door so he wouldn't awaken his family. He faced the room. He'd thought he'd heard a soft, shuffling sound, like the noise of a box or something solid being pushed along the floor.

Its emptiness met him face on, its windows looking black against the night, its walls like four hands cupping him, its closet door wide open to its sterile interior, its adjacent bathroom darker. He walked around the room, feeling its walls with his hands, running his fingers along runnels in its plaster, looking for something, some hidden button or device that might open the chamber that had taken his boy into it. He found nothing. He searched the closet with equal intensity. Again, nothing.

"I know the sound came from you," he whispered to the room. Although his family slept within twenty-five feet, he felt alone, stranded in here. Angry, he hastened to its bathroom. He almost turned on the light, then had a notion to leave the light off and to look into the mirror.

CHAPTER
8

The tub shone like dull alabaster, the toilet sitting prim like an ivory sphinx. He spun to face the mirror.

Cory stood there, facing him from the opposite side of the glass, his fingers moving along the surface and making soft squeaking sounds as if trying to find a way out. His eyes were focused on something beyond Robbie. Then, he began to cry. "Daddy?" he asked. "Mommy?"

"Cory?" Robbie rushed at the mirror, fingers crunching hard against glass to reach his son. Instantly, Cory blinked out, his image replaced with Robbie's stark, horror-etched reflection.

"What the *fuck*?" he yelled. Robbie slapped the mirror hard with his hands and felt a strange kind of tickling on one side of his face, the sensation of fine filaments brushing over his skin as if something had passed him in the dark. He pulled his hands back and the mirror stuck to him with the movement, glued against his skin like wet material – a thin veil of silver that clung like cool jelly before retracting. He yanked his hands back and watched the mirror ripple, then go still. Mesmerized, he poked it with a finger. It was hard, silver glass again.

"I'm not dreaming," Robbie said. "I know what I just felt." A dank aroma of old wood, dust, and something else, something rancid like long-dead mouse bodies, blew at him and he knew without doubt that not only was the house dangerous, but that something within *this* room served as its core energy source, a malevolent pivotal point, a portal to something sinister. It was an innocuous room in a house that didn't feel right; it wasn't the traditional creepy basement, wasn't the lonely attic – the familiar tenets of 'bad places' in too many horror films. An empty bathroom at the end of a corridor…

Something cold swept over his feet. He looked down and saw that, in the minute he'd been captured by the mirror, the tub had filled with stagnant water that bubbled up from the drain, foamy and black, the bubbles bursting with the stink of methane gas. The sinister water trickled over the edge and onto the tiled floor. Robbie felt *things* move in that water and something stung his bare feet.

"Get off me!" He slapped at the light switch in the bathroom. Light spilled on. The tile floor was clean, white, devoid of water. The tub was stark, sterile. His feet were dry, untouched. He stared at the mirror. He saw a man with a night's worth of beard-growth whose dark blue eyes formed pinpoints of terror. He tore through the empty bedroom and ran towards the door, expecting it not to open. It opened and he stumbled into the hallway, urine-yellow light spilling out behind him. Cole stirred in his bed and Robbie heard his mattress squeak as he got up. His form filled his doorway, his longish hair looped in messy cowlicks.

"What's wrong?" he asked Robbie. "You look spooked. What are you doing in that room?"

Robbie hurried past him and burst into the main bedroom, feeling for Cory. He found him cuddled against Tanya. He felt warm, soft. He heard Cole approach their door.

"Dad," he whispered. "He's fine. You're having a bad dream."

Robbie stood, hands shaking, the spit in his mouth gone dry.

"I'm awake," Robbie said.

"*Now* you are," Cole kept his voice low, "but you must have been sleepwalking and dreaming about looking for Cory. I don't know what's with you and that room. It's just a room."

Robbie walked back, his voice low but firm. "I looked at every inch of that frigging room today and I'm telling you, I didn't miss him. He wasn't in there."

"Then he must have snuck past me and Chris," Cole said. "It's not like we were just watching our door. Take a chill pill." He turned towards the empty room with its dull light.

"Don't go in there," Robbie said. "I'll shut the lights off."

Cole looked quizzical. "If there was something so bad about that room, it could come out into the rest of the house any time, right?"

His words scared Robbie more than Cole could know. "Do you feel something wrong with it?"

"No. I think you just got scared today and you're relating it to this room."

"I'll shut the lights out in there," Robbie said.

"I'll go with you."

Robbie saw he really wanted to do it.

"Okay. But I don't want you coming in here by yourself."

"It's supposed to be our study," Cole argued.

"Maybe we'll use one of the attic rooms instead."

"And what'll you do with this room then?" He looked like he was ready to laugh. "Seal it off?"

Robbie started at the words.

"Don't push me," he told him. They walked into the bathroom together and Cole made a face at Robbie in the mirror.

"Just a stupid old mirror," he said. "It's fuggly."

"Fuggly?" Robbie asked.

"Friggin-ugly," he said. "Actually, it's the other F-word, but..."

"Ah. I tend to agree. I'm going to try and talk your mother into putting a new one up in its place."

Cole shrugged. He walked out and Robbie shut the light off. Cole trudged back to his bedroom and closed his door. Robbie left the dark room and glanced back into the dim cavern.

"Don't ever touch my children," he whispered to it. That rank smell again, like desecrated things. He made a point of remembering to give Des Hawkins a call tomorrow. He wanted to know about this room; if anything bad had ever happened in it; anything: a senior dying in bed, an accident—any blighted history that could suggest why this space felt so wrong. Normally, he'd laugh at such notions, but not now.

He went back to bed but didn't fall asleep. He watched the sun creep up as a reflection on the opposite wall, saw the corridor leading to *it* gradually lightening, studying for any sign of a shadow or sound that might try to make a move towards Cole's bedroom across from it. Nothing occurred, yet the feeling of impending doom remained.

* * *

At 8:00 AM, Robbie got up. Tanya rolled over in bed, smiled at him, and leaned to kiss Cory on the forehead.

"How'd you sleep?" Tanya asked. "You still look tired."

He shrugged. "First night disorientation," he lied. "You?"

"I slept like the dead."

He shivered at her words.

"I'll convince him into his own bed tonight," she continued. "Every time I went to roll over, I'd feel his knees or his feet in my lower back."

"He's right next to us anyway. We'll hear him if he gets up." He dearly wanted to believe that and thought about how he'd thought he'd seen their sleeping son's frightened image in that foul mirror last night. He showered, dressed, and joined Tanya and Cory in the kitchen a few minutes later.

CHAPTER
9

Cory, still in his pajamas, ate a bowl of cereal while fiddling with a small toy truck that he pushed along the tabletop.

Robbie grabbed coffee and sat down opposite him.

"How'd you sleep, Cory?"

Cory glanced at him, his eyes heavy with the early morning.

"Okay, I guess."

Robbie tried hard to not look like he was observing him. "Just okay?"

Cory shrugged. "I guess. I dreamed of our old house, and that you were looking for me in it."

Robbie started. The coffee sloshed, almost spilling over the edge of the mug. "What do you mean? I *was* looking for you yesterday afternoon." He pondered; should he push the point or not? "Where did you go to play yesterday, bud?"

Cory stopped pushing the car and looked at his father. "I don't know."

"You don't know?"

"I was in my bedroom and I had to use the bathroom. Cole was using the big bathroom, so I went to the other one."

"The other one in the guest bedroom?" Robbie gripped the mug.

"Yeah," Cory said, resuming the pushing of his toy. "And then I woke up on the floor when you found me."

Robbie felt his gut plunge. He chose his next words with care.

"Cory...I want you to think carefully. Do you remember where you explored inside the house? I'm not upset with you. I'm just wondering if there are any neat places that I haven't discovered yet."

Cory looked at him, confused. "No—I was going to the bathroom and then…"

Robbie glanced over his shoulder; Tanya had left the kitchen to carry a load of laundry down to the basement. "And then *what*?"

"I looked at the mirror."

"What happened with the mirror?"

"I don't know. I saw the bathroom, except the bathroom in the mirror was different…there was candy on the other side. I wanted to touch it. I…I don't remember."

Robbie felt sick. "Candy? What kind of candy?"

"Lollipops," Cory said. "Different colors with white sticks. They were sitting on the counter in the mirror."

"But you didn't have real lollipops with you?"

"No." Cory stopped pushing the truck. "Did I do something wrong?"

"No, son, but do you remember what happened after you saw the lollipops? Did you touch them? Try to remember."

Cory's lower lip trembled. "Are you going to be mad at me?"

"No. I just want you to remember what happened."

Cory started rolling the truck, hard this time, back and forth, the toy clinking against the porcelain bowl. "They were real. I got the red one. I was in the other bathroom, but I could still see ours through the mirror."

Gooseflesh broke out on Robbie's arms, neck, and shoulders. "Do you remember feeling the glass when your fingers reached the mirror?"

Cory shook his head. "I don't remember. Is there something wrong with the mirror, Daddy? The lollipops were real. I ate the red one. I don't remember what happened. I was in their bathroom, and I heard you call me. Then you found me."

Robbie couldn't drink any more of the coffee. A shiver broke through him, making him shudder. He looked at Cory.

"When you say *their* bathroom, who are you talking about?"

Cory stared at him. "Wherever that other room is. I don't know how I got there. I saw the lollipops and I felt scared when I saw our bathroom on the other side, and then I just woke up."

"Daddy wants you to promise me that you won't go in that bedroom or bathroom again until I take care of some things. Just use the regular bathroom. Promise me?"

Cory banged the truck into the bowl. Whack, whack, whack, the sound of it making Robbie's jaws tighten. The air in the kitchen went tight and still.

"Promise me."

"Okay. I won't go in there."

They stared at each other.

"What's the matter with that room, Daddy?"

He could sugarcoat his words but his son still knew that something was wrong.

"I don't know, Cory," he said. "But I'll take care of it."

Cory's next words shook him.

"Is there something wrong with this house? If there is, can we leave?"

The truck hit Cory's bowl; bang, bang, bang.

"Cory, stop hitting your bowl with that truck!" His words came out sharp.

The truck stopped.

"No. The house is fine. The mirror is old and maybe it's cracked or loose or swings open somehow. I'm going to take a closer look at it. Just don't go near it again."

"Yes, Dad." Cory looked like he might cry. Can I go now?" He'd lost interest in eating any more of his cereal.

"Yeah," Robbie said.

Cory walked away from him. Robbie listened to his son climb the stairs, a part of him wanting to rush after him to make sure he didn't go near 'that room,' while knowing that he also couldn't overreact, lest he truly frighten his family. He heard the washing machine come on in the basement and Tanya loading clothes into the dryer.

"Don't fuck with my family," he said into the room, to the air in the room, to the house. He got up and found Des Hawkins' business card and made a call.

* * *

Tanya placed wet laundry on top of the dryer, then loaded a basket of whites into the washer. She got a kick out of the dumb waiter but hadn't reconciled with the idea of opening a door and tossing linens into a chute yet. Maybe it would eventually grow on her. The basement was humid and smelled of wildflowers and mold. She heard Robbie and Cory's muted voices and smiled. Her boys had so much *room* to move about in this property! She sighed, contented, making a mental note to contact the local schools and see about getting the boys registered for the autumn. She heard Cory's footsteps skitter away a minute later, then Robbie making a phone call.

She hummed a little while she added soap to the washer. She shut the washer lid, turned around to go upstairs, and stopped, her gaze taking in something in front of her on the concrete floor. She paused, her mind trying to make sense of what it saw in the morning light flooding through the basement's windows.

"Oh…my gosh, gross!"

She looked at the mutilated body of a large field mouse lying in a shadow near the wall. Tanya crept forward for a closer look. The mouse had been ripped clear along its middle, like someone had taken a blade and gone to town with it, leaving lacerations that allowed its blood and entrails to bloat.

"What the hell?" she said. Sure, an old place would have the occasional mouse; not that she cared. But this mess? The mouse looked *shredded*.

She glanced around, wondering if something feral had made its way into the basement, possibly through the crawlspace beneath their kitchen. She'd get Robbie to clean this up. She took a slow circle through the basement, peeking into corners, the storage room with its dusty shelves and milky, filtered light, the furnace room where the furnace sat hunched like a sleeping bull. All windows were shut, none broken. A filament of cobweb spun in the air.

She was alone down here, and yet felt suddenly watched. Panic sent her rushing up the flight of uneven wooden stairs. She shut the door to the basement with a small bang. She found Robbie sitting at the table, his call ended.

"Who were you talking to?" she asked.

"I had a couple of questions for Des Hawkins. What's up? You look a little flustered."

Tanya walked over to the coffee pot and poured a mug. "There's a dead mouse downstairs in the laundry area that you're going to have to clean up."

"Mouse?" Robbie shrugged. "We're bound to have some."

"It's mutilated."

"What?"

It's *mutilated*. Torn apart like something took teeth to it."

He stared at her.

"I'm not kidding," she said. "Look for yourself."

Robbie made his way down the stairs, his feet loud and banging.

"Damn!" he said a moment later.

"Do you think the former owners had some kind of terrible trap that it got out of before it died? Something that would mangle an animal like that?"

"I hope not," Robbie said. "Anyone who would devise something that wicked needs to be shot."

"Maybe we have a stray cat," Tanya told him. "I thought I heard something run through another room."

Robbie shrugged. "I don't know how it would have gotten in. I'll look around. In the meantime, toss me a roll of paper towels, would you?"

Tanya complied. Robbie bent to clean up the remains of the mouse.

"Quite the house-warming present," she said, doing her best to lighten the moment.

"Yeah," Robbie mused. "Ruined mice and phantom lollipops."

"Pardon?"

"Nothing. Just mumbling to myself."

* * *

He tossed the bloodied wad of towel into a trash can and walked around the basement, refusing to be held hostage by this feeling of trepidation.

I own you, he thought, regarding the house. *I've paid hard-earned bucks to be here and I'm staying. Don't challenge me.* He grasped a broom in case a stray cat or some other form of wildlife should leap out at him and strode through the basement, the broom grasped like a battle sword. Nothing occurred. A couple of spiders in webs scurried away from his presence.

He paused and watched the quiet basement for a minute, feeling the bub-bub, bub-bub of his pulse thrum in his veins. His questions to Hawkins had been tentative, but inquisitive. Had the former couple mentioned anything *odd* happening in the house?

"Odd?" Hawkins had asked, sounding part defensive, part amused.

Robbie persisted. "Did they have kids?"

"No." Hawkins was quiet for a moment. "They'd had a baby, but they lost it."

"Lost it?"

"Crib death, about three months ago. Listen, it's not the type of thing people talk about, or their agents, when you put a house up for sale. Stories like that don't make for good business. I'm sure the sad memories are a main reason that prompted them to move."

"They had no other children?"

Hawkins cleared his throat. "Only the one. Why do you ask?"

Robbie had chosen his next question with care. "Are there any spots in the house that a child could get into, like actually into the structure of the house—between walls or floors? Any trap doors?"

Hawkins response had been immediate, quizzical. "No. Nothing that I'm aware of and I've seen every room and closet in that place. Why do you ask?"

Robbie sighed. "My youngest took off on us for a couple of hours yesterday. We looked everywhere for him and couldn't find him, inside or out. Then, I found him in the bathroom off the guest bedroom after already having searched in there, half asleep and drywall dust on him as if he'd crawled into a tight space somewhere."

He didn't dare mention anything about the lollipops.

"Is that old mirror secured to the wall?"

Hawkins was quiet.

"I don't know what your boy may have gotten into, Mr. Parker; perhaps one of the old closets that hasn't been used in a while, or exploring the cupboards in the bathroom. Plaster walls can create a bit of dust. Maybe he was curious, crawled into a cupboard to explore and fell asleep. There are no known crawlspaces in the house. As for the mirror, it's an antique that was put up when it was built. It's secured solidly. Why do you ask? Has it come loose?"

Robbie sighed. "Just thinking of replacing it. It isn't my cup of tea."

Hawkins laughed at this. "Well, it's your place now. You can do whatever you want. If you discover some kind of hidden interior crawlspace, it'll be news to me. Please let me know if you do. Otherwise, it's a grand house. Beautiful place. You and your boy must have somehow just missed paths. He may have been elsewhere, then stumbled back into the bathroom, half asleep."

"Yeah," Robbie said, thinking about Cory's words. *Lollipops. Different colors, with white sticks. I got the red one. Is there something wrong with this house?*

Crib death.

"What room was the baby in?" Robbie asked.

"Pardon me?"

"You said they lost their baby to a crib death. Which room did the baby sleep in?"

He heard Hawkins' breath whistle through the receiver and wondered if the man rolled his eyes at the question.

"The bedroom beside the master room," he said.

Robbie realized it was the room that Cory had chosen. Terror flooded through him.

"That's a sad story," Robbie said.

"Sorry to have to tell you," Hawkins' said, "but you asked. Stuff like this happens, and who knows why? I don't think they could stand to be in the house anymore; the sad memory of it. They wanted a fresh start. It's an old house, Mr. Parker. If you were to look into its history, chances are you'd discover that other things have happened there over the past century. People died in their homes back then; wakes were held—"

"I know," Robbie cut him off. "I just thought I'd ask about the house, for safety reasons. Sorry to have disturbed you."

"Not a problem," Hawkins said. "Once the place is fixed up the way you want it to be, I'm sure it'll grow on you. It's difficult to make a new move. Things take time."

"Yeah," Robbie said. "Thanks."

"Feel free to call me if you have any other questions or concerns. I like to make sure my clients are happy."

"Sure."

He hung up and drummed his fingers for a moment. Crib death; the same room that his youngest son occupied.

"Crib deaths happen quite often," he mumbled.

Then Tanya came upstairs with the story of the mouse.

CHAPTER
10

Cory sat on the edge of his bed, his stuff spilling from boxes, and stared at the window. He wasn't sure if he was happy being here. He missed his old room with its Harry Potter wallpaper and posters. He listened to Chris and Cole prepare to go to town together. They loved him, but they didn't always want him tagging along, especially if they wanted to talk to girls. He felt at odds, and now that he was away from friends he'd had in his old neighborhood, he realized that he knew no one here and probably wouldn't until school started at the end of the summer.

He sighed and lay back on his bed, grabbing a comic book. After ten minutes, he was bored almost to tears.

Cole stole a peek at him. "See you later, Cory. Be cool."

"Yeah." Cory let his shoulders slump. The front door opened and shut. The house fell quiet.

Cory thought about the conversation he'd had with his father. *You and your brothers are not to go into that bedroom or bathroom. The mirror is old; maybe it's cracked or loose. Daddy will take care of it.*

He tried to remember what had happened after he'd seen the lollipops in the mirror and the feeling of curiosity when he'd reached forward to touch the reflection of something that wasn't in the room with him. His fingers outstretched, he'd felt the cold kiss of glass against his fingertips. Then…the details came back to him, knocking the breath from him and making him sit up.

* * *

His fingers had gone through the mirror. What was hard turned suddenly soft and he was inside a room exactly the shape of the one he'd just left, only on the other side of the looking glass. This room was from a long time ago. It contained a claw foot tub, a wooden stand and washbasin, and several melted candles. His hand grasped the lollipops as he looked back at his parents' bathroom through the mirror. The air in this room was dusty, stale, like air that had been locked up for a long time. When he pushed his hand against the mirror, it stayed firm this time. That frightened him. He wasn't sure how to get back now. An idea had come to him; he'd just walk through this other house and find the door to the outside, then he'd run back to his real house, but not before first taking one of the lollipops--a red one--as if holding something as natural as this could act like some kind of a safety net.

He walked through this other bathroom and into the same-shaped guest bedroom as in his parents' house. This room contained a wooden four-poster bed with a quilted comforter. A highboy with polished drawers and brass handles stood opposite. An intricately carved rocking chair waited in a corner, and a low table and fancy stool in the opposite corner. The table contained many glass bottles of perfumes, the glassware hand blown glass, some looking like sea shells or tiny magic lamps with stoppers; clearly, a woman's room. The room smelled faintly of the perfumes, talcum powder, and something else. Something almost spicy and not quite nice.

He wondered if the mirror had been some kind of a door that had allowed him entrance into a house built next to theirs, and that by reaching for the lollipops, he'd somehow pushed a small button behind or actually in the glass. He knew that someone was inside this other house. He could feel their presence. He wasn't sure whether to call for someone to help him, or just try to get out of here on his own.

He stepped into the corridor. The air continued to smell bittersweet. The light that filled the windows was a pale white haze. Cory stepped over to the window and looked outside. He saw clouds or mist moving past the glass. He felt as if he was inside a house that floated somewhere up in the sky.

He headed along the corridor, peeking into what was supposed to be Chris's and Cole's rooms. These also contained furniture from another era; the same high four-poster beds, one with a small footstool beside it in order to reach a mattress almost as tall as him. Flowers in vases filled with water almost glowed in this odd, white light.

He reached his own bedroom and stopped to look inside. He saw a baby's crib, its white bars containing blankets and cushioning. He heard a baby's cry but couldn't see the child. The room smelled of powder and sour milk. A mobile with thin filaments holding tiny, colorful butterflies twirled slowly over the crib. Music accompanied the movement of the mobile, notes that sounded like water droplets hitting a firm surface. He heard the baby laugh and wanted to walk into the room to see the child. Even the company of a baby would be better than being alone here. A footstep along the ceiling above let him know that someone was in the attic.

He glanced into the main bedroom and saw another high bed, this one made of brass bars and thick with blankets. More antique furniture, the curtains drawn so that the room was dark. A smell of medicines floated at him: eucalyptus, rubbing alcohol, the miasma of many pills within bottles.

"Jeffery?" an old woman's voice called from the bed. "I feel so sick. Help me."

The covers moved and Cory saw the shape of feet, twin points sticking up beneath the material, shift position. He backed away. The squeak of a footstep in the attic, coming down the stairs now.

* * *

Cory rushed down the main stairs, past a parlor with high-backed sofas, polished tables, and oil lamps that gave the air a sooty scent. A fire popped in the fireplace. A player piano began to play by itself, its roll music punching the melody out with gusto.

"Mommy," Cory ran for the front door. He tugged and it opened. He rushed onto the porch and saw only white mist, thick as smoke, everywhere. He grabbed the handrail and took a step downward, tentative, his foot feeling for the ground. He reached out and felt nothing.

Nothing but air.

He dipped down so that his leg swung far lower than he knew where the ground should be and still felt nothing but air within this mist. He didn't know what was out there. He realized that, if he stepped off the end of the step, he might fall into nothingness—he wouldn't know where his real house might be, if it was out there at all. He had to go back to where he'd come in; to try and return through the mirror.

He hurried back up the stairs. The player piano continued its jovial song, something fervent and in a minor key, the ivories pressing then rising, pressing then rising like rippling teeth. Upstairs, the baby began to cry. He was halfway along the hallway when he felt watched. He turned. It was an old man, thin, palsied scalp, the skin under his eyes bagged and almost purple, clad in a burgundy smoking jacket and proper trousers, the chain of a hand-watch swaying as he walked, stepping into the landing.

"I didn't mean—" Cory began, but the man walked right through him. Cory felt a moment of damp, as if he'd been hit with a gust of rain-filled wind, and the man reached the doorway to the main bedroom.

"Jeffrey?" the aged female voice called out again. "Help me."

"I'm here, Isabelle," the man said. Then he turned and looked directly at Cory. "I put the lollipops there for you," he told him. "You can help yourself anytime. Feel free to visit. It's a nice place here. I'm going to get my wife some water now. Come back again."

"How did you do that?" Cory asked.

The old man, his skin so transparent that Cory swore he could see the man's teeth and gums shining through his cheeks, smiled and held a thin finger up to his lips. "That's our secret," he said. Then he shut the bedroom door. Cory listened to the woman in the bed begin to cry; then what sounded like rough, coughing sounds issued from the room. Then all went quiet.

Cory hurried back to the man's bathroom. The other lollipops still waited on the counter where he'd left them, and now three balloons floated in here too; red, yellow, and blue, what he recognized as the primary colors from his school art class. The red balloon said 'Hello', the yellow one said 'Little' and the blue one said 'Friend.'

Cory smiled, but he wanted to go home. It had been interesting and the old man had seemed nice enough, although odd (and that trick he'd done!), but he wanted to get back to his parents' house. This bathroom contained no light, only that strange white glow. Its window was old, chipped wood, its sill thick with heavy dark paint, its glass crawling with flies. The sound of the baby crying drifted to him from down the hall, followed by the maddening whirl of its mobile. He recognized the song now from his own childhood. It was *Mary had a Little Lamb*. Someone walked into the baby's room, *shushing* to comfort it.

He ate the red lollipop, then approached the mirror. This mirror was exactly like the one in his parents' guest bathroom. He touched the glass. It was hard, cold, unrelenting. He wasn't sure which part he needed to touch in order to go through again. He heard his name being called from somewhere in his real house. He pressed with both hands, panicking.

* * *

"Daddy!" he called out. "I'm here!" His father's voice faded for a minute.

Cory started to cry. He slapped his hands against the mirror, wanting only to go home. Okay, the mirror was strange and this other house next to his was very odd, even if the old man had seemed nice enough and they left balloons and candy. Maybe they were lonely. But he wanted out. Everywhere he slapped along the glass, the glass refused to give. He could see the bathroom in his real house through the glass; he was separated by a thin, yet resistant medium.

Minutes passed. He wept, frightened now. His stomach growled. Desperate, but not knowing what to do, he leaned against this side of the mirror, his face wet with tears, knowing that his real home was just on the other side. He heard the old man's voice in the guest room behind him.

"You don't have to go. You're welcome to stay here. We have lots of room for company. You can visit your family as much as you want from here. I can show you how, if you'd like to stay."

Cory turned. The old man smiled. His odd pale eyes glowed a little. He smelled of the medicines from the bedroom. "My name's Jeffrey. The baby might like a big brother like you. You could learn how to play the piano together. We're happiest when new people stay. It's nicer for us all."

"I don't want to," Cory said and ran at the glass. Something gave, the feel of damp elastic, and he felt himself pulled through a tight, warm tunnel as Jeffrey rushed up behind him, his old man fingers cold and grasping at his ankles. Cory landed with a thud on a floor. He sat, disoriented, sunlight far too bright in his eyes and stared around himself. He saw his father rush into the room a moment later.

"There you are! What are you doing in here? I've been looking for you for almost an hour."

The taste of the stale red lollipop in his mouth, the sugar old with time. The feel of the old man's hands on his ankles. Had the man been pulling him, or pushing him out? Cory wasn't certain.

Hello, Little, Friend.

CHAPTER
11

He tossed the comic book away as the details came back to him. He didn't mind the idea of visiting as long as he could always come back here at the end of each visit.

Strange old man.

He hadn't liked the old furniture or the stale smell of unmoving air. Yet, he was curious to know more about this other house and he *had* been invited to visit. *How* that house was there, and the weirdness with the mirror was the most frightening part to him. It was sunny out and he decided that he'd find his football and go kick it around the driveway. He didn't want to go back to visit today. He felt it better not to tell his parents about Jeffrey. If he wanted to visit them, he'd have to be quiet and the best time would be at night, when his parents and brothers slept. Something about Jeffrey and his family felt sad, lonely, and needy. He almost felt sorry for them. Almost. For now, the day beckoned. He grabbed his football and carried it downstairs.

* * *

His father was on the front porch, securing a loose floorboard with a screwdriver. He glanced up at Cory.

"Football." His father smiled. "Good choice. I can get a goal post set up this afternoon, if you'd like."

Cory grinned. "Sure." He looked up at the house and beyond it, wondering where Jeffrey's house might be and why he couldn't see it from out here. He reasoned that the other house must be built *inside* his parents' house somehow. He thought of the mist outside its windows and how, when he'd stepped out onto Jeffrey's front steps and had felt for the ground, there hadn't been any solidity; just opaque vacuous space.

"Whatcha' going to do with the ball for now?" Robbie stopped working with the screwdriver. He stood up and tested the board with one foot, satisfying himself that it was secure.

"I dunno. Kick it around." Cory shrugged. He kicked the ball high into the air before grasping it again.

"We'll look into a team at school, if you'd like," Robbie told him. "It could be a good way to make some new friends."

"I guess."

"You seem a little bummed," Robbie said. "What's up?"

Cory fiddled with the ball, not really interested in kicking it around anymore. "I'm never old enough to go out with them."

"Oh...I hear you. I was the youngest kid at home too. I know how you feel."

"Did Uncle Tim always leave you behind?"

Robbie grinned and sat down on the top step. "Most of the time. A fifteen-year-old didn't want a ten-year-old tagging along when he hung out with his buddies or wanted to keep an eye on a pretty girl. But he did make some times special just for me, like your brothers do on occasion."

Cory squinted into the sun. "Was I an accident?"

Robbie's grin faded. "No! Of course not."

"How come I came so much later than them then?"

Robbie rolled the screwdriver back and forth in his palm. "You were a gift that came later so that, as our first two were growing up so fast, we could still have all the joys of a little one around. No one is ever an accident, sweetheart. We couldn't imagine life without you."

Father and son looked at each other.

"I'm sure you'll make at least one good friend within the next week or two," Robbie continued. "Take a walk up the road and see if you can spot any kids playing. Boy, girl, it doesn't matter. Ride your bike around a little bit."

"I suppose." Cory sat down on the step. He wanted to ask his father how another family could be living inside their house, but he thought back to this morning's breakfast conversation and knew that he couldn't mention a word of it. Maybe, if he got to know Jeffrey better, he would invite Jeffrey over to visit. His father always held a respect around older people, and Cory felt that his father would probably like Jeffrey once they got to know each other. Jeffrey could bring his wife, and the baby. His mother would like the baby, Cory reasoned. She always went gushy over them in stores.

"You need air in the tires?" Robbie asked, breaking Cory's thoughts. "Let's go get your bike out of the barn. I'll pump up the tires. I saw a corner store just two blocks up the road. I'm sure it sells treats and comic books. You worked hard setting up your room yesterday. That's worth a few dollars for treats. Deal?"

"Deal," Cory said. He put Jeffrey out of his mind. The old man would be busy taking care of his sick wife and doing whatever he did in there. He accompanied his father to the barn and watched as his father added air to his front tire.

"We can turn this barn into a play area too, up in the loft," Robbie told him. "We might even get a few chickens so we can have our own eggs."

"Really? Can I have one as a pet?"

Robbie laughed. "I suppose."

He handed the bike to Cory, then dug into his pocket and extracted a five-dollar bill. "There you go, bud. All yours. Have fun. Just keep us updated so we know where you are."

"Thanks, Dad." Cory rode along their driveway. He glanced at the house and saw Jeffrey's form standing in the attic window, watching him. Jeffrey waved. Cory, on instinct, waved back. When he looked back at the attic window a few seconds later, Jeffrey was gone, the window a dull square slate against the frame.

* * *

Tanya walked through the bedrooms as Robbie fiddled with porch repairs. She made their bed, then went into each of the boys' rooms to straighten bedcovers and start unpacking boxes. Cory had left his covers tossed back, an open comic book face up on the bed. She'd seen him step outside with his football and heard his and Robbie's voices drifting up through the open windows. Her poor wee one. She wondered whether they should have had another baby shortly after Cory had been born so that he could have had a sibling closer in age to himself, but that was a moot point. You don't have a baby when your youngest is almost ten, and besides, she didn't think she'd have the energy to mother an infant at this point in her life. She was thirty-eight years old. As soon as they got settled, she'd get back into her web design work. She thought she might like to take the smallest room on the main floor as her office where she could set up her desk, her computer, all of her books and manuals.

She began hanging up his clothes in his closet. She paused, remembering how they'd found him yesterday—dazed and coated in plaster dust and cobwebs—and took a moment to inspect the inside of his closet. She ran her fingers along the thick plaster walls, glancing up at the ceiling. She saw nothing out of place; no tiny door, no entrance into a crawl space. She shrugged. He could have fallen asleep in here, heard his name being called, and stumbled from room to room looking for them. A kid half-asleep could be pretty darned disoriented. She put the thought from her mind, loving the brilliant sun streaming through his window.

She finished hanging up his clothes. A watery melody came to her along the breeze. It lasted seconds, a muted wind chime sound, only familiar. She sought to identify the tune. It had been from "Mary Had a Little Lamb." She wondered if the former family had left a set of chimes outside somewhere, although she'd never seen a set that could elicit a melody like that. The sound stopped as quickly as it had begun.

She continued with her tasks. It was starting to look like a room. She placed his lamp on the desk and bent to plug it into a nearby socket when she heard a baby cry. Her maternal instinct made her straighten up. She would have sworn the cry had come from inside the room. Tanya walked over to Cory's window and glanced into the yard. She saw nothing. She knew she'd heard a baby cry.

"I'm not going crazy," she mumbled. "I heard a baby."

She checked the other bedroom windows, thinking a neighbor with a baby might be close outside. She saw no one. She stood in front of the spare bedroom, and on impulse, stepped into it.

This room had an odd, almost held-breath feel about it that she attributed to its not having any furniture. Flies buzzing in the warming sun drew her attention to the bathroom. Tanya saw two new flies moving up and down the panes in an attempt to reach the outdoors. She opened the window, drew the screen back, and let them out.

"I'm sure there'll be more of you." She regarded the old mirror. It was four feet high and five feet across, expanding over most of the wall. It had a heavy, ornate gold painted frame common to turn-of-the century fare. It could use some cleaning, but she liked it enough. She saw a scattering of fingerprints on its glass. She used the palm of her hand to smudge them away, then noticed that some of the fingerprints seemed to be *in* the glass itself…as if someone had pressed from the other side.

"Strange," she muttered. Must have been a manufacturing defect from all those years ago. She'd have to point it out to Robbie. Maybe they wouldn't keep the mirror, heritage or not. "We can probably get a good price for you," she murmured. She left the bathroom, and never saw the shadow that stepped across the glass the instant she left, its fingers touching from the other side.

*   *   *

She became engrossed in tidying Cole's and Chris's rooms and forgot about the baby's cry and melodic chimes. It must have been sound traveling from a nearby house, the effects probably more immediate because of the direction of the wind. Robbie came upstairs and popped his head around the corner.

"Up for a tea and a sandwich?" he asked.

She tossed a stray hair from her eyes. "Sounds good. You making it?"

"I can do that, m'lady," he bowed. "Cory took his bike up to the corner store to get a treat. Poor kid doesn't know what to do with himself."

She placed some items on Chris's dresser, then walked towards Robbie. "I know." They walked towards the stairwell together, then descended to the kitchen.

"I know it's not quite 'home' yet, but by the end of today we'll have the basics set up in each room. By next week, I'll have curtains up and will have painted at least two or three rooms." She set the teakettle on to boil. "It's going to be cozy. Funny...I went into the spare bedroom, just to take a look and decide how I might want to fix it up for the boys—I let some flies out through the bathroom window and noticed fingerprints all over the big mirror. I went to rub them away, then saw that some prints are actually on the other side of the glass. Isn't that odd? Someone must have touched the glass just prior to it being coated all those years ago."

Robbie, who had been casually laying out slices of bread along the counter, stopped in his movements. "Inside the glass?"

"Yeah. I rubbed and rubbed, but they're actually on the other side of the glass." She saw the look of horror on his face and stopped. "What's wrong? You look as if I'd said I saw a hand waving at me from the other side."

He shivered. "I don't think I want the boys using that room as a study. I don't like that damned room. It just doesn't have a good feel. I hate that mirror."

Tanya laughed now. "Oh, come on, Rob. It's the only room in the house that's still completely empty. You were just shaken up because we couldn't find Cory yesterday. He crawled out from under a bed or something where he'd fallen asleep."

"We don't know where he went," Robbie cut her off.

Tanya sighed. "There's nothing wrong with the room, hon. It's this big empty cavern, but once it's painted, with nice blinds and furniture and homey things, it'll get a lived in, good feel to it again. I can make that bathroom really cute, too. I'm just not convinced I want to keep the antique mirror. It's too big and gaudy and I'd actually like to modernize the area."

"I'm thinking of taking it off too," Robbie said. "Maybe we should just keep the room as a guest bedroom, for when our parents or friends come to stay with us. The kids can each have a desk in their own room, or for that matter, up in the attic, away from the rest of the house."

"I suppose," she said. "Hurry with those sandwiches. I'm hungry!" She laughed at him again. "We do almost have more house than we need, but better than being cramped. Especially when grandchildren finally come along."

They ate their sandwiches.

"I suppose part of the attic would be a better study area for all of them," she agreed. "We could turn it into a whole recreation area in that one spot, with a loveseat and a games table and such. Funny, but while I was cleaning Cory's bedroom, I swore I heard a baby cry for a few seconds. That, and what sounded like a music box or chimes."

Robbie coughed hard, almost choking on his sandwich. His face turned red and his eyes watered as he fought to catch his breath. Tanya, half concerned, half amused, rubbed his back.

"Are you going to be okay? What did I say? I said I thought I heard a baby, not that I wanted another one."

He shook his head and took a long moment to regain himself. He stared at her.

"What?" she implored. "You're looking at me like I've said something insane. I figured it was just the sound of a neighbor's baby carrying along the breeze. The room does look like it was for an infant, though…that pale pink paint."

"They lost their baby," Robbie said, his voice flat. "Hawkins mentioned it to me on the phone this morning. I'd called him with a few questions about the place." He decided to fib. "I'd asked him if the former owners had had kids and if they knew of any kids Cory's age who might live along the street. He said they'd had a little girl, and they'd lost her. Crib death. She was only a few months old."

"Jesus," Tanya said. She placed her half-eaten sandwich down on her plate. "That's terrible. How sad. Was that the baby's room?"

Robbie nodded. "Yes. We'll get it painted and fixed up for Cory. It's sad, but it's something in the past. We can't let a sad memory affect our future here."

"Yeah," she said. "Time for happiness in this house again."

"I agree," Robbie said. He clinked the edge of her tea mug with his. "Cheers to that!" They laughed again, but it felt strained.

CHAPTER
12

Cory pedaled. A high, white cumulus cloud banked to the southeast, promising another banger by early evening. A couple of little kids about three years old stood on the sidewalk and watched him as he rode past, one with a finger thrust into his nostril, his booger-picking stance stilled as he observed Cory with curiosity. Cory dismissed them: they were way too young to even think about hanging out with.

He reached the corner store, a small wooden structure that reminded him of a local fishing shack his father used to bring him to back at their old town, and leaned his bike against the side wall. A few adults lingered about, one in front of the magazine rack, another choosing lottery tickets, another trying to make a decision over various jars of jam. A middle-aged woman sat behind the counter, her hair dyed a florid red. She glanced at him. "Hi, son."

"Hi," Cory said. "Do you have comic books?"

"Over there, by the magazines. Lower shelf."

Cory perused the contents for a minute. He decided upon a new *Spiderman* comic. He walked back to the counter where a bunch of loose nickel, dime, and quarter candies waited in open cardboard boxes.

"You want candy?" the lady asked him.

"Yes, ma'am," he said. She handed him a small brown paper bag. He spent another minute deciding over the selection. The bell over the door jingled. Cory saw a girl of about ten or eleven years old walk into the store. She was pretty, with shoulder-length dark hair and freckles over her nose. She walked up to the red-haired woman and asked for a paper bag.

"You look like you're out of breath, Gina," the woman told her.

"I ran here," the girl said.

"Why? We're open all day, honey."

The girl giggled. "Nothing better to do." She looked at Cory who flushed at her attention and looked away. He saw the lady smile.

"You new in town, son?" the lady asked.

Cory felt his face heat up more. "Yes, ma'am. We just moved in yesterday morning."

"Ah, the big house at the end of the road," the lady said and her smile kind of faded. Suddenly, it seemed as if he'd caught both of their focus.

"Yes, ma'am," Cory repeated. His parents had insisted he refer to adults as 'ma'am' or 'sir'; not that his brothers did it anymore, much to their father's angst.

"That's the—" the girl started, but the lady gave her a sharp look and shook her head. The girl shut up.

"What?" Cory asked.

"She wanted to say that's the house that took a long time to sell," the lady added quickly. She gave Gina a look of consternation. "Big place. Not everyone wants a house as big as that, but obviously your family did. Do you have brothers and sisters?"

The answer seemed logical enough to Cory. "I have two older brothers, ma'am."

"You can call me Mrs. Rideout," the lady told him. "You can even call me Anna, if your parents allow you to refer to adults by their first name. I'm easy, son. You do whatever's comfortable for you. Gina lives just up the road too. I'd say you're both about the same age and likely will be in the same class this autumn."

"Maybe," Cory said. Gina studied him for another minute, clearly not shy like he was, then began selecting her candy.

"I'm ten," she said with authority, as if being of an age that commanded two numerals instead of a single digit somehow provided her with the right to flaunt more audaciousness.

"I'll be ten in August," Cory said softly.

"Cool," Gina said. "You like these little licorice balls? They change colors."

"I took some of them," Cory said.

"Good taste," Gina told him. They both laughed. Maybe she wasn't so bad after all.

"What are you doing after you buy your stuff?" she asked.

Cory felt his face go warm again. "I dunno. Ride home, I guess."

"You want to come over to my place? We have a swing set in the back yard."

"Sure. I'd have to let my parents know where I am."

They paid for their candy and Cory followed her outside.

"You have a bike?" he asked her.

"At home," she said.

"I'll just push mine and walk with you." He strode alongside her, not sure of what to say next.

"That house you live in has been for sale a lot," Gina said. "The last people were only there for a year. My parents talk about it all the time. Everyone around here does. Something bad always happens to each family that moves in. Anna didn't want me to say anything."

"Then why are you saying it?" he asked. "What do you mean something always happens? What's happened?"

Tina bit into a chocolate bar. "The last people lost their baby. It died in its bed. Before them, the father fell from the loft in the barn and broke his back and neck. He died a few days later. I don't remember stuff before that, but I heard that the house has had lots of families. Fires, accidents…someone killed themselves there. People got murdered."

"That's gross," Cory said. He gripped the bars of his bike, feeling unease push into him. He thought of Jeffrey and made a note to ask the man about this stuff. Given Jeffrey lived so close by, he'd know about these things.

"Every family who's bought that house always ends up selling it soon after," Gina continued. "People around here take bets how long they'll last. Some say six months. Some say less. My mother says that's wrong; it's like playing with bad luck or something."

Cory wasn't sure what to say. "My parents love it."

"I've never been inside it," Gina said. "I'm almost too scared to visit it."

"So, you'll never come over to play then?"

She shrugged. "Maybe. I'm curious about it, though."

"My father's going to clean up the barn and turn the loft into a clubhouse for me. It'll be cool. I can't help it that some man fell. You have to be careful climbing ladders."

Gina kept walking. "Yeah, or hang onto them when someone pushes you."

"Who?"

She stared at him. "Do you believe in ghosts? Dead things that maybe aren't completely dead?"

They both stopped walking.

"How can they be dead if they aren't completely dead?" Cory wanted to know.

"They don't go away to wherever they're supposed to go," Gina continued. "They hang around. Yours isn't the only house in town that's called haunted. There are a few others too. I don't understand how that can be. I wonder what they do?"

"Who?"

"Ghosts. I don't know what they're supposed to look like."

"I don't know either," Cory said. He'd have to ask Jeffrey about that too. He couldn't mention such a thing to his parents, especially with his father so uptight about that room.

"I don't want to talk about it anymore," he told her.

Gina stopped in front of a small farmhouse, its front yard bordered in a dark brown wooden fence. "This is where I live. It's old, but it isn't haunted."

Cory sighed and glanced down the road at his house.

"I'll come over," Gina promised him, "but I don't know if my parents will want me to. I can say that you live on another street."

"What happens if they find out where I really live?"

"I'll say that I got mixed up with your address," Tina decided, "but that we'd become such good friends, I wanted to visit you, and that your house is really okay."

"I think it's okay," Cory said. "You don't think the house is going to eat you up, do you?"

Gina laughed at this. "No, silly!"

* * *

Gina had him wait on the sidewalk. "I'll tell them that I'm going with you to play at the park. I'll just say you're a new boy at school. It's not a real lie because you will be new this autumn, right?"

Cory shrugged. "I guess so." He waited, his thoughts taken with her words while Gina went inside. He stared at his house in the distance, high and square and dark in the sun, its stone walls looking mossy from here. Nearby, the old red barn. *Fell from the loft. Broke his back. Dead.*

"People slip," he whispered. Gina reappeared, followed by her mother, a thin, blonde-haired woman with a tired, but gentle, face.

"This is Cory," Gina said.

"Hello Cory," Gina's mother said. "I'm Mrs. Dewar. When did you move to town?"

Cory hesitated. Gina widened her eyes at him.

"Uh, just a little while ago," Cory said.

"Where do you live?" Mrs. Dewar asked.

"Over there, behind those houses," Cory nodded down the road. "Not too far."

"That big stone house up the road that just sold?"

Cory's mouth fell open. He didn't want to lose Gina as a friend, but he felt afraid to lie. He shifted his feet. "Yes, ma'am." Gina's face curled in irritation at him.

Mrs. Dewar's expression changed. It looked part irritated, part nervous. She looked at the house, then back at him. "You're welcome to play here, Cory, but I don't want Gina going to that house. It has nothing to do with you son. I just don't like the house. Mind my words, Gina." Mrs. Dewar turned and went back inside, leaving Gina on the porch. Gina strode towards him.

"What'd you tell her that for?"

"What did you want me to do? Lie? She'd really not like me then and never let you play with me."

"I want to see the inside of your house," Gina insisted. "Now I'm really curious…"

"It's just a house."

"I'm going to have to sneak over," Gina continued. "Maybe I'll try to stop by tomorrow. I'll just tell my Ma that I'm going over to the library. There's a reading group there in mornings."

"You'd lie?" he asked.

"I want to see that house," she said. "I'm a bit scared, but you'll be there. And your parents, right?"

"Yeah."

"It should be okay then. I'll come over tomorrow morning."

"Okay. I'll see you then."

He got on his bike and rode away, feeling excitement at having made a friend, but unease over her stories. Before he left the vicinity of her house, he looked over his shoulder and saw Gina's mother standing behind a set of sheer curtains, watching him go.

CHAPTER
13

Cory rode his bike over to the barn. It was empty, his father back inside the house. He glimpsed at the old wooden ladder leading up to the barn's loft. Its rails were thick, but uneven. A person would have to grip the sides and hang on as they rose up to the loft that sat at least eight feet above the barn floor. Miss one rung and it would be easy to slip, your hands coming loose in a moment of panic.

He set his bike against the wall and approached the ladder. He reached out with one hand to touch it. The wood felt warm, dry, and splintery in spots. Cory gave the ladder a shake. It didn't budge; it was anchored to the barn floor, and thick bolts secured it to the edge of the loft. He saw chunks of hay spilling over the loft and sunlight trailing through a dusty window. Cory pushed himself onto the first rung. He didn't think his parents would care if he explored here. The rung felt solid; he jumped a little, still feeling safe. It held firm. He relaxed and brought his opposite foot up to the second rung, then the third. Now four feet up from the barn floor, his stomach turned at the prospect of falling. Distance winked at him, the floor cool and dark, promising that, should he plummet, he'd be guaranteed a good bruising, if not a sprain or broken bone. Six more rungs waited. He took another step up and wondered where on this ladder the man had slipped. Cory stared at the floor, looking for any signs of old dried blood.

Finally, he reached the edge of the loft and peeked over, his mouth open with anticipation, wondering what he might find up here: the face of the dead man waiting for him, grinning his dead skull grin, asking him if he, Cory, might like a game of checkers?

He thought of Jeffrey again and wondered if the man could somehow sneak into his parents' house?

"Stupid," he said. "Her stories are getting to you." Gina. He hauled himself to the loft and stepped away from the edge. The barn's ceiling sat several feet above his head. He walked to the milky window and peered out. He could see fields and woods from a new angle here. Bales of dusty hay leaned against the far corner. It could be a neat place. He turned to walk back to the ladder and stopped, a scream formed in his throat.

A thin man, balding, his skull and flesh broken along the left side from cheekbone to temple, brain matter and blood leaking down that side of his face, observed him.

"Hello, Cory," the man said. "It's a long way down." Then he blinked out of sight.

Cory felt the scream lodge against his tongue, thick and salty, refusing to budge. He couldn't breathe. When he did finally open his mouth, all that came out of him was a loud 'puh' noise, the release of held oxygen, his fright so extreme that he could barely inhale. He stared at the top of the ladder, afraid to go near it and peek over the edge, lest the bleeding dead man pop up again from below like some decomposing Jack-in-the-box. His thoughts rolled over. He couldn't stay here. He had to look. He had to see what might be there.

"Mister?" he called out to the man. *It's a long way down.* Would he have seen the guy if Gina had never mentioned anything about death and ghosts to him? He must have imagined it, but it had looked very, very real.

Silence; warm, pressing as humidity built with the day. Cory counted to three, then forced himself to walk to the edge of the loft and peer at the barn floor almost ten feet below, waiting for the dead man to be sprawled there, arms and legs cast out from his body like bent bicycle spokes, guts soaking into the rough wood floor. He saw nothing other than a sunbeam filtering dust through the air. Then, just as suddenly, he was overtaken by the sensation that he was about to be shoved, hard, from behind. He whirled. Again, nothing. Almost weeping, Cory curled one leg over the edge and found the top rung of the ladder. He hung on, but hurried down and jumped the last two feet to the barn floor. He ran, forgetting his candy and comic book in the bicycle basket. Only when he reached the front porch and door of the house did he glance back. He saw the dead man watching him from just inside the barn's open door. The man's willowy body, his front coated in gore, slipped back into the shadow of the interior.

Cory, lips shaking, let himself inside and shut the door behind him, Gina's words following him like skeletal fingers prying for a grip.

* * *

They saw him walking by the kitchen.

"Hey sport!" Robbie called to Cory. "How'd your outing go?"

"Fine," Cory said and kept walking. They heard him patter up the stairs towards his room. Tanya looked at Robbie.

"Go and see what's up," she said. "He still seems out of it. When the boys come back, I'm going to ask them to spend some time with him."

"Yeah," Robbie said. "That's a good idea."

He found Cory lying on his bed, his face turned to the wall. "What's the matter, bud?"

Cory shrugged but didn't look at him. "Nothing. I'm tired. I'm going to have a nap."

"In the middle of the day? Did you get yourself some treats?"

Cory turned to look at him. His face looked part hopeful, part resentful at Robbie's presence. "I got a comic book and some candy."

"Where are they?"

"I left them in my bike basket. I forgot them there."

Robbie sat on the edge of Cory's bed. "Why don't you turn around so that I can see you while I chat with you?"

Cory shrugged and rolled onto his back, to stare at his ceiling.

"Did something happen that upset you while you were out? You seem bothered."

Robbie thought he saw that kind of vacuous expression in his son's eyes that was filled with everything and nothing at once.

"I don't know if I like it here," Cory said. "I miss our old house."

Robbie let out a chuckle. "Ah, sweetie, it can take a while to get used to being in a new place. I'm a little homesick too, but Mom and I are working hard to make this feel like our home. We did a lot of work in the kitchen today. We'll start on your room soon. Maybe you'd like to tell us how you'd like to decorate it and we can start looking at paint colors and other things later this week."

Cory shook his head. "I don't care about the room."

"Well, it *is* your room, and it's bigger than the one you had in the old house."

"I'd rather have my old room back."

Robbie sighed and stood up. "Don't be bummed about the move, Cory. I'm pretty sure you'll meet at least one or two good friends before the summer's over. We're going to have a barbecue out back tonight. I'll make a bonfire pit and we can roast some marshmallows. What do you think?"

Cory shut his eyes. "I suppose."

"It'll get better soon," Robbie told him, kissing him on the forehead. "I promise you. By the end of the summer, it'll feel like home."

He got up. Cory said something that made him stop.

"Dad?"

"Yeah son?"

"Do you like this house?"

Robbie looked at him. "We bought it because we liked it. It has more room than the old one, which is pretty important to three growing boys who all enjoy lots of space."

"I don't think I like it."

Robbie leaned against the doorframe. "Why do you say that?"

"It feels weird."

"It's still new. Give it more time. Have your nap, if you're tired. The Internet company said they'll be here tomorrow, so you'll have your computer back up and running again."

Cory seemed to cheer up a little at that. "Really?"

"Definitely, sport. We'll come out of the Stone Age soon enough."

Cory laughed at this, and Robbie was glad. "We'll have fun tonight."

"Okay," Cory said.

* * *

Robbie walked back downstairs, musing over his son's words. He had to admit he felt a kind of eeriness about the house too, the news from Hawkins about the former couples' baby, and Tanya thinking she'd heard a baby cry in Cory's bedroom. And the mutilated mouse in the basement. They were well overdue for some positive stuff to occur. He strode back into the kitchen, determined to fix what needed fixing, put their mark on the house, manipulate it into being their own. No more bad memories from other families or sad stories from real estate agents. He couldn't blame Hawkins for not having mentioned the crib death; it wasn't exactly a selling feature. It was in the past. With that, he set back to work.

"He okay?" Tanya asked.

"He'll be fine. He's just homesick. He perked up when I mentioned that we'd have Internet by tomorrow."

Tanya smiled. "What would today's kids do without computers? Remember how we used to pass our time with board games, just hanging out, telephone calls?"

"Oh yeah, I remember my two-hour-long calls to you that would tie up the phone line. It drove my parents nuts. They used to tell me that exercising my jaws wasn't an adequate pastime. Grant you, the said the same thing every time I went into the refrigerator. I disagreed highly, of course. So they started letting me have the second car a lot more often, so that we could see each other and I could eat out."

"We were so bad," Tanya laughed.

"Bad to the bone," he said. "You game for a barbecue tonight? I'll make a fire in the little fire pit for marshmallows, and take out some of those steaks? Maybe Chris and Cole can take Cory back into the downtown core for a bit after supper—show him some of the area. We can sit in our deck chairs and admire the stars."

"And the mosquitoes," she said. "The mosquito tent is still packed away."

"We'll survive."

"I am so happy," Tanya said. She walked over to him and kissed him full on the mouth. "I love the house. I know the kids feel displaced, but it'll grow on them. It's all going to be good."

"Of course it is," Robbie agreed. "How can it not with us adding our touch to it?"

CHAPTER
14

Gina swung on her backyard swing set, alone in the yard while her mother stood inside, washing dishes, and her father sat in front of the television. She'd been born in this town and although she had a couple of friends, she only saw them on occasion once school was out. She was an only child and a lonely kid. They lived at the opposite end of Amberstead, too far to walk or even bike. She kept her eyes on the old stone property where the new kid, Cory, had moved in. The house looked dark and brooding as the sun hit its opposite side, throwing her view of it into shadow. Its chimneys poked into the sky like daggers. Its barn sat quite far from the house, in a field whose eastern edge was ringed by thick woods. The barn looked black without any interior light.

She swung back and forth, her legs dipping down as she retrograded, and sticking out straight as she moved forward again.

A dull green light popped on in the barn's upstairs window. It flickered a little like cold fire. A similar light appeared in one of the house's attic windows. It left the attic window, a watery green ball, and floated along through the waning evening sky until it disappeared inside the barn. Then a moment later, two glowing orbs, round like distant dinner plates, floated back to the house and disappeared down one of its chimneys. Gina's legs froze. The swing came down hard, making her heels scrape the ground. She knew what she had seen, what had looked to her like floating balls of verdant electricity.

"Ghosts," she said. So, the stories were true. She'd never actually *seen* anything until now. She wondered if something might happen to Cory's family. A shiver tickled her arms, making the hairs stand up despite the warmth of the evening. Her curiosity grew, and yet she felt afraid. It was a feeling akin to having friends dare you to walk a rickety bridge; she wanted to visit the new boy, but she understood that the place prevailed in its spiritual activity, and that the spirits there were aware of her growing curiosity about them. When she'd been a bit younger, she'd had a friend who used to walk with her along the path beside that house; a girl who always disappeared the moment she reached the edge of the road. Her name had been Wanda. One day Wanda just ceased to appear.

"Gina."

She whirled on the swing to stare in the direction of the voice. It was Cory. He stood behind her. Although he looked at her, he seemed to look beyond her too, as if he was trying to see something on the other side of her.

"What are you doing here?" she asked, startled. How had he gotten here without her seeing him? Perhaps he had jumped the fence, afraid for her mother to notice him.

"I can go wherever I want," he said. "So can you. Will you still come over tomorrow?"

She couldn't get up from the swing. The wood felt different, everything buzzed as if the air around her had changed and become alive with soft electricity.

"Yes. I will."

"You promise?"

"Yes," she said.

He didn't say another word. He turned and walked back towards her house, squeezing through the shrubs.

Gina broke out of her paralysis and ran to the spot where he'd stood. She peered through the shrubs. He wasn't there. He couldn't have reached the street that soon.

"Cory?" she whispered, fierce. "Where are you?"

The night fell quiet around her, broken only on occasion by a sound from the nearby kitchen as her mother finished cleaning the supper dishes.

* * *

With steaks set to sizzling on the barbecue, potatoes baking on the side, and a pot of corn on the cob boiling, Robbie unscrewed a bottle of beer and took a long, grateful mouthful of the foamy liquid. Chris played a game of Frisbee with Cory out in the field. Cole sat in a deck chair, engrossed in his cell phone and text messaging some of his old friends.

"Everything cool back in the old place?" Robbie asked.

Cole stretched, glanced up. "Yeah, I guess."

"What do you think of downtown Amberstead?"

"It's all right."

Robbie flipped steaks. "You like it enough here?"

"It'll grow on me."

"We're going to give you guys part of the attic for a study and recreation area," Robbie continued. "Mom will turn that last bedroom into a guest room for when the grandparents or other folks come to stay."

Cole shrugged. "You don't like that room, do you? You think it's haunted or something."

Robbie almost dropped the steak. He caught it at the last second and hurled it back onto the grill. "I didn't say that. I'm just not sure where your brother went for over an hour the other day. And he appeared in that bathroom after I'd been in there just minutes earlier."

"So, he crawled out from somewhere between your first and second visit, that's all," Cole said.

"Cole, there was nowhere in that room for him to crawl out from. There's no opening, crevice, crawlspace, or hidey hole that I can find—I've checked everywhere where he could have remained hidden while I'd looked for him."

"Somewhere else in the house then," Cole said, "and he managed to stumble into the bathroom at the last minute. It's an old house. Maybe he'd snuck into that thing you call a dumb waiter, in the kitchen."

Robbie's brow rose at this; the boy had a point. He'd never thought of that. Yet, there was very little room in the dumb waiter, other than straight down.

"That's possible, although he would have landed in the basement, not the upstairs bathroom."

Cole waved a hand. "He probably didn't want to get in crap with you if you found him there, so he ran back upstairs."

"Did he tell you that?" Robbie prodded.

"No. I just know the kind of thing I'd have done at his age."

Robbie felt a little better. "I'll have to ask him about the dumb waiter."

"Don't," Cole said quickly. "You ask him, he'll deny it. Just look there the next time you can't find him."

Robbie grinned. "Ya think?"

"Yeah."

Robbie flipped the last steak. "I had some reservations about this place...its age, its size...but I think it's going to be all right."

"Well, I'm done this year anyway, and then it's outta here for me, so it doesn't matter."

"College boy."

"That's right. School, and then 'cha-ching!'; bring on the money, baby."

"You're gonna do well."

"Yes, I am," Cole joked. "You can turn my room into a shrine for me, celebrating my brains and beauty."

Robbie laughed hard. "I'd like to say the humor comes from my side of the family, but I'll go for the brains instead. That leaves beauty and humor to your mother."

"She wouldn't be happy with that," Cole said.

"Nope; women want it all. I'm just the stud."

Cole grimaced playfully. "Hey, that's gross!"

"Food's done!" Robbie yelled. "Come get it!"

CHAPTER
15

"Isn't this a great night?" Tanya asked them. "Wonderful weather, good food, a fantastic new house." She looked at Robbie. "You seem more...upbeat."

"I've got my second wind back," he told her. "Beer helps."

Cory picked at his steak.

"You not too hungry, hon?" Tanya asked him.

"Nope."

"Did you fill up on candy earlier?"

He was apathetic. "It's still in my bike basket."

From across the yard came the sound of little kids splashing in a pool, followed by the sound of a new baby crying.

"There's your baby," Robbie told Tanya.

"Poor thing's probably uncomfortable with the dampness," she said.

Cory's head twisted at the wailing. He put his fork down, his interest in supper gone.

"At least finish your corn, son," Robbie told him.

"I'm not hungry." He looked a little sad.

"You'll make friends soon," Chris said. "We've only been here two days."

"Your brother's right," Tanya reached over and gave Cory's arm a gentle squeeze.

"I met a girl at the store today," Cory said.

Robbie smiled. "Really? Someone your age?"

Cory nodded. "She's ten. Her name's Gina. She lives up the street."

Tanya beamed. "Well, invite her over to play."

"She said she might come over tomorrow."

Tanya and Robbie looked at each other, relieved.

"That's great," Robbie said. "There you go. Your first friend here."

Cory fiddled with his fork. He went to say something, then stopped.

"What?" Tanya asked.

"I don't want a play area in the barn." Cory looked at Robbie.

"You don't have to play there if you don't want to. I just thought you might like me to fix up the loft."

"No."

"You don't like the barn?" Tanya asked Cory.

"It's creepy," he said.

Tanya and Robbie giggled, but Cory looked bothered. Chris carried his plate back to the house.

"You coming back?" Tanya asked him.

"Nah. I'm going to watch a movie on my computer. Thanks for supper."

They turned their attention back to Cory.

"I was going to build a safety rail around the loft and angle a set of stairs out from it, rather than a straight up-and-down ladder." Robbie said.

"I don't want it."

"That's fine. If you really don't think you want to play there, we'll use the space for something else." Robbie cast Tanya a questioning look.

"Can I leave the table?" Cory asked. "I'm going to go read my comic books."

"Put your plate by the sink," Tanya said.

They watched him walk inside the house. Cole got up too.

"Keep an eye on him when he goes in," Robbie asked Cole.

"Dad, he doesn't need babysitting. He's just being a baby, is all. He'll snap out of it." Cole walked away, almost disgusted.

"Kids," Tanya said. "I suppose we can keep tools and stuff in the loft."

"He'll change his mind. He's just being a bit silly. Oh, and Cole made a good point earlier. He thinks Cory may have climbed into the dumb waiter and probably fell a ways down into the basement. Maybe stunned himself a bit, heard us calling, ran upstairs and ended up in the bathroom. It would explain the plaster dust and cobwebs. It's the one place we didn't look. He was probably still in the shaft when I went down into the basement and was nervous about letting me know where he was."

Tanya's eyes widened. "I never thought of that. We should close that thing up."

"I think I will."

"I guess that explains why we couldn't find the little bugger," she laughed.

"And maybe that's why he suddenly doesn't like heights and isn't interested in the loft," Robbie added. "There are logical explanations for everything."

They clinked beer bottles. Robbie lit the campfire and they sat back to enjoy it, feeling somewhat relieved.

* * *

Cory lay on his bed, agitated. Cole stuck his head around his doorway a moment later.

"You want to watch the movie with us? It's the original *Halloween* film."

"No."

"What's got you so bummed out? You said you made a friend today. Lighten up."

Cory shrugged.

"Stay out of the laundry chute," Cole told him. "They don't know you were in there, but I do. That's where you disappeared, wasn't it? You idiot!"

Cory pushed himself up on his elbows. "I never went in the laundry chute. Why would I?"

Cole snorted. "Liar. Why couldn't they find you then? And where else would you get coated in all kinds of crap? You went into the room down there," he motioned with his chin towards the guest bedroom, "because you wanted them to think you'd hidden in there, except Dad had already looked. You got them into a tizzy over you."

"I never went into the laundry chute!"

"Sure," Cole grinned. "Sit by yourself, if you insist." He walked away. Moments later the soft sounds of a film started up.

Cory fumed, but worse, he felt sick with his secret. How could he ever have any of them believe him, even if he could bring himself to tell them the truth? He lay back on his pillows, frustrated.

"Psst!"

Cory twisted his head towards the doorway again, angry, ready to tell Cole to frig off and leave him alone, but instead, he saw Jeffrey's lanky old man shape standing there, his thin hair shining like spun silver in the watery moon light.

"I know how you feel," Jeffrey whispered. "Come back down to the other room, step over for a visit, and we'll talk."

"They'll notice I'm gone," Cory said, his voice low.

"Your parents are engrossed in their campfire and your brothers will be tied up for the next two hours watching that movie. You can be back here in a few minutes. You hear them calling you, you step back out again."

"How can I climb through a mirror anyway?" Cory insisted. "I don't understand."

Jeffrey smiled. "It'll make sense to you soon. You want friends, don't you?"

Cory nodded.

"So, you found friends. Come over any time. Even that little girl you met today. She'd like it over here."

"How do you know about her?"

"I saw you walking with her on the street." Jeffrey grinned. "You think I stay inside all the time?"

Cory nodded. It made sense. He thought about the dead guy in the barn today.

"Jeffrey?"

"Yeah kid?"

"Is there something wrong with the barn?"

Jeffrey studied him. "Things are only wrong if you let them be. I'll see you in a couple of minutes." Jeffrey slipped past the door. Cory sat on the edge of his bed, thinking about Jeffrey's words. How could there not be something wrong with a bleeding dead guy popping up on a ladder?

Cory took his shoes off so that he wouldn't make any sound. He scooted past Chris and Cole who were too engrossed in the movie to bother noticing him. He peeked through the corridor window. He saw his father standing by the campfire, poking logs with a long stick while his mother reclined in her chair with a glass of wine. They were occupied. He hurried through the empty room. Even the air in here smelled a little different, like leaving a city behind and catching the first aroma of a nearby ocean, only this didn't smell like kelp. It had an odd scent, almost dusty and sweet. He reached the bathroom with its filtered light and looked at the mirror. He saw his face, his expression curious and eager, his eyes a little scared. Today, instead of lollipops and balloons, he noted that Jeffrey had left several new comic books on the counter on the other side.

He touched the mirror, feeling its cold, hard surface stick to the ends of his fingers. Then, that odd, wet warmth like touching uncooked meat and suddenly his hand pushed through. Cory climbed up onto the cupboard and squeezed through the glass. It slid over him with the sensation of tepid, wet skin and then he was in the other bathroom again. He looked back at the room he'd just vacated. He touched the mirror; it was still gummy.

"I'm glad you decided to visit."

Cory whirled and saw Jeffrey standing in the doorway, watching him. "There's a *Batman*, a *Fantastic Four*, and a *Strange Tales* there." He nodded at the comics. "I'd like to introduce you to some of the others who live here. Come on; we're having supper downstairs. We've put on a great meal."

"I can't stay too long, and I just ate," Cory sputtered. "If my father starts looking for me again and can't find me, he'll be pissed."

"Time works differently here," Jeffrey said. "What can feel like hours here is only minutes in your house."

Cory hesitated, puzzled, then followed Jeffrey through the room. "Why can't I see the outside when I look through your windows? Everything looks like fog."

Jeffrey hesitated.

"I will explain things to you in time. Come have dessert."

Cory followed him. "I'm not really hungry."

"Not even for ice cream?"

Cory brightened up. "Well, I guess I can eat some of that."

"Thought so," Jeffrey said.

CHAPTER
16

They arrived at the same style of kitchen as Cory's house. A group of four adults sat around a long wooden table, one a woman who looked odd to Cory with her hair tightly coiled around her head and her lips painted a dark red; she held a baby over her shoulder, patting the baby's back as it fussed.

"Everyone," Jeffrey said, clapping his hands. The room fell quiet. "This is Cory. He just moved in with his family. He's been nice enough to come and visit us."

Cory felt himself blush, but looked at each of the people.

"Such a cute little boy," the woman with the baby said.

They all laughed. Cory relaxed a little. They seemed like nice folks, although *different* in a way he couldn't quite understand. Everything about this side of the property felt unusual to him. The air seemed lighter. His ears hummed, as if some faraway machinery ran a steady engine.

"Would you like some ice cream, Cory?" an old woman asked. "I'm Ida, Jeffrey's wife."

"What kind do you have?" Cory asked.

"Whatever flavor you'd like." Ida smiled at him. "What's your favorite?"

Cory smiled back. "Strawberry."

"Oh, that's my favorite too!" exclaimed the woman with the baby. The baby fussed and the woman jiggled it a little. "And I'm Ruth. This is little Tamara."

Cory saw that the baby was very young, maybe just a few months old; a little girl dressed in pink pajamas. The woman pushed a pacifier into the baby's mouth and the baby quieted down. A man who looked to be in his late thirties and clad in a man's silk dress shirt, dark vest, and heavy trousers lit a cigarette. His hair was greased back from the front of his head.

"Leonard here," he said. Something about him held a hard edge. A scar floated under his left eye, like a ragged crescent moon. The last person at the table was a quiet, timid looking woman who appeared to be in her late twenties. She fiddled with a cloth napkin, sometimes looking at the group, at other times staring about the room as if lost in thought. Her dark eyes met Cory's, looked away, then stole back to him.

"Madeleine," she said.

Leonard with the greased-back hair stared at Madeleine and gave her a wink. Madeleine blushed and looked away. They were, in Cory's opinion, a very odd family.

Ida spoke. "Maddy, would you be so kind as to get Cory a dish of strawberry ice cream from the icebox please?"

Madeleine hesitated, then got up without a word and walked over to a wooden box with doors. She opened the doors and reached in, pulling a glass pot from the inside and setting it down on the cupboard. She scooped a large ball of pink ice cream into a delicate-looking glass bowl—the kind of bowl that Cory's mother called 'her good China'—and carried it over to Cory.

"Here you are," Madeleine said. Her voice sounded sad and sweet. Cory reached out for the bowl. His fingers touched Madeleine's. Her skin felt icy from the scooping of the ice cream. Something about her made Cory feel very sorry for her.

"Thank you, ma'am," he said.

"You can have as much as you want," she said.

"Come sit at the table with us," Ida patted a vacant chair between herself and the odd man with the dark vest.

"Go on," Jeffrey encouraged him.

Cory did as he was told. He took a seat, aware that they all watched him as he tried the ice cream.

"This is the best ice cream I've ever had," he admitted.

Ida beamed. "I made it myself."

"Made it?" Cory asked.

"Of course," Ida replied. "If you want ice cream, you have to make it."

"My mother just buys it at the supermarket."

"Supermarket," Ida mused.

"It's *their* way of doing things," Jeffrey countered. "You know that. We've visited their place before."

"Oh, I know," Ida waved her hand at him.

Cory thought of Gina's words earlier.

"Is our house haunted?" he asked.

Ruth paused, her patting hand going still against the baby's back. Ida's fork froze in mid-air. Jeffrey cleared his throat. Leonard cackled with laughter, as if it was the funniest thing he'd ever heard. Madeleine flushed deeply.

"Why do you think that?" Ida asked him. She glanced at Jeffrey, then at the others around the room, as if his question had amused her.

Cory felt a little stupid. "A girl I met at the store today said every family who moves into my new house always has something bad happen to them."

"Did she?" Jeffrey asked, his face more curious than concerned. "People in small towns love gossip. Boredom fuels that gossip. This is an old house. Things are going to happen over the years. That's not unusual."

Ruth leaned closer to him. "It's a nice house. Do you like it?"

Cory answered automatically. "It's all right. I miss my old room."

Ruth nodded. "Well, if you stay with us—" Jeffrey's eyes flashed at her, and Ruth stopped talking. The baby fussed again.

"What she meant to say was if you visit with us, you won't feel so lonely and you'll soon not miss your old room," Jeffrey finished. Ruth shook her head as if irritated and walked towards the kitchen entranceway. "Like I said, invite your new friend over with you. Then you'll have lots of friends. Eventually, you can even invite your whole family."

"I'm putting the baby to bed," Ruth said, "and then I'm retiring for the evening."

"Good night, then," Jeffrey said to her. They listened to her high heels clack up the stairs.

*　*　*

"You want to see something interesting, Cory?" Jeffrey asked. "Come here with me for a moment. Come step out onto the back porch."

Cory hesitated, remembering the impenetrable fog he'd encountered, and the lack of solid ground off the last step.

"No, it's all right. Things are clear tonight. Come—look for yourself."

Jeffrey opened the door to the verandah while Ida nodded at him. "He's about to show you something special," she winked.

Cory followed behind Jeffrey's footsteps onto the exact same porch layout as his parents' home, only much more old-fashioned in décor. A door stood in the center of this porch: a tall, painted, wooden carved screen door, its design ornate with flowers, vines, and leaves.

"If you could imagine being anyplace right now, where might you want to be?" Jeffrey asked.

Cory paused. "I don't know…my old house, I guess."

"Your old bedroom, right?"

Cory nodded.

"Push the door open and take a look. Go on."

Cory glanced between Jeffrey and the screen door. He could see a lush green yard filled with mature trees, but curious, he did what Jeffrey instructed. As he pushed the screen door open, the backdrop of lawn and trees fell away and, instead, he saw the image of his old room appear in the ever-widening gap between the door and its frame. There was all his bedroom furniture in his old room, looking exactly like it had before the movers had arrived and packed everything up.

"How can this be?" he asked, a little frightened, yet fascinated. "Is it real?"

"Of course it's real." Jeffrey stood beside him. "In our world, you can have whatever you want...whatever you can imagine. That's what I meant when I said you don't have to feel so lonely anymore. You can be wherever you put your mind. It's even better than playing make-believe because, here, whatever you think about can actually exist. Go on; step inside your old room. Everything's safe. I'll walk in with you, if you want."

Cory reached up for Jeffrey's aged hand. His skin was cold, hard in spots with calluses, his bones protruding against the fragile skin. They walked into Cory's old bedroom together. The screen door remained open, as if caught on a breeze. He glanced back and saw Jeffrey's family sitting around their kitchen table, watching them. They smiled and waved. The strange man, Leonard, gave him a 'thumbs-up' salute.

"Is that neat, or is that neat?" Leonard called.

Cory let go of Jeffrey's hand and slowly walked around his old bedroom. He touched his bed covers; they were real. He felt the solid boards of his floor beneath his feet. There was his window, which had overlooked his old street. He ran to it, peered out, saw some of his old friends playing, and a neighbor hauling a can of trash to the curb.

"Hey! Eric!" Cory yelled through the window. The boy named Eric paused in his playing and looked around himself, confused.

"He might hear you, but he won't see you," Jeffrey cut in.

"Why not?"

"It *is* a secret. We only show our secret to special people who are willing to visit us. Now...that new girl you met today? Gina is her name. She lives up the road from you."

"How did you know that?" Cory felt a whisper of unease roll over his skin. "Do you know her?" He supposed Jeffrey would if they'd all lived in the same neighborhood for a while.

"Yes," Jeffrey continued. "Shut the door for a moment; then open it again. You'll see her playing on her swing. She's outside, swinging by herself in her back yard."

Cory pulled the screen door shut, then slowly opened it again, watching the regular yard fall away, to reveal Gina moving back and forth like a pendulum on her swing. She looked quiet and lonely.

"Why don't you go say hello? Don't stay too long; just pop over and let her know that you haven't forgotten her. Ask her to stop by sometime."

"What happens if this door shuts while I'm there?" Cory asked.

Jeffrey smiled. "Nothing. You just open it again. However, I'll hold it open for you. You'll be able to see me standing here, but she won't—because she doesn't know about the secret yet. I'll wait for you to come back. Go on. Try it out. You'll see how much fun it is to be able to do whatever you want, whenever you want."

Cory hesitated, then stepped into Gina's yard. He stood for a moment, smelling the night air, seeing his own house in the distance. He felt a little heady with vertigo, yet alive with an adrenaline rush.

"Gina," he said. He watched her whirl with surprise, to stare at him.

"What are you doing here?" she asked.

It *was* real. He glanced back and saw Jeffrey smiling his approval. He allowed himself to stay for a few minutes before Jeffrey motioned that it was probably a good idea to say goodnight and come back. As he returned to Jeffrey's porch, he saw Gina run after him, then stare through him, as if she couldn't see him any longer.

"Cory?" she called.

"Hurry back," Jeffrey called. "You'll see her tomorrow."

CHAPTER
17

"What do you think of that?" Jeffrey asked as they returned to his kitchen. "You can see anything in the world when you come to visit us. And you get your favorite ice cream."

"It's pretty neat," Cory agreed. "I just don't understand how it can be."

"All answers will come in time. For now, just feel happy. We love company. And look: your ice cream hasn't even melted while you were gone."

A voice came to them all. Cory recognized the sound of his mother calling.

"Cory? Cory! Answer me."

"She's standing at the bottom of her stairs," Ruth intoned from above. "Best send him along before she starts looking again."

Jeffrey stood. "Let's hurry you back before your mother starts worrying.

Cory spooned the last of the ice cream into his mouth and set the bowl on the table.

"Did that like a champ," Leonard cackled, opening a long thin silver box and extracting a dark-papered cigarette from its interior. He lit it with a metal lighter that elicited a long, orange flame. "See ya around kid. Night visits are always easier; your parents won't try to stop you if they're sleeping." He gave Cory a wink. "We're always here. So is the ice cream."

Cory stared at him. He wasn't sure how he felt about Leonard.

"Madeleine's not interested in you," Cory blurted. He wasn't sure what made him say it. Leonard inhaled deeply on his cigarette, held the smoke, then blew a series of smoke rings into the room. One of the smaller rings passed through a widening, fading loop. He grinned.

"That so? You know women better than me? Are you a ladies' man?"

Madeleine looked almost pained. She clasped her hands and stared down into her lap.

"Cory!" Louder, closer.

"Better hurry," Jeffrey rushed him along.

They passed the room that matched Cory's in his new house. Ruth sat in a wooden rocker, rocking the baby to sleep. The rocker's runners made soft creaking sounds along the wooden floor.

"Bye, Ruth," Cory said.

"Oh, you'll be back," she crooned, "for the best strawberry ice cream in the world. Won't he, Maddy?" The baby rested upon her shoulder. They hurried past the other bedrooms. Shapes of people lingered in them, their backs to the door, their conversation muted. One of the men turned to glance their way and Cory felt a burst of shock when he recognized the face of the dead man from the barn. He wasn't all busted up here. Weird.

He and Jeffrey reached the bathroom and stood in front of the mirror. It looked solid. Cory reached with one hand and felt it. It was hard and cold.

"I can't go through," he told Jeffrey.

"Do you want to go through?"

"I have to get home."

"Then set your mind and touch it again."

Cory stared at him.

"Go on," Jeffrey said. "She's halfway up the stairs now."

Cory sighed and touched glass. His hand pushed through what looked and felt like gelatinized water.

"Easy as pie. If she asks why you're in here again, tell her the other bathroom was being used and that you couldn't wait."

"Okay. Thanks for the ice cream."

"Not so lonely anymore?"

"No, sir."

"Good boy. Come back soon."

Cory almost fell through the sticky substance of the mirror, crawling hands-forward across his parents' bathroom counter. He thudded to the floor just as his mother's footsteps reached the doorway of the spare bedroom.

*   *   *

"Cory? Are you in here?"

"I'm just finishing up on the toilet." He quickly undid his belt, flushed the water in the bowl, and edged towards the bathroom doorway. His mother inched into the room.

"What are you doing in this bathroom again?"

Cory felt his face flush. "Chris or Cole was in the other one and I had to pee."

He saw his mother let her breath out. "I'd rather you not come into this room."

"It's just a room," he said. "I needed to go badly." He heard Chris and Cole's movie playing along the hallway and prayed that one of them *had* used the other bathroom recently, otherwise he wouldn't be sure what to say. He wanted to tell his mother about Jeffrey and his family, but something made him hold back.

"What's that on your face?" she asked. She wiped his cheek with one finger and he saw a bit of reddish-pink liquid on her fingertip.

"Candy," he lied. "I was just eating some of my candy."

"Sticky-faced kid," his mother laughed. "Smells like strawberry. Hang on." She returned to the spare bathroom and paused, looking around.

"What?" he asked her. "I flushed."

"I know," she said. He saw her move back to the bathroom and look at the mirror. His heart sank. What would she do if she saw Jeffrey standing on the other side?

"I don't like that mirror," she said. "I usually like antiques, but I don't care for that one. Your father and I will look for a new one next week. There's just something about it…"

He felt a teary sense of panic come into his throat.

"I like it," he said.

"Well, I don't. It's too old, filmy, and frankly, a little creepy." She ushered him along the corridor. "You don't want to watch the movie with them?"

He shook his head.

"Then come back outside with Dad and I. We're roasting marshmallows."

They walked towards the top of the stairwell. As they started down, his mother ahead of him, Cory glanced at his bedroom. Jeffrey stood inside the doorway, watching him. He winked and put his finger up to his lips.

"You did good, Cory," he mouthed silently. "She's not ready yet." Jeffrey slid back behind the wall. Cory paused. Was the guy going to be waiting for him in his room when he came back?

His mother heard him stop and looked around. "What?"

"Nothing."

"Come enjoy some marshmallows and the campfire."

His father pushed marshmallows onto the end of a long wooden skewer and nodded for Cory to sit near the campfire. Cory took a seat, his thoughts scattered. Things at Jeffrey's house still didn't make sense to him. But he understood that adults held more answers than kids did and that Jeffrey or one of the others would eventually explain how solid mirrors could turn soft like putty and how they could live in a house whose entrance Cory could not see except in the bathroom mirror. He sat woefully, aware that his parents watched him, their eyebrows raised to each other over his sullen mood.

CHAPTER
18

The doorbell rang the next morning. Chris answered the call, wearing a pair of baggy pajama bottoms and a loose rugby t-shirt. He saw a skinny adolescent girl who stood a foot shorter than him, looking up at him from the front step.

"Is Cory here?" she asked.

"Yeah. He's up in his room. Go right on up the stairs and turn to your right. It's the first room along the hallway."

He watched her with curiosity as she stepped into the foyer, her head twisting around to take in the house. Her eyes were a wide, clear blue and she looked a little daunted by the place.

"What?" he asked her. She stopped her staring and turned to look at him.

"Is there something wrong?"

"No," she said. "It's a big house."

"Too big, if you ask me," he said.

"Do you like it?"

He shrugged. "It's okay, I guess."

"I wonder if you'll like it later on."

"Why wouldn't I?" *Strange little girl.*

"I'll go find Cory," she said and scooted up the stairs away from him.

Chris returned to the parlor where Cole was playing a video game. Their parents had gone into town to buy groceries and wouldn't be back for several hours. They'd been instructed to stay home until their parents got back.

"Who was that?" Cole asked, somewhat bored. He scored another two points, his thumbs working magic over the controller.

"Some girl looking for Cory."

"Cory? He scores a chick before we do? No way!"

"She's hardly what I'd call a catch. Scrappy looking little thing. She walks in and looks around the place like she's never been inside a house before."

"Maybe she lives in some shitty apartment or trailer," Cole yawned. "Who cares?"

They heard the girl's voice mingling with Cory's upstairs. Chris got up and shut the door to the living room to tune them out.

* * *

"He's not dead."

Gina stared at him. "Yes, he is. He smashed his head on the barn floor and he died several hours later. My father was one of the people who came over here to help when his wife ran outside, screaming."

Cory sat in the middle of his bed, cross-legged. Gina sat on his rocking chair, watching him.

"You were the one who told me that this place has things happen in it. I saw him. I was in the barn loft and he crawled up the ladder to talk to me. He had guts leaking out of his head and he told me to watch my footing."

Gina looked intrigued, but scared.

"Maybe my story scared you and you just imagined it. Why did you come over so late last night?" she asked. "And how did you get back to the street so fast?"

Cory's mouth worked. "Can you keep a secret? You can't tell anyone. You have to promise me."

"Sure. What is it?" She sat forward, fascinated, excited.

Cory got up and gently shut his bedroom door so that Chris or Cole wouldn't overhear them. "My family doesn't know about it yet. We have people who live on the other side of our house. They're really nice...well, a few are kind of strange, but most of them are nice. One of them is an old man named Jeffrey. I went over yesterday and met them all. I had ice cream there—the best

I've ever tasted. They said I could invite you over, if you wanted to visit."

Gina stopped rocking. "*Where* next door? Is it the Wilson's over there?" She pointed to the house to the right, the one with the kids' toys in the backyard. "There's no old man there."

He glanced at his bedside clock. It read a quarter after ten in the morning. They'd have enough time before his brothers would call him down to lunch.

"No." Cory felt a little impatient. "I'd have to show you. It's really neat. Follow me, but be quiet. I don't want my brothers or parents to know about it yet." He opened his door and motioned Gina to follow him to the spare bedroom.

Gina hesitated, then stepped after him.

"Why is this room still empty?" she whispered.

"Because it's going to be the spare bedroom and my parents don't have any furniture for it yet. I want to show you something."

He walked ahead of her until they both stood in front of the big, hazy mirror. She looked at herself, then glanced at him. When her head turned, her reflection didn't move with her, but Gina didn't see it. Cory jumped a little.

"What?" Gina asked and stared at herself. "Why are we in here? It's a big old mirror. What's so special about it?"

"There's a house on the other side of it. I saw the guy in the barn, in that other house. He's not dead in there. He's fine. He looks like he never had an accident."

He saw Gina's mouth twitch a little, as if she wasn't sure whether to laugh or mock him.

"In *there.*" She nodded at the mirror. "How can he be inside a mirror?"

"Touch the mirror," Cory urged her. "This is the secret. I've been over there twice. They're pretty neat. I just don't know how you can walk through a mirror."

Gina looked dubious and frightened.

"Touch it!"

She leaned forward, tentative, until the tips of her fingers pressed hard against the mirror's smoky surface.

"So, I'm touching it," she said. "Now what?"

He felt disappointment and embarrassment that nothing had happened. He pressed one of his hands against the glass and felt it resist: hard, cold.

"Okay, so we're both touching the mirror," Gina said. "What's this got to do with people who live somewhere inside your house?"

An idea came to Cory. "Take my other hand."

She blinked. "Why?"

"I don't know. It just feels like the right thing to do. If we each touch the mirror and hold onto each other, it's like it makes things more powerful."

"What are you talking about?" she asked, but did as he requested. Her free hand went through the glass with a soft squelching noise, the sound of icing being squeezed from a linen bag, and she disappeared up to her shoulder. At the same time, Cory's right hand did the same thing. In the next instant they felt themselves lifted and sucked forward so that the front ends of their bodies were inside the room Cory recognized as Jeffrey's lavatory. The air in here was cooler, sharp, while their legs remained in the other side, floating in the air of Cory's house, which was warm and humid.

"What's happening?" Gina screamed, her face registering terror. She squeezed Cory's hand hard, wrenching the bones together. Then, they came all the way through as if birthed, and fell to the floor on Jeffrey's side.

"Ow'! I've hurt my knee..." Gina rocked back and forth, pressing her left knee, her face crunched against tears.

"It's okay. We're here."

"*Where* are we?"

A woman's soft voice answered them from the next room.

"In our house. It's so nice of Cory to invite you over. Are you okay?"

Ruth stepped into the small room, her crisp grey skirt matching her jacket, a fitted outfit cinched tightly at the waist. Sharp black shoes with laces and thick heels adorned her feet over heavy-looking hosiery. Her dark hair was swept up in a 'do that looked gelled into curls near her cheeks and her lipstick was a fresh, claret red. Gina stared at her, forgetting about her knee.

"You look different," Gina said. "You don't look like everybody else."

Ruth laughed. "And neither do you. We all look like ourselves."

"I didn't mean that," Gina interrupted. "I meant you don't look like people from our town."

Ruth studied her, then reached a hand out to help Gina up. "I've lived in this town all my life, just like you have."

Gina hesitated, then reached and grasped Ruth's hand. Ruth gently hauled her up from the floor. "I'll get that cleaned up for you. Come downstairs. We have plenty of that strawberry ice cream, Cory."

Cory went to follow and saw that Gina wallowed behind.

"We can come back soon. We go back the same way we came in—through the glass."

"I don't understand," Gina's voice trembled. "It doesn't make sense. How can we walk through something solid?"

"It's only solid until you touch it. Then it changes."

"*How*?"

"I don't know. But you don't have to worry, and they told me that, when I'm ready, they'd explain why things work like that here. Come on. You're with me. We'll be fine."

Her lips trembled, but she followed him and Ruth who waited in the upper corridor, her mouth curled in an amused smile.

* * *

The doors to the bedrooms were shut this morning, probably because everyone was sleeping. Ruth ushered them down the stairs.

"This house looks exactly like yours, except it looks like something from long ago. And *where* is this part of the house anyway? You can't see it from outside." Gina twisted her head to take it all in.

"I think it's inside our house," Cory said.

"But it has windows."

"It has an outside, just like yours," Ruth said. "You saw it last night, Cory. You stepped into our yard. It's a grand place, Gina."

"Why can't we see your place from the street, then?"

"You'll eventually understand why," Ruth said.

They reached the kitchen, which was empty of others this morning.

"Take a seat and I'll get you some of that ice cream." Ruth left the room.

Gina sat beside Cory, moving her chair closer to his. "I don't know if I like it here," she whispered. "It feels weird. It's like being in an old movie in black and white film. You know, how people dressed and talked from a long time ago. My parents rent them. They like Humphrey Bogart and Lauren Bacall."

"Who are they? Why do they rent stuff like that?"

"They're actors. I don't know," Gina stared around the kitchen, at the high wooden cupboards and an old stainless steel stove with copper doors and lids. "My father says his parents always watched them. He grew up watching them."

Cory lost interest. "This place is full of antiques. They must have a lot of money."

Gina shook her head. "My ears feel full, like when they get water in them and when you breathe in..." She took a deep breath. "It feels almost like I can't get enough air into my lungs. I don't think I want any ice cream. I'd like to go back to your house."

Ruth returned, carrying two bowls piled high with pink ice cream.

"Just eat some to be polite," Cory whispered.

"Where's Jeffrey this morning?" Cory asked. "Everyone's gone."

"Everyone's out doing what they're supposed to be doing," Ruth said. "We lead busy lives. I stay behind to look after the baby. Someone has to, you know. Enjoy."

"Ruth?"

Ruth paused in her step. "Yes, love?"

"Can I show Gina what Jeffrey showed me last night? Out there?" He motioned at the back porch and its odd screen door, which displayed a brilliant summer day of greenery on its other side. He saw Ruth hesitate.

"I suppose," she said. "Jeffrey is usually the one who likes to do that." She cocked her head as the baby cried upstairs. "I'll be back in a few minutes. Don't go too far through that door." She hurried away quickly. Gina watched her go. She didn't touch her ice cream.

"She has a baby?"

"I guess so. She's always holding it and taking care of it."

Gina sat quietly. She prodded at the ice cream with her spoon. She watched it and noted that it didn't melt, not even after what felt like minutes passing.

Cory ate a few mouthfuls, then put his spoon into his bowl. "I'm not as into it today. I hope she doesn't mind. If my mother was here, she'd tell us to eat it all, just to be polite."

"I don't want to touch it."

"It isn't poison. I had some last night, and I'm still here." Cory shook his head at her. "You don't have to treat them like this. They may like old stuff, but everybody's different."

"Something about here isn't right," Gina whispered. "I feel like she can hear us talking, even though she's upstairs. It feels like we're being watched."

They glanced around.

"You want to see something neat that Jeffrey showed me last night? This is the real secret part."

"I don't know if I want any more secrets," Gina said. "I want to leave."

"We will, but you have to see this first." He took her hand and led her up to the screen door.

"It looks like your backyard, only different." Gina peered around herself. "I don't get this. How can it be a house inside a house, but it has a yard that we can't see from your house? I feel like I'm in a dream. Let's go back."

"Okay, we will, but this is the best part."

Gina's breath became fast, scared. "Hurry. I'm afraid that if she comes back, she won't let us go home."

Cory waved his hand. "Ruth won't hurt us. Imagine your house," he told her. "And your yard."

"Why?"

"Just imagine it in your head. We'll both think of it at the same time, okay? Just do it."

She sighed. "Okay, I'm imagining my house."

Cory opened the screen door and they saw the front of Gina's house, its flowers looking parched in their window boxes, her bicycle lying on its side on the front lawn where she'd left it the night before, her mother sitting inside the small, screened porch, reading a paper and drinking a cup of tea.

Gina's mouth fell open. "Being here is like being awake in a dream."

"Come on. We'll walk over to it." He took her hand and led her down the steps and onto the street directly in front of her house. She stooped, reached down and touched the road; her finger came up dusty.

"I can't believe this," Gina said, except now she sounded a little more excited and less scared.

CHAPTER 19

"I don't want my mother to see me," Gina said. She scooted behind a cluster of trees on her neighbor's lawn. Cory ran with her, giggling. The neighbor, a heavy middle-aged woman, paused in her lawn watering to glance around.

"Hi, Mrs. Dylan," Gina said. The woman didn't answer. She stood with water issuing from the end of her hose, her face confused.

"What's wrong with her?" Gina asked him. They watched the water hit the side of her house, soaking a window and creating a muddy current in the soil of her garden.

"I don't know. Let's go." They ran between the two houses until they reached Gina's back yard where her swing set waited.

"How can you just step out from someone's porch door and be all the way over here?" Gina wanted to know. "What kind of a secret is this?"

"Beat's me, but it's too cool. Jeffrey showed me this last night. I even got to go back to my old house. I was in my bedroom, looking out my window at my friends playing in the street."

"That's impossible."

"I swear, it's true. We can go back and you can imagine something else if you don't believe me. You'll see for yourself."

"Let's go inside for a minute. I'd like to get a drink of juice. You thirsty?"

"Yeah."

They let themselves in through the back door of Gina's house. A large orange cat lounging on a kitchen chair stood up on all fours to hiss at them, its hair rising into a ragged tuft along its back. It took off into another room as if it had been doused with water.

"What's with your cat?" Cory asked.

"That's Bobbins. He can be weird at times."

They let the back door shut softly behind them. Gina took two small glasses from the cupboard and filled them with orange juice. They gulped the liquid down.

"Gina?" Her mother called. "That you, hon?"

"Yeah," Gina said. "I'm going back out to play."

"Gina?"

"Yes!" Gina yelled, irritated. "Let's go back out, otherwise she'll find an excuse for me to stay in."

They stepped out, leaving their glasses in the sink and making their way over to the swing set.

"At least swinging will give us some breeze." Gina settled herself onto one of the swings, taking it higher and higher each time. Cory didn't feel much like swinging. He took a seat on the one next to her and twirled himself around, allowing the chains to interlock, then unlock again.

"We should head back there soon," he said.

"We can just walk up the road to your place."

"I think we need to go back through Jeffrey's house first."

"Why? I don't like the place."

"I think it's the only way to get back to my house."

Gina laughed. "You just walk up the road and in through your front door. I don't want to go into their house again. That woman...her lipstick almost looks like blood."

Cory rolled his eyes. "I think they're just lonely for company."

"I'd still rather not go back there. Maybe they're magicians or something."

"Maybe." They watched Mrs. Dylan drag her garden hose along the side of her house. "That would make some sense."

* * *

Linda Dewar placed her teacup on the table and listened as the back door of her house open and shut. Her husband, Rod, was at work. It had to be Gina, back from the library, although the reading group was to be going on for another hour. Perhaps her daughter had become bored. It happened sometimes. All these years later, she wished she'd had another baby, someone who could have kept Gina company. Too late now.

"Gina? That you, hon?"

Silence, other than the impression that someone had just stepped inside the house. She stood up. "Gina?" She saw their cat, Bobbins, fly towards her, moving in a curve around the stairwell, his tail thick like a section of fire hose.

"What's gotten into you?" she mumbled. She stood by the door, looking in through the screen at the dimness of the corridor. She swore she'd heard the back door open and shut. She let herself inside. A delicate shiver danced up both arms, lifting the hairs along the skin as if something in the house was different. Linda made her way into the kitchen and glanced around the room. It was empty.

"Gina? I heard you come in." She waited, then irritated, moved towards the hallway, wondering if the girl had gone upstairs to her room. She caught sight of dishes in her clean sink. She walked over. Two small glasses with remnants of orange juice sat there. She'd just washed up all the dishes before she'd gone out onto the porch. So, Gina had come in with a friend, gotten drinks, and they'd left again without saying hello. She wondered who Gina'd brought home. She didn't have many friends. Occasionally, one of the kids from school might come around to watch a television show or to work on a homework project during the school year, but mostly, Gina was alone, a quiet girl who spent a lot of time reading, playing out in the yard by herself, writing in journals and tinkering on her computer. Sometimes it made Linda feel sad. She loved her daughter more than anything else in this world. The fact that the child was growing up so fast made her feel teary at times. She walked back to the stairs and called her. "Honey, are you up there?" Silence. She sighed and climbed the stairs. She found Bobbins crouched beneath a basket chair at the far end of the hall. He hissed again and dashed past her, growling.

"What has gotten into you?" she asked him. The cat tore down the stairs, his growl a low whimper. On impulse walked into Gina's bedroom, which faced the back yard. It was a small room with an angled ceiling. Her daughter's bed sat kitty-corner to the higher wall, its comforter decorated with several big, colorful cushions and some of Gina's favorite stuffed animals. A soft cover book lay, spine-up, in the center of the bed. Linda walked over to see which one it was: one of the *Twilight* books. She smiled. The girl was smart, pretty, but shy. Who knew what she'd grow up to be? Sometimes, Gina'd talked about becoming a teacher. She was bright with words and ideas and she possessed a vivid imagination. She was too preoccupied with ghost stories, vampire stories, and tales of the eerie. The girl was drawn to the topic of the macabre. It wasn't Linda's idea of reading material, but then, Gina was her own person. The book brought her mind back to the boy who'd shown up at the house yesterday afternoon. Cory something. Quiet young fellow, but living in that house! It gave her a chill. Even when she'd been Gina's age, that house had come with a history.

She and her girlfriends would walk past it on their way to school because the fields behind it had once contained a footpath. And then odd things had begun to happen on that footpath when she had been fifteen. A couple of girls had complained about strange men appearing on the path behind them, asking them to come over to the house and visit some time. One of the girls had been groped and the man who did it had never been found or charged. The girl, a kid Linda remembered by the name of Amy Dickson, had told the police that the man who'd grabbed her had been old. Old as in elderly the police had wanted to know? No, Amy had insisted; he'd looked old, like he'd been from another time. The police shook their heads, but had conducted a search around town for any man of that description. They'd written her statement off as the imagination of a hysterical young woman.

But Linda remembered one time when she'd walked home from school alone along that path. It had been autumn, late

October, and the house had risen up in view, stark against the backdrop of half-bare trees, its many attic windows peering in all directions, their glass and frames staring at her like an ephemeral beast. She'd paused to stare, curious about the house, but afraid of it. It had been one of those times when the house had sat empty between its last fated residents, waiting for another sucker to purchase it. She'd stared at its vacant windows, wondering about its empty rooms; how the shadows would elongate as the sun slid past them on its apogee from dawn to dusk. How anyone's footsteps would echo through its corridors and against the starkness of its high-ceilinged, empty rooms. Its basement would be a damp whisper. Its attic would be a held breath. She and the house watched each other. Ridiculous, she'd thought. Houses can't stare.

But this one could.

She'd felt its eyes on her and she'd picked up her pace, moving past it, glad when its trees finally cut it off from view. She'd crossed the road to keep her distance from it, but before it had fallen out of sight, she'd glanced back. She'd seen an old man's face framed in one of the upstairs bedroom windows, watching her. He'd smiled and waved.

She ran home, sobbing, because she'd recognized the man in the window. His name had been Jeffrey William Hopkins, and he'd been born in that house. He'd lived and married in that house. He'd killed his daughter Madeline in that house for trying to run away with a man whose character Jeffrey hadn't liked, but he'd had money and power as one of the town's bankers and his jail sentence had been relatively light. He'd also been involved in gambling and criminal elements, and he'd owed debts to questionable characters, one of whom had gone missing shortly before Jeffrey had died. His wife had disappeared and he'd told everyone around town that she'd left him. Her body was later found buried beside her daughter's, beneath soil inside the barn, five feet beneath one of the animal stalls. He'd perished in that house, falling down the long set of stairs leading from the second story to the main floor. She knew his face because her parents had talked about him, the stories around him; they had kept newspaper clippings with his photographs.

He'd been dead for over twenty years on the day Linda had seen him smiling at her from that empty upstairs bedroom window, and when he'd waved, she'd felt the scratching dry skin of his fingertips linger against the nape of her neck, a gentle pulling to come over...come visit.

She'd not walked that way to school again and, years later, she'd almost wept when her own husband had purchased this house, on this street, just up the road from *it*. He didn't believe her story. He said she'd probably seen some real estate agent checking out the condition of the house, and nothing more.

"It's just a rambling old house with a bad reputation, thanks to Hopkins," he'd told her.

"Why do bad things happen to all the people who move in there then?" she'd demanded.

"I don't know," he'd shrugged. "Shit happens to people."

"In the same house?"

"Maybe it just draws unlucky people. It's not our problem, Linda. We don't live in it."

"Thank God for that," she'd whispered.

CHAPTER 20

Linda picked the book up off the bed and set a loose piece of paper into it to set the page location, then laid it on Gina's desk. She stood in front of the window, and glanced into the brilliant morning yard, her mind on the gardening she still needed to do out there. She saw both swings on the swing set move back and forth, except they moved in opposite directions from each other. Then they gradually stilled. She felt a burst of sour panic cut through her stomach.

"Gina?" she called through the open window. That same melancholy feeling crept back to her, the kind that always made her want to cry whenever she thought of Gina growing up and moving away from home--this idea of somehow losing her daughter to the world out there. She was growing up, her little girl was. Almost a teenager. She had to cut her a little more leeway. As for the swings, maybe a storm front was coming in, pushing hot air ahead of a cooler system behind it. She peered at the sky, which was a transparent blue. The bad feeling wouldn't go away.

"I love you," she said into the room. Okay, time to stop being weepy, as her husband would call it. Go downstairs, wash the two glasses and decide what she would make for supper. Linda headed back down, noting that Bobbins now crouched beneath the living room sofa, his eyes wide, dark orbs, watching her. He hissed again.

* * *

Mrs. Dylan dragged the section of garden hose along the side of her house towards her back yard, her head tingling with a headache that had come on suddenly while she'd watered flowers in her front yard. For a reason she could not explain, the day had become *different* at that moment, as if the air had thinned and had denied her enough oxygen. She'd felt the passing of a pocket of cold within the humidity, an anomaly of temperature so out-of-place that she had been unable to swallow for a moment. She would have sworn she had heard someone call her name. It had been the voice of a child. Then the cold passed and the heat of the day flooded back. She continued watering, trying to place the owner of the voice. A child...a girl.

"Gina Dewar," she said. "That's who it was." The voice had sounded as if it had come from right beside her, and yet the girl had not been anywhere in sight. Mrs. Dylan had glanced up at the Dewar house. The girl must have called a greeting as she had passed by a window. As for the cold pocket, who knew?

She reached her backyard and started the hose again, determined to get the remainder of her flowers soaked before the sun peaked at high noon. The sound of creaking swing chains from the Dewar yard caught her attention. Ah...the girl was out back, playing before the day became too hot.

Mrs. Dylan went to wave hello to Gina. She saw two swings moving on the set, one lifting high, rolling back, lifting higher, then back again in a steady arc. The other spun around like a top, paused, then retrograded in the opposite direction. She saw dust kicked up from the ground where feet may have dragged, had children actually played there. Yet the swings moved by themselves. She gripped her hose, feeling its hard rubber press into her palms. That acute stab of cold air returned, enveloping her like a cloying bubble. A miasma of something rank, a placid yet definite stink of something gone *off*, drifted past. She thought she heard children giggle. The swings continued to move despite the breathlessness of the day.

"Oh my," Mrs. Dylan uttered. Nausea hit her hard in the gut. Colors faded, bird calls muting. Then, the swings slowed and came to a stop. The day held its breath. She sensed movement ease past her and with it, the cold trailed out again. She stared at the swing set whose seats hung like nooses from their chains. She had not fainted in years, but she felt the blackout coming with the speed of a train. The last thing she saw before everything went dark was the detail of her lawn rising up to greet her face; the minutia of grass blades, some yellow and parched, some green. She hit hard.

* * *

Mrs. Dylan paused in the yard and stared at them, but didn't say hello. She seemed to look through them.

"What's with that old lady?" Cory asked. "Is she not all there?"

"She's usually friendly." Gina raised a hand and waved, then used her feet to dig into the lawn to stop her movement. Mrs. Dylan didn't acknowledge her.

"Maybe you should tell your mother."

"If she sees me, she'll want me to stay in. She thinks I'm at the library. She won't let me go back to your place. We should go before my mother sees us out here."

They ran alongside the yard, past Mrs. Dylan. Gina waved again and the woman still refused to acknowledge her. She stood there, gripping her hose, her eyes focused on the Dewar back yard.

Cory laughed at this. They hurried towards his house.

"Let's try to just go back to your place," Gina said.

"All right."

They reached the mid-part of the road; Cory hit something that felt spongy, like slamming into a volleyball net, only cool, sticky. It sent him sprawling backwards, his arms looping to regain his balance.

"What the hell?" Cory said. He could *see* the road clearly, and yet something in the air would not allow him to pass beyond this section of the sidewalk. Gina stopped beside him, her face curling with unease.

"What's wrong with you?"

"I just walked into something." He put his hands up and felt the air grow thick and solid despite its transparency. It felt like he was pushing his hands into cold, wet steak. He pulled his fingers back and they were coated in a translucent slime. "What's going on here?"

Gina put her hands up now too and the look on her face told him that she felt the same thing. They moved over onto a lawn and the clamminess followed them like an invisible border.

"It won't let me go past it." He glanced at her and felt fear for the first time. They could see the world around them, yet could not reach anything beyond this point. A woman moved towards them on the sidewalk, walking a small dog. When the woman and dog got to within twenty feet of them, the dog, a beagle, went crazy. It yanked back hard on its leash, howling and shrieking as if it had been attacked. The woman cried out in surprise.

"Marty, what's the matter with you?" the woman admonished the dog, doing her best to drag the animal forward along the sidewalk, but the dog dug in with its paws, its collar cinched into its neck, its skin bulging and its eyes bugging with terror.

"Of all the stupid things," the woman continued. "There's nothing there."

She could not encourage or force the dog any further along the sidewalk. She ceased yanking on the leash and glanced around her for whatever may have set the animal off. She pulled the dog across the road to the opposite sidewalk and, although Marty the dog still balked, his hair bristling along his spine, he allowed himself to be pulled forward from that distance. Once they had moved further up the road, the dog visibly relaxed.

Gina and Cory watched them go.

Gina put her hands up. "It's still there. Why could that woman walk through it, but not us?"

"She crossed the street." Cory let a car drive by, noticing it passed through the veil without a problem, and ran to the other sidewalk. He tried to push through and it still resisted. He walked back slowly, running his hand along something unseen yet resilient the entire way.

"There's a wall between us and there," he whispered. He turned and ran in the opposite direction, back towards Gina's house. He got to within the same distance and encountered another invisible barrier. He began to cry. "Something's wrong. It won't even let us go back to your place." The wall of resistance spread across both sides of the road for as far in either direction as they'd attempted to feel it.

"Why did it let me go home?" Gina asked.

"I don't know. We got there but your neighbor didn't see us. That woman with the dog didn't look at us, either."

Gina's fists clenched in terror. A young man wearing a set of headphones and pushing himself along on a skateboard started up the road towards them. He passed through the first barrier without a problem. Cory ran towards him.

"Hey, can you help us? Can you bring us up the road there?"

The teenager slowed a little on his skateboard, letting it roll to a stop. He pulled an earplug from one ear and seemed to listen to the day. He didn't look at Cory.

"Hey!" Cory screamed and grabbed the boy's right arm. The boy pulled his arm back and stared at his skin, his expression puzzled. He rubbed at his skin, shook his head, pushed his earplug back into his ear and kicked the skateboard back into motion. He passed through the second barrier.

"Nobody sees us," Cory whispered.

Gina fought tears. "I think it has something to do with your neighbor's house...by walking through his back door, things have changed. What kind of a secret is it? What does it do?"

Cory felt horror. "It's magic. It can bring you anywhere you want to go. You just have to think about something and you're there."

"But the world isn't the same as it usually is," Gina wept. "Everything's different. Nobody sees us. I want to go home. I don't want to play anymore." She went to run back to her house and hit the invisible wall. She tried to run across the road several times, only to be bounced back by something she couldn't see.

"Let me go home!" she screamed, hysterical. She stamped her feet, her arms rolling, her fingers clawed and tearing at nothing. "I want to go home! I *want-to-go-home!*"

"Okay, okay!" Cory reached her and grabbed her. She spun and slapped him hard in the face. "Why the heck are you hitting me? It's not letting me out either!"

"This is your fault! You wanted to show me that house. You wanted me to keep this secret. I just want to go home…"

Cory could barely breathe. "You wanted to see my house."

"And your house is *fucked,*" she shrieked, frenzied. She hyperventilated.

"We'll go back the way we came. That's what we'll do. We'll just walk by Ruth and go back through the mirror."

"I don't want to see that woman again."

"Just take my hand. We'll go together. It's the only way."

"Who's Jeffrey?"

"He lives in the house. He's the one I met first."

"How does the door work?"

"He never told me how it happens. He just showed me," Cory said. "And he comes into my house. He walks in any time he wants."

"That's not right," Gina said. "Neither is his house. Do you see their house from here? There's your place…where's his?"

They saw nothing beyond Cory's house.

CHAPTER
21

Jeffrey's porch door waited in its sunny garden. They approached the door and it swung open to greet them. Jeffrey stood on the other side, his face neither frowning, nor smiling. He watched them.

"You showed Gina the secret," he said.

"I don't care about your secret. Gina wanted to go home, but it wouldn't let us out of the street. Nobody sees us...even when we talk to them."

"Their world is so much slower and denser," Jeffrey sighed.

"Whose world?" Gina asked.

"*Your* world." Jeffrey's face grew solemn. "There are some things that I'll explain, but not yet. Here, you can stay up as late as you want, have as much candy as you want. You don't even have to go to school anymore. It can be better. Come and have some ice cream. It is a hot day out there. We can talk a little more inside."

"I don't want to talk," Gina said. "I'm leaving."

"Well, my darling," Jeffrey told her, "I don't think that's going to be possible."

For the first time, Cory smelled something on Jeffrey, a kind of mildew. It puffed off him, from his breath, his skin, his clothing. His lips looked a little too purple in this light, his skin pale, his veins a turbulent blue beneath waxy flesh. His old man jacket and pants hung from his body like rotting curtains in an abandoned hotel Cory had once seen on a highway.

"Come on, Gina," Cory said, pulling her by the hand and hauling her past Jeffrey, through the kitchen and up the stairwell.

Their feet pounded as Jeffrey came up behind them, slowly, but with determination.

"You'll find that she won't be able to pass back through the glass," Jeffrey said. "We've made the decision. No one will believe you if you try to tell them what happened, Cory, no matter what you say. When she disappears, you will look guilty. They will know she came here to see you...to *your* part of the house. You'd best keep your mouth shut."

They ran to the spare bathroom and reached the mirror, seeing Cory's house on the other side. They slapped their hands against the mirror, screaming.

"Mom! Chris!" Cory beat his fists alongside Gina's, feeling the mirror remain solid. They heard Jeffrey step behind them.

"You can go. She cannot. Accept the fact, boy."

Ruth hurried into the room, holding the baby over her shoulder. "What's the commotion here? You woke the baby."

Gina turned and stared at the infant in Ruth's arms. Her face went white.

"That's the baby that died a few months ago," she whispered. "It's not your baby."

"You can see the baby is happy enough. And so will you be." Jeffrey reached for her.

"Don't touch me!" Gina shrieked, kicking at him.

Cory renewed his fury against the mirror. Suddenly his fists went through and he felt himself lifted and over something; his upper body protruded out into his parents' house. He felt Gina grab his ankles, the sound of her voice piercing, begging him to wait for her. He hit his face, biting his lip and drawing blood. Dazed, he stood up and whirled to stare at the looking glass. It had solidified but he could see a remnant of Gina and the others behind the glass, wisps of pale shadow just behind the silver lame. He heard the baby cry and heard Ruth croon to her, echoing like a discordant melody in his head. He heard Gina's nails scrape against the opposite side of the glass as she sobbed, and then all went quiet. She was alone, caught in the secret, a place of never-ending strawberry ice cream, of a yard and road that allowed you restricted travel, of a place that let you see people who lived in the town, but who could not see you. Cory ran, sobbing. He reached his bedroom and threw himself onto the bed, panicked, drawing the comforter up to his neck. His gaze roamed over to his beside clock. It read 10: 20. They had been gone a mere five minutes.

"Gina," he whispered. "Gina."

He heard footsteps coming up and saw Cole.

"What's the matter?" Cole asked. "You sick or something?"

Cory ran to him, sobbing, and clung to him. Cole, shocked, brought a hand down to caress his younger brother's hair. "What happened?" he asked. "Did you fall? Why are you bleeding? Where's your friend?"

Cory couldn't speak. He could only cry.

* * *

Cole called his parents who were just leaving a specialty grocers and about to head home.

"Cory's hurt himself," he said. "He hit his mouth and he's crying, but every time I ask him to tell me what happened, he won't. I think he tried to play in that dumb waiter again and fell, and he's afraid he'll get in trouble for it."

"Oh dear," Tanya muttered. Her voice faded a little over the cell phone. "Are his teeth okay? Are any loose?"

Cole paused. "I'll look." He had Cory sitting on a stool in their kitchen, a cold cloth held against his mouth. "Mom wants me to check your teeth to make sure you didn't hit any of them."

"I didn't," Cory tried to not cry, but couldn't stop.

"Let me look anyway." Cole checked his teeth, then picked up the phone again. "His teeth are okay, but he's really shaken up." He glanced at Cory. "I know you were playing in that stupid chute again and this time you fell. Why don't you just admit it?"

"I wasn't," Cory said.

"Right."

He listened to something his mother said, nodding. "Okay. I'll tell him."

Cole put the receiver back into its cradle. "Mom says you're not going to be punished for being in there, but you're not to go in there again, for any reason. Dad said he's going to seal the thing shut because of this." He pulled the cloth away from Cory's mouth. "Try to stay out of trouble, okay? You want something to eat?"

Cory shook his head.

"Cat got your tongue, huh? I think your friend went home because she had more sense than you do."

Cory cried harder.

"Maybe you should go lie down for a while. You're acting like a big baby." Cole rejoined Chris in the parlor. Chris had come in to see Cory, shaken his head and said 'brat' and had gone to sit down again, more amused by Cory's swollen lip than anything else.

CHAPTER
22

Linda Dewar began to worry when the time slid past one o'clock in the afternoon and Gina hadn't returned home. The reading group at the library began at 10 AM sharp. It ran until noon. Even if Gina had stayed an extra few minutes to peruse new books, she should have been home by now. The library was a ten minute walk away. Linda found the library's phone number on a sheet of paper and dialed the place. A woman with a perfunctory voice picked up at the other end. She recognized it as belonging to one of the book matrons, Glenda Peterson.

"Glenda, it's Linda Dewar. Yes, nice day. Is Gina still at the library? Has the reading group gone on longer than usual?"

Linda gripped the receiver. "What do you mean she wasn't there? She specifically told me she was on her way to the group!" Linda listened, her stomach clenched. "Can you look around and see if she's in the building? Maybe she didn't attend the reading group, but she's probably sitting at a table, reading. Sometimes she does that."

She waited while Glenda put the phone down. Seconds dragged into minutes.

"Come on, Glenda," she hissed. Finally, she heard the receiver scrape the desk as Glenda picked up again.

"She's not here, Linda. I never saw her. She may have come in and left without my noticing her. I'm sure she'll arrive home soon."

"I hate it when she does this," Linda said.

"Well, they all do it, especially towards the teenage years," Glenda's crisp voice softened a little. "Does she have a cell phone?"

"We haven't let her get one yet," Linda said. "Now I wish we had."

"I'm sure everything's fine," Glenda assured her.

"I guess," Linda said. She put the phone down and stood for a moment, her knuckles pressed against her mouth. A small mouse of panic ran from her gut to her throat.

"One day you'll know what it is to be a mother, Gina," Linda spoke aloud. "Until then, you don't know how much a parent can worry."

* * *

Gina dug her feet into the floor as Jeffrey and another man with odd slicked-back hair and what looked to her like gangster clothing pulled her along, out of the old lavatory and back into the upper hallway.

"You'll enjoy being here," Jeffrey told her. "It'll just take some getting used to. You can go home and see your family any time you want. You just cannot live there anymore, and they may not see you. Still, it's really the best of both worlds."

"I want to see my mother."

"Oh, you can," Jeffrey crooned. "You can walk into your room, sleep in your bed...play on your swings. You can even hug your mother."

"Then let me go."

"Okay," Jeffrey agreed. "You can let go of her, Leonard. She'll be fine."

The man named Leonard released her other wrist. "We have to finalize her being here; she's still in limbo."

"I know that," Jeffrey said. "I'll take care of it."

He walked with Gina back to the screen door. "Go home and see your mother. Just come back later." He opened the screen door and the yard swept out and twisted around the house towards the street.

"I won't come back," Gina told him, her voice shaking, but her anger determined.

"I'm afraid that isn't a choice." Jeffrey remained calm. "Go. You'll feel better when you see that you can visit them any time."

Gina ran through the yard and around the house. She felt the quality of the air change, from cool to warm again and suddenly she was out on the street where she and Cory had been caught within folds of something invisible. She held her arms in front of her, afraid of slamming into the sticky air again, but felt nothing. She reached the opposite side of the street from her house at the same moment she saw her mother step out onto the front porch, her face tight with worry.

"Gina!" her mother called. "Gina!"

Gina soared into the road and felt herself step through something sticky at the same moment a car turned a nearby corner, picking up speed. She felt the air around her ripple, a kind of elastic shiver and something silky moved over her skin, a membranous sensation of having slipped through a firm, wet hole. She stumbled out of it and into the center of the road as the car bore down on her, its brakes screaming. Yet her eyes remained caught on her mother's, those few seconds as her mother's mouth opened in a pre-scream, her hands flying up to her face, Then the car hit and everything went dark.

* * *

Gina woke up. She became aware that she sat in the middle of the road. She stood up and stepped back to examine the accident scene. She saw her mother huddled over her body, blood pooling everywhere, her mother wracked with sobbing. A man squatted beside her mother, his face wet with tears.

"She just appeared in the middle of the road suddenly. I don't even know where she came from. I never saw her run into the street. I'm so, so sorry."

He and Gina watched Linda rock Gina's body. Gina brought a hand up to her own cheek and felt her skin. Her skin was dry, clean, unhurt.

"Mom?" Gina said. "I'm okay. I'm right here."

Her mother didn't look up. She kept rocking the body and weeping.

"Mom!" Gina yelled. "Look at me!" She touched her mother's shoulder and felt the warmth of her mother's blouse and skin against her hand, but still her mother did not look up. A police car pulled into view.

"Mom!" Gina screamed. "I'm right here!"

She felt someone place a hand on her shoulder and spun to see the old man, Jeffrey, standing beside her.

"She'll ache for a long time, and then she'll come to an acceptance. You will always be able to see her any time you want, but she cannot see you. That's part of the secret."

"Why can't she?" Gina wept.

"Because you're no longer mortal. Theirs is a temporary state."

"What does mortal mean?"

Jeffrey patted her shoulder. "It means being alive in a body."

"But I'm right here, in my body."

"In a different way."

Something dawned on her then and she looked at him with horror. "Am I a ghost? Are you what's wrong with that house? Is that your secret?"

"I don't see there being anything wrong with it. Like I said, you can go home and live in your house there any time you please. You don't have to live with us, but you can always visit."

"Why did you do this to me?"

"We need your energy. Things get a little...stale...after a while."

"I hate you," Gina told him.

"Oh, the new ones always feel that way at first, but eventually even that wears off and becomes very old," Jeffrey said. He started back towards his yard. "When you get bored at your house, you can come back over to visit. We even have a library, filled with books. And we'll always see and hear you."

She watched him walk away, whistling. She turned back to the scene in the road. She watched her mother being held by a police officer while another covered her body with a blanket from the trunk of the cruiser. More police cars arrived and officers held the gathering small crowd back. Her father arrived home, frantic, weeping. Gina sat with her parents on their front porch and watched them sob, saying her name over and over again.

"I'm right here," she kept telling them. Frustrated, she went inside and up to her room, where she lay on her bed and stared at the ceiling. She glanced at her books, toys, games. She was home, but she wasn't. For now, this would have to do. She supposed it was better than not being able to be here at all. Fear gripped her. She listened to her parents sob, knowing that all her words of assurance that she was still very much alive would not be able to reach their ears. She'd thought that dead meant *dead*; that you became nothing, gone, out of existence. This was not the case. Things were just different in a way she couldn't comprehend, but at least it wasn't as bad as she'd thought it might be. She just wished they could see her, feel her touch, and hear her. She got up one more time and went to them. They sat huddled on the sofa, weeping over old photographs of her as a baby, as a younger child.

"It was all great times," she said, sitting beside them. She saw her father glance up and around the room for a moment.

"I thought I heard her voice," he wept. "Oh my baby, come home to us."

"I am, Dad," she said. She sat next to them, comforted to be near them, but frightened by the void she now felt in this new, odd world.

* * *

They heard the car hit something that sounded like a dull thud akin to a sandbag being struck. Robbie was sitting on the back porch, trying to leaf through a magazine but unable to concentrate. He and Tanya had questioned Cory about the dumb waiter chute when they'd gotten home, but he'd not said anything. He sat before them, visibly frightened and too quiet. In Robbie's mind, Cory almost looked like he was trying to fold himself up inside himself, the way some flowers will draw their petals in during cold evenings.

"You can't go in that chute. It's an eight foot drop to a concrete floor in that basement, do you understand me?" Robbie had urged him. "I know it seems like a fun place to play because it's different, but you could be killed. That is the second time you have done this. Why?"

Cory had looked at him with cry-swollen eyes, his arms wrapped around his knees, hugging himself. "What's it like to die?" was all he'd said.

Robbie and Tanya had stared at him.

"What a thing to ask!" Tanya had exclaimed. "I don't want you to find out by falling in that thing. We are sealing the door. That's the end of it." She'd glanced at Robbie, shaken her head, and had gone downstairs to fix herself tea, upset with the whole affair.

"What's really bothering you, son?" Robbie had persisted. "You seem so...I don't know...out of it. Is something else on your mind? Did you and your new friend have a fight? She'll get over it and come back over, I assure you."

"I don't want any friends coming over."

"What? Why not?"

"I just don't."

Robbie sighed. "Listen; you'll make more friends. Life will get better. Just give things time. Will you look at me please?"

Cory raised his eyes again and Robbie saw something in them; something that reached out and twisted at his heart—unadulterated terror in his boy's eyes.

"Everything is fine, son. Everything's good. Gina will be back."

The kid looked like someone who desperately wanted to believe his father's words, but couldn't. Robbie reached out and hugged his son to him.

He went downstairs and found Tanya sitting at the counter, drinking tea, her face tense.

"Chris says Gina came over to see Cory around 10 AM this morning and that they'd been playing upstairs. He says the kid must have gone home without them noticing. He and Cole were in the parlor playing video games. Cory must have gotten bored and gone exploring for something to do after she left. However, he's really shaken up by something. He won't say what."

"That thing he said, about what it might be like to die...why would he ask us such a thing?" Tanya's eyes searched his. "Why is he even thinking about it?"

Robbie waved his hand. "He fell in the chute. It scared him. He might have thought he was going to die. He's had the morning to think about it. He's at that age where the realization that we *can* die has sunken in."

"The loss of innocence," Tanya said.

"Yeah. Something like that." Robbie rubbed his eyes and plucked a magazine from the counter. "I'm going to go sit out on the porch. Join me?"

"I will. I'm going to take some chops out to thaw for supper first."

"See you out there," he said, standing up and giving her a kiss before leaving the room. He'd been out there only ten minutes when the sound of a collision came to him. He stood straight up, dropping the magazine. Whatever had happened had occurred near their house. He was halfway through the yard when he saw Tanya run from their front door, her hands coming up to her mouth at the sight of something having taken place further up the road.

*   *   *

Cory wept. He cried until no sound came out of him and still he wept, his body shuddering. Tanya held him to her.

"It was a terrible, terrible accident. Her poor parents. It is okay, honey. I'm so sorry you had to see that." Cory had come out of the house behind Tanya, drawn by the sound of a woman screaming: Gina's mother. They'd been some of the first people to run towards the woman named Linda Dewar and to try to comfort her until the police arrived. Naturally, she had been inconsolable, rocking her poor baby's body in her arms while the shocked driver had sat down hard in the road, pale, broken by what had just occurred.

"She just appeared in the road out of nowhere," he kept repeating over and over again.

When the police had arrived, only then did Robbie walk back home, carrying his emotional son and consoling his broken wife; what they had witnessed was any parents' worst nightmare. It was one of those horrible moments when no amounts of 'I'm so very sorry' phrases could help in any way. The mother of the girl had just had her heart ripped out of her life; her daughter, Cory's new friend, gone just like that.

Robbie had stumbled home, numb, and had collapsed on a chair in the kitchen. Cory lay against Tanya on the sofa, both of them weeping, weeping, weeping. The day grew dark around them despite its sun and heat.

"What is dead?" Cory asked. "What is it?"

Robbie had come into the room to sit with them. He and Tanya stared at each other. He didn't answer for a long moment and then, when he did, he chose his words with care, aware of how they could impact on a young mind.

"It's when the person is no longer in their body."

"Where do they go?"

Robbie wiped at his mouth, distraught. "I don't know, son. Nobody knows for sure. Most people believe in heaven, a beautiful place where we all go when we know it's our time to go home. Why did you ask about it earlier?"

"I don't know," Cory wept.

Tanya wrung her hands. "It doesn't matter. He couldn't have foreseen this. That poor woman. That poor family. Gina was their only child."

"What's home like in the place where you go when you die?" Cory persisted.

"I don't know, Cory. I guess it can be anything you want it to be. It's supposed to be very beautiful. I'm sure that wherever Gina is now, she's being looked after."

Cory looked at him. "Does that place have a screen door on its back porch?"

Robbie stared at him. "What? What do you mean?"

Cory looked away again, broken. None of it made any sense. The day felt like jelly slipping into a dark drain.

CHAPTER
23

Night; the sky was clear and star-studded, the house silent other than the occasional chirrup of a cricket outdoors. The clock in their stove face read 3:18 AM, its digital numbers square and glowing an unearthly green. It had taken Tanya and Robbie a long time to fall asleep, but finally they had after they'd each gotten up and checked on Cory and then the other boys, almost afraid to leave their children.

Cory slept on his back, his tears dried, his mouth open. He'd cried himself to sleep.

Now something woke him up, a soft sound beside his bed. His eyes came open in the dark. He became aware that someone stood beside him, watching him. He rolled his head around to see who it was, expecting it to be his mother or father checking on him.

Gina stood there, her face whitewashed by moonlight. She wore the same clothes she had earlier today before she'd died. She wasn't cut up and broken like she'd been at the accident scene. She was wholesome, clean, although her face looked sad.

"I miss you," she said. "They can't see me at home. Only that other family can and I don't like them that much. They keep telling me that I'll get used to them. I won't. Can you come over, please?"

She walked away from him and up his hallway towards the spare bedroom. Cory watched her reach the open doorway of the empty bedroom. She paused to look back at him.

"They want you to come over," she said, her voice more inside his head than resonating along the corridor. Then she entered the bedroom.

Cory hesitated and glanced into his parents' room. He heard his father's snoring. His mother's form was still. Cory padded past his brothers' rooms and into the empty bedroom. Gina had already gone ahead to the mirror.

He reached the mirror and stood in front of it, seeing his reflection only. He touched the glass.

"Gina?" He kept his voice to a whisper. Okay; so maybe this was death. At least she was still here for him. He brought his hands to the glass and pressed hard with his fingers, feeling for the familiar 'give' that he'd come to expect. Jeffrey had always let him come and go and now that he knew he could still see Gina, he felt better.

The glass didn't give.

"Gina…"

Then he saw her standing on the other side of the mirror, her fingers pressed to match his on the glass, her eyes wide. *Help me.*

"What do you want me to do?" he asked. He saw a dark form step behind Gina and yank her back from the mirror. A scuffle followed and both forms disappeared back into the depths of Jeffrey's house. Cory hadn't been able to discern if the form had been one of the men or women.

"Leave her alone!" Tears rode the edge of his voice. He pounded his fists against the mirror and felt the glass give a little. The first inch of each fingertip sunk into what felt like warm, silver mud and then his hands pushed through. He'd bring her back into his parents' house. She'd be safe here. He felt certain of it. First, he had to find her. Then he'd tell his parents the truth about Jeffrey and the mirror and he'd make them stop.

* * *

From the time her first son had been born, Tanya never fully slept without one ear 'attuned' to the sound of her children at night. Call it a mother's instinct, but she'd awaken over the softest cough or the sound of a footstep making a board creak along a floor.

She sat upright in bed, the tone of Cory's voice resounding on the edge of her sleep. She hurled the bedcovers back and hurried into his room. His bed was empty.

"Cory?" She flipped on the light switch in the bathroom. Not here, either. She poked her head into Cole's, then Chris's rooms to see if Cory may have slipped into bed with one of his brothers, something he'd do from time to time when he'd had a nightmare. Both of her sons were asleep, but Cory wasn't with either of them.

She stepped back into the corridor, heart pounding, wondering if he'd gone downstairs. She was about to start back that way when she heard Cory say, "Leave her alone."

Tanya ran towards the spare bedroom. She hurried into the bathroom in time to see the lower half of her son's body hanging out of the antique mirror.

Hanging out of it, as if he were caught within it. Her mind tried to comprehend the impossible, but this was overridden by her maternal impulse to protect her son. Something had him.

"Cory!" she screamed. She grabbed onto each of his ankles and tried to pull him back. She saw the mirror ripple as if it were made out of thick, almost plasticized lead that adhered to the contours of his body like rubber. She heard other footsteps rushing along the corridor, heard Robbie's, then Chris's voices calling her name.

"In here!" she screamed. Something had Cory on the other side; it hauled and Cory sunk into the mirror to just below his knees, slamming her hard against the bathroom cupboard as she tried to secure her grip on him. The light in the bathroom flashed on and Robbie rushed in just as Cory was pulled again, his ankles sliding from her grasp. She, Robbie, and Chris stood in shock and horror as they watched Cory's feet slip from her and through the glass, to disappear. The mirror shivered, like a pond recovering from a dropped rock, and went still.

"What the fuck?" Robbie shrieked as Tanya fell backwards, sobbing. Robbie pounded on the mirror, his fists raining blows over every segment of the glass. It was solid, unbreakable, unrelenting in any way.

"Where is he?" Chris yelled, panicked. "How can he go through glass? What is that thing?"

Robbie picked up a clay vase of dried flowers and hurled the vase against the mirror. The vase exploded into fragments, but the mirror did not crack.

"I should have known something was wrong with it. I should have said no to this house," Robbie raged.

"What do you mean something was wrong with it. What are you talking about?" Tanya sobbed. "Where's our boy?"

Robbie was on the counter now, his hands yanking at the mirror frame, doing everything in his power to disengage it from the wall. Chris joined him, followed by Cole when he'd come into the room. All three of them used their weight and strength to try to pull the mirror and frame from the plaster, to no avail.

"It...must be riveted...to the fucking plaster," Robbie panted, his face a mix of rage and fright. He examined the frame. "They've used screws and anchors to secure the thing."

"You saw what I saw," Tanya said. "He went *through* the damned glass!"

"I know that!" Robbie screamed, regretting it when he saw her recoil, but they all stood there, a family in their new home, having witnessed their youngest son and brother enveloped by what was supposed to be a solid object—a man-made piece of framing and wood and silver-backed glass. It had not swung open. It had not cracked. It had *softened* enough to allow him passage through, and then had re-hardened immediately. No law in physics, no sensible explanation existed that could account for what they'd just seen occur.

"It has to come off," Robbie said. He rushed downstairs to the kitchen where he'd placed his electric screwdriver from a job earlier in the day and carried it back to the bathroom. He got onto the counter and proceeded to remove screws that held the heavy mirror to the plaster wall. Chris and Cole got on each side and carefully wedged the mirror away from the wall. There was nothing behind it except old plaster and dust. They hauled the mirror onto the bathroom floor and examined every facet of it;

sides, back, along the edges where glass melded with the frame. There were no buttons, levers, or anything that could possibly explain what they all knew they had just witnessed.

"Where is he?" Tanya wept. "Where's our Cory, Robbie? I feel like we've all woken up in some kind of a carnival fright house. First that little girl. Now this."

"He has to be in the house," Robbie said. "I know what we all *think* we saw, but there has to be some kind of rational explanation."

They looked at each other.

"I know what I saw, Rob. I had his ankles as he slid through," Tanya said.

"I saw him go through the mirror, too, Dad," Chris added. "We all did." He shuddered, his face waxen and horrified as he stared at the looking glass. "How do we get him out of there?"

Robbie slid down against a wall and sat on the cold tile floor. "I don't know. I don't understand how such a thing can happen, so how the hell can I reason how to undo it?"

"You do think he's in the mirror," Tanya prodded.

"I don't know how, but his absence has to do with that mirror, yes."

"And what if we can't find him?"

"Then we call the police."

"And how are they going to get him out of there? They won't believe us! They'll have us all locked up as insane or charge us with a missing child." Tanya glared at him, tears streaming along her cheeks.

"Do you have any better ideas?" Robbie yelled back.

"Mom, Dad, calm down," Cole cut in. "Fighting isn't going to find him. Chris, come with me. We'll take a look around the house again."

"I'm not going anywhere," Tanya wept. "I'm going to be here for him when he comes back."

She watched them step out of the room. Robbie glanced back at her.

"I love you. I don't know what's going on, but things are going to be okay. We'll find him. When he's back, we're getting rid of that mirror."

* * *

4:12 AM. Tanya sat with the light on in the bathroom. Robbie and her two older sons had conducted their search, to no avail.

"I can't get my head around this," Robbie said. "I'm sure there's some kind of pathway in a wall somewhere, something that has created some kind of optical illusion with this mirror. He opened something, crawled through...we just don't know what."

"I suppose," she said. "I'm sure if I wait here, he'll come to me."

"I'm going to look around again," he said. "I'll be back in a few minutes."

A soft wind picked up. She sat with her housecoat pulled over her knees, looking at her reflection in the mirror, looking for any sign of her boy.

"I know you have him in there," she told the mirror softly. "And I'm getting him back. I will not stop until I have him. Understand that. If I have to destroy you to get him, I will." She got up and shut off the overhead light, throwing the room mostly into darkness, other than from the glow of the moon. Now her form looked like a shadow in the looking glass. She felt fear, but more so, the determination of a mother. She also felt guilt because she'd wanted an old house, this house, and now their son was missing and in such an extraordinary way that no one in their right mind would believe them about what had occurred. That was the hard part. Telling anyone about this would only make things worse. They had to find him themselves. And then they would leave. As much as she thought she'd love this house, she couldn't live here any longer, even with this mirror removed, and ever look at this room the same way again.

Frustrated, she got up and using her hands and wit, she felt along each of the room's walls, starting with the wall that had held the mirror. She moved from wall to wall, locating nothing. She tried the taps in the tub and sink, thinking perhaps they hid some other purpose, some kind of spring that would open a magic door. Nothing occurred. Angry, but exhausted, she went back to her spot and sat down again.

A young girl stood in the center of the mirror's glass, looking directly at her. A dull yellow light appeared behind her, as if she stood in a room that was backlit. Tanya gasped and recognized her at once. It was the girl who'd died in the road yesterday: Gina Dewar.

"He's here," Gina told her from the other side of the glass. She appeared scared and kept glancing back over one shoulder. "Your mother's watching us. She can see us."

"Gina?" Tanya stood up and rushed towards the mirror. "Honey, are you alive?"

"Shh! They'll hear you!" Gina motioned for someone to step forward. Cory came into view in the glass, to stand beside Gina.

"Cory...how did you get in there?" Tanya whispered. "Try to touch my hands."

She placed her hands on the dark mirror and felt only cold, smooth glass. "How did you go through? Tell me."

"I just touch the glass and wait and it lets me through," he said. "Gina's here, Mom. She's real."

"But they took a lifeless body away," she said. "How can this be?"

"Put your hands up to mine," Cory said.

Tanya did as she was told, matching her hands to Cory's. She forgot about calling her husband or other sons. She felt afraid that, should she disrupt the moment, she'd lose him again.

"Now just wait," Cory said.

Then she felt it; a warm, almost tingling sensation along the palms and undersides of her fingers. Suddenly the glass gave with a gentle sponginess and her hands broke through so that she felt hers clasp Cory's. She let herself fall forward, a gentle almost flowing motion, and within seconds found herself stumbling into a room that looked very similar to the one she'd just left, only darker, older in style. She stood up and brushed herself off, then grabbed Cory to her.

"Oh my God, I didn't know what had happened to you," she hugged him to her. She became aware of the girl, Gina, standing nearby. She stared at the girl. Tanya shook her head and reached out to grasp Gina's hand. Gina stepped back.

"I can't go with you." She glanced over her shoulder again.

"This has to be some miracle," Tanya said. "You're alive and your parents are going to be so happy to see you. You must come with us."

"She can't, Mom," Cory said. "The house won't let her out of here. Only me."

"What *is* this place anyway?" Tanya looked around herself. "It looks like our house only older..."

"It is your house, sort of," a man's voice said behind them. Tanya whirled. Gina rushed towards Tanya. Tanya went to hug her and felt the girl move through her like a cool breeze; it was the feeling of an electrical current passing through her body and then Gina was gone.

"Where did she go?" Tanya yelled.

"Back to her parents," the old man stepped into the room. His facial skin was the color of wet plaster, his lips almost ruby, his eyelids bagging over his cheekbones. His neck bulged with what looked like a large, dark growth from one side and when he turned his head to regard Cory, Tanya saw that a piece of wet bone protruded through the bloody skin. She fell back, pulling Cory with her. This man looked like he was dying.

"Cory, come now," she said, turning back to face the mirror. She saw her bathroom through it, opaque and gradually brightening as the morning sun came up.

"He can go home, if you wish to stay instead," the man told her.

"I will not, and neither will my son. Who are you?"

"His name's Jeffrey, Mom. He lives here with his family."

"Our family grows a little at a time. New people are both invited and required. I am not making a request. Him or you."

"What exactly are you asking of us?"

Others moved into the room behind the man named Jeffrey. There were women dressed in an era from the forties and fifties, one of them only in her early twenties. A gunshot wound allowed blood to trickle from her forehead into small rivers along her face."

"Madeleine!" Cory called out. "What happened to you?"

"She didn't listen," Jeffrey said.

The other woman in a sharply fitted suit carried an infant dressed in a pale pink sleeper. "All this commotion all the time," she complained.

"Be quiet, Ruth," Jeffrey snapped. "We're in the middle of a negotiation. So what will it be, Mrs. Parker? You or your boy? One of you can leave, and one can stay. I'm being generous."

A man with a fedora and a loose suit jacket extracted a cigarette from an antique cigarette case and used a matching lighter to bring it to flame. Tanya watched as the cigarette smoke furled *through* each of them, twisting and coalescing as if interwoven with them.

She understood, suddenly, especially the baby. The baby…realization dawned on her.

"You took their baby," she spat, frightened, yet disgusted. "You would stoop as low as that to a child and a young couple? You deprive another couple of their only child—that poor little girl—and now you dare to try and take my son?"

"Your son can go, if you stay. Or you both stay," Jeffrey said.

"We make lovely strawberry ice cream," the dead girl named Madeleine told them. "It's your son's favorite."

"And you can visit any place you want, any time, as long as you always come back," they all chorused, as if in a rehearsed speech. They stepped closer and she smelled them now; cloying, the under-aroma of things going soft.

"What you're doing is wrong," Tanya said. "You're killing people and you're depriving them of a rightful death. This isn't what death is supposed to be. You're a cold pocket of disease."

She felt a small hand come into hers just then; cold, not-quite-solid in the way a silk scarf might feel, and looked down. She saw that Gina had crept back and stood with her.

"I don't like this house," Gina said to her.

"I know, honey," Tanya said. She turned and looked at Cory. "Sweetheart, listen to me. You go back home. You go find Dad and your brothers. You stay with them. You tell them what happened. Go now."

"Are you going to come home too?" Cory asked.

"I'll always be with you," she said, doing her best to contain her tears. "Hurry now."

Cory stepped back to the glass and placed his hands on it. "I'll wait for you."

Tanya forced herself to smile as she watched her son climb through and disappear through the silver. Then she saw his form through the glass, on the other side. He stood up, disheveled, and called out to his father. A moment later, Robbie hurried into the room and she watched as her husband scooped their son up into his arms, jubilant.

"There you are!" Robbie cried out. "Where were you?"

"In the mirror, with Mom," he said, and she watched Cory point at the glass. Robbie's mouth fell open with horror.

CHAPTER
24

Tanya pretended to play their game. She held Gina's hand as they followed the others downstairs to the kitchen of this astrophysical house, its composition a dark vibration of its physical component's past, and she understood. It was an old house. It came with a history, some of its former residents not-so-nice. She'd gone to university before she and Robbie got married and one of her electives had been a metaphysical course, its study having focused on life-after-death ideologies. At the time, she'd seen the course material as somewhat nebulous, an interesting time-passer in an otherwise practical academic program.

She saw now that the discussion of lower astral levels had been correct. This house was nothing more than a sprocket of dark space along the subway line to a proper death, and fear could keep her here; fear or ignorance. She felt fear about leaving her family behind but understood now that all would come together again at a distant point like the stitches of pattern forming a cohesive fabric, if only she stood her ground and kept moving. Bring the girl and the baby with her, back to the place where they now needed to go. She would open the door and those with the desire to follow would do so. The others could stay behind in the place they had created—a diseased version of their former home with its dank shadows, needing the energy of new souls to fuel their own dim lights.

"And you say that, should I open that porch door, that the children and I will be able to go home?" she asked Jeffrey. She'd taken the baby from Ruth who stood in the background, looking a little lost and over-protective. Gina held her other hand.

"You can see your husband and sons anytime," Jeffrey said, a little cocky for her. "They just won't be able to see you. I consider it a good compromise. We benefit from your energy, and you get to live forever."

"Live forever," Tanya said. "Sure. So, you consider this home then?"

"Yes, we do," Jeffrey said, proud.

Tanya turned away from him. "Shall we go home?" Tanya asked the children.

"I can go see my parents any time, but they can't see me," Gina said.

"I know," Tanya whispered. "But things will get better, in time." She would have to allow the image of peace in her heart to override her fear, and they would have to keep walking. She shut her eyes for a moment and imagined the place that she'd always envisioned as Heaven: it didn't matter how you pictured it as long as your heart felt clear and good, and your intention was strong when you did so. She recalled part of the content of the course: *...for in the spiritual world, the mind creates reality. If you think fear, you will create fear. If you focus on joy, you will create a place of joy. This world consists of a higher vibration, ruled by thoughts and intent.*

She saw the yard stretch out ahead of them and began walking with Gina, while carrying the baby.

"I'm taking the children out for some air," she told Jeffrey. "We'll be back."

"Of course you will," he said.

"Cocky bastard," she muttered under her breath and kept walking. "He thinks I'm as ignorant as he is."

"You see that light at the end of the yard, near the road?" she asked Gina.

It looked almost like the rising sun, only whiter, larger, and it undulated a little.

"Yes," Gina said. "Where are we going?"

"Home," Tanya said. "Don't feel afraid. Just hold my hand and keep walking with me. It's a beautiful place with green hills and clear blue skies. Everything you could ever want is there, and everyone you have ever loved, or will love are there, or will be."

Gina nodded. "Yes. What about the baby?"

"We're all going home," Tanya said. "Gina, do you know anything about Heaven?"

"Only what my parents told me when my Grandma Dewar died last year. They said she waits for us in Heaven."

"Yes," Tanya said. "They were right."

They approached the light, which felt almost tropical, yet soothing, brilliant, yet not blinding. The town fell away from the edges of this light and from deeper in the light, first one, then another, and then another figure emerged and stepped towards them. Their ears buzzed a little.

Tanya felt Gina's hand stiffen around hers for a moment, then the girl let go of her hand and ran towards someone stepping towards her.

"Grandma Dewar!" Gina cried out.

Tanya wept with relief and joy when a great-grandfather came forward for the baby.

"Thank you for looking out for her," the man said, his eyes a kind dark blue.

"I'm always a mother," Tanya told him.

"Are you joining us?"

"I have something else to do first, and then I will."

* * *

"What is that mirror?" Robbie sat Cory on the edge of his bed. "I'm not angry at you, son. But Mom's gone now and we need to get her back. You have to tell me how that mirror works."

Cory cried a little. He thought of Jeffrey's words: *he can go home, if you wish to stay instead.* "He told Mom that I could go if she stayed instead. He won't let her go."

"*Who* won't let Mom go?"

"Jeffrey."

"Who's Jeffrey?"

Cory looked at his father. "I don't know. He's an old man who lives in that mirror, with his family. They invite new people to stay with them, but I didn't want to live there. It felt weird, even if I could visit our old house."

Robbie shuddered at the words. "What do you mean you could visit our old house?"

"When you go through Jeffrey's back door, you can imagine being any place you want to be, and suddenly you're there. Except the people there can't see you."

Robbie's forehead beaded into a sweat as new fright overtook him.

"And what did Mom say when Jeffrey told her this?"

"She told me to come home and said she'd always be with me."

Robbie's fingers tightened into clenched fists.

"Come downstairs with me. You're to stay right beside me at all times, do you understand?"

Cory nodded. "What's wrong, Dad? Mom will come back here. I always did, even though they didn't want me to go."

It was now almost 6 AM in the morning. Robbie didn't care about the time. He found Des Hawkins' business card and dialed the man's number, letting the phone ring until Hawkins' picked up.

"It's Rob Parker calling. I've had an incident at my house and now I want some clear answers out of you. Did this house ever belong to an old man by the name of Jeffrey or Jeffries?"

A long silence on the phone, then Hawkins said, "Yes, it did. Why do you ask?"

"There's a mirror in our spare bathroom, and something's not right with it," Robbie stormed.

"Jesus," Hawkins' said. "I'll be right over."

CHAPTER
25

Hawkins hadn't shaved and his eyes had the scared look of a rabbit in the road with a tractor-trailer bearing down upon it.

"He was the second owner of the house," Hawkins explained. He recited the story to Robbie. "His wife, his daughter, and finally him, the first two murdered by him, his wife when she tried to leave and he thought she might talk…as for him, some say it was an accident. Others around here say he might have committed suicide. A few even say he was pushed."

"Pushed by whom?"

"His angry family?" Hawkins' countered. "Yes, the house has a history. Nothing you can prove, nothing tangible that science can place a cool, laboratory finger on. People buy the place and something happens. Something that frightens them and they leave. Often, someone in the family dies. A crib death, a barn fall, a slip from a roof while laying shingles, a kitchen fire one time. I've sold the place twice. Other agents have sold it a few times. Most agents won't touch it. They won't even walk in here."

"So why do you keep selling it again and again when these things continue to happen?" Robbie forced himself not to yell. "Now my wife's missing. You may think I'm crazy, but our son somehow passed through that mirror in the spare bathroom. My wife had him by the ankles and he still *floated* through the thing. He doesn't understand how or why. He's just a kid. What is wrong with that mirror? Where's the hidden device that opens something near it?"

Hawkins' looked like he wished he was in a bar, throwing back tequilas.

"I don't understand the mirror," he said. "I know that other owners hated it. They would try to take it down, and it would go right back up on its own. They'd remove it from the house...one family even carried it out to the barn and left it there, and it was back up in the bathroom the next morning, fully secured to the wall. The woman with the baby, the last family, wanted the house put up for sale when the woman walked into that room with the baby one morning—she'd been rocking the baby and she heard voices in the room. Her husband was at work. As soon as she and the child looked into the mirror, she said she saw the faces of other people looking back at her and the baby. Someone in the mirror, a woman from another era said to her 'what a sweet baby.' The woman almost fainted as she ran from the house with the baby, terrified. Her husband coaxed her back inside. When he went and examined the mirror, he saw nothing; experienced nothing. He tried to convince her that she'd imagined things because of her fatigue being up half the night with a newborn.

"And then the child got caught between the crib mattress and the bars a few days later. They were hysterical, naturally. The woman kept ranting about how she could still hear the child cooing in that room, and how, when she'd go to see the mirror, she'd see the other woman holding her baby and saying 'Melissa's fine. She likes it here.' They put the house up for sale that same week. The woman had a nervous breakdown. She still thinks her baby is somewhere in this house."

Robbie fell back hard against the chair. He pulled Cory to him.

"Why did you agree to sell the house?"

"What else are we going to do with it, Mr. Parker? No family is going to walk away without getting their down payment back. I have no right to walk in here and burn it down or condemn it. Nobody does. You try talking about this stuff outside of superstitious gossip circles or séances and people think you are crazy. What would you have me do? The family wanted the house up for sale. They wanted to be gone, pronto. I did what they asked. And I know you're going to ask the same thing of me, aren't you?"

"I can't live here anymore," Robbie admitted. "Yes, we want to put it back up for sale, but I'm going to take my family out of here while we wait for it to sell. We'll stay with my parents. I don't even want our furniture. I'll auction it off. I want nothing that has been inside this house. It's wrong. It's evil. No one else should fall victim to it. What you're telling me confirms that, Mr. Hawkins."

Hawkins reached inside his coat pocket and extracted a package of cigarettes. "I'm going to step outside to have a smoke. I'll list it for sale this afternoon. You may take a bit of a loss on the property or you may just break even on your costs."

"I don't care at this point. I just want out of here. Now...what do I do about finding my wife? Where the hell in this house do people go?"

Hawkins' looked at him. "I can't answer that for you, Mr. Parker. I haven't a fucking clue and, frankly, I'm not sure that I would want to know. You might want to ask a psychic or a priest. No one's ever been able to get rid of that mirror."

They stared at each other.

"I'm sorry," Hawkins continued. "I'm just the real estate agent."

* * *

Hawkins was good to his word. He had the house listed for the same price they'd purchased it and a 'House for Sale' sign up on the front lawn by late that afternoon. Robbie signed all necessary paperwork. Hawkins was also right about the mirror. After Hawkins left, Robbie had gone back into the spare bathroom. The mirror was fully mounted again on its wall, as if it had never been pried loose.

"Did you two put the mirror back up, Cole?" Robbie asked his older sons. He looked at Cole, then Chris who appeared surprised.

"No," Cole said. "We never touched it."

"Neither did I," Robbie murmured. "We're leaving. You're all going to Grandma and Grandpa Parker's house this afternoon. The place is up for sale again."

"*What?*" Chris spat, his eyebrows raised. "Why? What about Mom? Where the hell is she anyway?"

"Because the place is bad," Robbie said. "We're moving. Pack what you need for the next little while and start loading it into the car. No questions asked. Just do it.

As for Mom, I don't know," Robbie said, "but I'm going to find her. In the meantime, you and your brothers will be away from here."

"You and she aren't having problems..." Cole asked. "Like marriage type stuff?"

"No!" Robbie exploded.

"Why would she just go away then?"

"She went into the mirror to get me," Cory said, matter-of-factly.

"Oh, for frig sake, more nonsense with that stupid mirror!" Chris fumed, spinning and walking away from the bathroom. "That is so stupid. It's a mirror, not a door. Is everyone going nuts in this house? You need your head examined, Cory!"

"You saw it for yourself last night," Robbie shot back as Chris bore into his bedroom. "You saw your brother's feet slide through!"

"I saw nothing," Chris yelled back. "It was a bad dream. We were all mostly asleep."

Cole looked at Robbie and his face registered both disgust and fright.

"What's going on in this house, Dad?"

"I don't know, son. I feel like I'm going crazy. I promise you, I am going to find your mother. You boys are staying with my folks. Let's get going. No more excuses, no more hesitating. Now!"

"Okay!" Cole scowled, but he and Chris began packing their bags.

"You stay right with me," Robbie hauled Cory along by his hand.

He called his parents next.

"Yes, for a few weeks, possibly longer until this place sells." He spoke firmly. "I know, I know, but the house was a mistake. I can't explain right now. I appreciate your being able to take us in. I'll tell you more when we get there."

He dropped the boys off just over two hours later. Chris and Cole stormed away from him, hauling their bags with them, refusing to look at him.

"What's wrong with the boys?" Doug Parker wanted to know.

"It's a long story, Dad. Keep the little one close to you. Do not let any of them wander off. Promise me."

"Robbie, what the hell is going on here? Are you and Tanya having...difficulties? Where is she?"

Robbie looked at the ground. He gripped the car keys in his fist, then forced himself to look at his father.

"I don't know where she is. I'm going back to look for her."

"Isn't she at the house?"

"Maybe," he said and walked away, ignoring the expression of confusion on his father's face.

*   *   *

Even with all the furniture in place, the house felt almost sticky with anticipation as he let himself inside. It waited. Somewhere in here he felt determined to find his wife, his love of over twenty years. He shut the door and did a cursory search through the basement, and then main floor, feeling watched as he did so.

"Tanya?"

Angry, he raced up the stairs, pausing to look at their marital bed where she'd slept beside him only hours earlier. His heart ached and his throat felt tight with panic.

He stepped into the empty spare bedroom and looked at the door leading to the bathroom. He saw a person's shadow move across the wall facing him and his hair stood up on end.

"Tanya?" He rushed into the bathroom, to find her standing in the mirror, clear as stones on a clean river bottom, facing him. She smiled at him, the same warm, enticing smile she'd always given him…the smile that had attracted him in the first place, and one hand up against the glass so that he could see her fingertips compress.

"I love you," she told him.

"Tanya…please come out of there."

"I can't, honey. Even they don't know I'm here right now. I got the children home safely—Cory's back with you; Gina is with her grandfather and the baby is with extended family."

"What baby?"

"The baby who'd died here; the ones they—" and here she nodded over her shoulder, "had taken for its fresh young energy. They are energy vampires. They take from the living to replenish themselves. It's a form of feeding and revitalizing."

"The Hopkins," Robbie said.

"Yes. They want to be here, in this house. It's a dark pocket between life and death. They killed the father after he killed them; shoved him down the stairs in this house, but the father's a control freak, even here. Jeffrey Hopkins. They've just re-created their own misery because they can't let go of it, and they're drawn to whoever lives or comes in this house. This mirror is their doorway between here and there."

"Then step out of the doorway!" Robbie pleaded. "Cory came back. He's safe with Chris and Cole at my parents' house. Just come home, sweetheart. Please."

He touched his hand to hers and for a moment, just a moment, he thought he could feel the heat from her fingers moving into his. She gave him that soft smile again.

"I can't," she said. "I'm already dead. I had to do it in order to save the children from them, otherwise they would have kept Cory, and Gina and the baby would have never been able to move into Heaven. I know you'll love the boys and raise them well, and I'll always be looking over you all."

"Tanya!" Robbie screamed. "What are you talking about? Then where's your body, if that's the case."

"Step outside and you'll see," she said. "I need to leave my body so that the law won't believe that I've just disappeared. I'll be following Gina and Melissa. I have loved ones there, waiting for me. My death will be deemed a terrible accident. You and the boys go on. I love you. I always will love you. When I'm gone, paint the mirror black. Use the paint in the basement. Paint it out and leave the house. You can't destroy the mirror. Cover it instead. You won't see me in it again. Go on…step outside to the front porch."

She faded out from the mirror, leaving only the silver glass reflecting the window back at him. Robbie wept, her words ringing in his ears. He hurried downstairs and onto the porch just as Hawkins' pulled up in his car again, another set of papers in his hands.

"I thought I'd bring you some copies of the listing agreement…" he stopped as the sound of glass smashing came from behind them. They both whirled in time to see Tanya's form plunge from the window that overlooked the loft in the barn. She hit the ground hard, bounced once, and was still.

"Holy shit!" Hawkins' exploded in horror. He stared between Robbie and the barn. "Isn't that your wife?"

"I came home to look for her," Robbie collapsed to the porch, his face crunching with emotion. "I just saw her in the mirror…"

Hawkins ran over to check on Tanya Parker. Robbie saw him lean down, feel for a pulse, then stand back up slowly, his shoulders heaving. He stared back at Robbie who sat, broken and beaten, on the porch of the house his wife had loved. He saw Hawkins' make a phone call. He sat numb, inconsolable as police and an ambulance arrived. He managed to give the same statement as Hawkins: she'd gone into the barn for whatever reason she'd had and must have slipped up in the loft—they both witnessed her fall. So did a neighbor in the next yard who ran over within the minute.

"What do you think she was doing up there?" an officer asked Robbie.

"Trying to sort things out," he sobbed. Only he would ever fully understand the truth of the statement.

* * *

His father came out to get him, and the two of them sat, crying, in the kitchen of a house once again up for sale. The police and ambulance had removed Tanya's body. Funeral arrangements had to be made over the next several days. People had to be notified. Robbie sat at the table, feeling ice grow in his chest, his eyes raw from weeping.

"How could this have happened?" Doug Parker asked. "She must have tripped on something up there; an uneven board, a clump of hay...my God. Abigail's comforting the boys. Naturally, they're hysterical. Come home. We'll discuss the furniture a little later."

"I don't want any of it," Robbie wiped his eyes. "I want nothing material that's been in this house."

"Dear, you'll want mementos when the worst of this pain passes."

"No!"

"Okay, let's just leave that for now. Come with me. You need family around you."

"Just give me an hour please. Let me sit with my thoughts for a little bit. I promise I'll accompany you then. I need some time to pack some clothes, gather any important papers..." He broke down, his head in his arms on the kitchen table. "Come back then."

"How do I know you'll be okay to be left alone?" Doug gripped his car keys, shaken and frightened.

Robbie almost said 'because I know their game,' but held his tongue at the last second. "I'm the only parent the boys have. I'm not going to let anything happen to me. One hour Dad. Please."

"Okay. I'll drive into town and get some groceries to bring home. I can barely function myself over this. One hour, son. I'm not leaving you alone after that."

CHAPTER
26

Robbie watched his father drive away, then he turned to face the house. Hawkins had returned to his office to list the property. The police and ambulance had left.

"I should burn you down, except I need my fucking money back to raise my sons! You're evil. You're all sick, you hear me? You're social fuck ups, even when you're dead! Murderers still, through a goddamned looking glass. I won't let you do it anymore. You took my wife. You took my heart."

He bore downstairs, Tanya's final words in his mind, and found a gallon of black paint they had purchased to touch up some wood paneling in the basement area. He carried the can upstairs with the brush and began his task: he started painting the entire surface of the malevolent mirror black. He coated it in a thick layer, and as he did so he saw *them* move forward from the other side, at first curious, then incensed.

"You took her, but you won't take anyone else," Robbie heaved. An old man, an old woman, two younger women, another man, what looked like a teenager...their forms like dark shadows, their presence as cold as an Arctic wind, whispering among themselves as to what he was doing

"You could be with her," the old man started to say and Robbie painted the last quarter of the mirror out, blocking them off. He heard them behind the glass, shuffling in there, the squeak of their fingers moving along the other side.

"As black as your souls," Robbie hissed. "I loathe you all forever."

He stood back and opened the window to allow a hot breeze to rush into the room. The paint began to dry in minutes. He left the mirror, looking like an ugly charred square on the wall, and retrieved clothing, important documents, money…and their box of photographs of them, as a family, taken over the last two decades. He shoved them all in a suitcase…turned, kicked the bedroom wall repeatedly until his foot ached…sat on the edge of the bed and wept…didn't care what Hawkins' thought of the mirror being painted. Robbie wondered if the next owners would remove the ruined mirror, only to find the ebony mess re-attached to the wall again on its own accord? It wasn't his problem. It couldn't be. He didn't blame the last couple for selling, or the families before that. He knew why. Self-preservation is a driving force.

His father arrived back as promised. Robbie locked the door, pocketed the keys to return to Hawkins later on, and drove away. They did not look back at the house as they swept past the 'House for Sale' sign freshly erected at the edge of the lawn by the road.

* * *

Hawkins' called Robbie and they agreed that an auctioneer would sell off the household goods; anything remaining would be donated to charity or trashed. The money from the auctioning would buy them new clothes and furniture. For now, Robbie told Hawkins, they had what they needed.

Hawkins pulled up to the again-empty house and left the car running so that he could attach a lock box with an entry key to the front door. It was his job as a real estate agent to take a walk-through, but he could not bring himself to do it right now. He attached the lock box and drove away. The day began to deepen towards dusk and as he glanced back in his rearview mirror, he thought he saw what looked like a small, greenish ball emanate from one of the house's chimneys and float towards the distant barn. He shuddered and stepped on the gas.

Night descended, this time with a three-quarters moon. In the darkened spare bathroom, the black paint had dried upon the looking glass. The mirror, an obsidian square that looked like the mouth of a mine shaft, shivered a little at this coating, cracking the freshly dried paint in spots. Paint chips, some as large as quarters, floated down to the counter and sink like chunks of soot. More loosened as the glass vibrated a little and soon a few widening spots of silver re-appeared. By the time anyone came in within the next day or two, all the paint would be off, a powdery mess that would have the agent cussing and cleaning up before the first showings would begin.

Jeffrey stood behind the mirror and peered through one of the widening silver holes. All they required was what they had always needed to see; who the next owners would be and which one might be most vulnerable. A kid was always easy. A mother very gullible. Every buying family usually had at least one of each.

Paint. As if that would have done anything to the portal. He smirked and shuffled back into the shadows of the house that mirrored the 'House for Sale,' knowing that time was on their side. So the woman had gotten away with the two young ones. They wouldn't make that mistake the next time; and there *would* be a next time on such a large house going for so low a price. Every time.

The End

Autopsy

Rolling gurney wheels make soft clicking noises much like
blood drops, trickling in increments along stainless steel drains
Reservoirs meant to capture the last tendrils of a life
Nail fragments, a dash of cartilage, sinew glowing rosy-white
beneath the merciless surgical lamp, the knife descends
Cuts
open, raw red zipper grinning, exposing minutia of flesh
Striations of muscle, musical notes helter-skelter along
bandwidths of bone
And entrails which spool out and over, bloating ribbons that
fall to the side, joining quivering liver and spleen
Filets of razor-thin memories laid upon the surgical glass
Life
is but a kaleidoscope of collected passing seconds
Death
is but the looking glass shattered into scattered fragments
Autopsy
A detailed glimpse of the many puzzle pieces
sewn tightly back together and buried deep with mortician's
thread

SMOKE
AND
LEAVES

By
Carol Weekes

Smoke and Leaves

I saw the outline of the carny rides as I drove past them, looking like black bones whose flesh had been picked clean. I should have just kept going on home, but something made me turn around and go back there. I needed answers. The show shut down at midnight each evening and they were here for another four days. My car clock read 2:14 AM. I'd worked until 12:30 AM and had hit a late night diner for a bite to eat, given my family had gone to bed hours ago. I felt eager to go home and check on them too—but first, I need to do this. We'd watch their line of eighteen wheelers pull into town, the sides of the trucks depicting florid paintings of the various acts of magic or illusion. Promotional posters would appear in windows, bulletin boards, stapled to telephone poles and blowing along the town's streets like oversized, garish stamps. And like a kid, always drawn to carnivals and wanting my son to experience the same kind of lurid thrill, I wanted to go. So we went together. It was a mistake.

I'm not sure what I expected to find as I turned onto the unpaved dirt road that led out to Barker's field where the carnival had set up their fairground this year. Their tents and trailers formed black pyramids and squares against the sky. I saw distant fires burning and knew that some of them would still be awake; warming their hands over heated oil drums and smoking cigarettes, maybe tossing back raw bourbon or gin straight from the bottle. On instinct, I shut my headlamps off and kicked the car into first gear so that I crawled along the road in the dark, using only the moonlight to guide me. I got halfway there and stopped, idling in the road, unsure as to whether I should proceed or just turn around and go home.

I couldn't shake the feeling I'd picked up after going to the carnival grounds last night with my little boy, this feeling that we'd been noted and followed by something eager, sinister, and hungry.

And I wasn't sure what I wanted to do about it. Ask them questions? Threaten somebody? I was fine until last evening, and then I'd felt as if I couldn't shake something an hour after we arrived at the fair. It had begun when Randy, my seven-year-old boy, had wanted to try his hand at some of the games in order to try and win a prize. Five dollars got us three tickets. He'd done well on the ring-toss and had won himself a bright pink stuffed gorilla in a cowboy hat with a plastic sheriff's badge, which had delighted him. Then he'd wanted to try his hands at the beanbag toss—the beanbags stitched out of odd, almost oily black cloth that had felt greasy when I'd touched one, and whose destiny had been the open, dark maw of a painted monster's mouth. The monster was some unidentified specimen with its black painted face looking like storm clouds and smoldering orange eyes. It had fingers depicted along the sides of the board in smudged tones, twisted, almost root-like fingers with charcoal, broken nails.

I hadn't liked the image at all. It seemed too ominous even for an adult-based form of entertainment, and certainly not for kids. But I'd bought the tickets anyway from a girl dressed up as a clown at a nearby booth and Randy had insisted he wanted to try the beanbag toss. He got three out of three bags into the monster's mouth while the carny worker, a reedy fellow with long grey hair that trailed past his shoulders and wearing what reminded me of a Victorian-era frock coat and shirt whose collar bore a deep red silk scarf held in place with a neck brooch, leered. I don't know why, but I instantly thought of the word 'abductor.' I wanted to haul Randy away by the hand, insisting that we go home, now. Dump the pink gorilla into the nearest trash can and drive home, shower, cleanse ourselves of this feel of some kind of pall, an almost moist sensation of fungal growth or sticking fog that had descended onto my skin.

"Three bags a prize does be," the carny worker bent down to address Randy. I thought I saw the man's eye color change for an instant, the eyes shifting from a pale blue to a grey so deep the irises and pupils merged. I shivered. "One for you, and one for me."

He opened a small wooden gate leading into the interior stall where the monster head (what looked to me like some hideous depiction of a cross between a storm cloud and a woods animal—wolf or coyote perhaps), loomed above Randy's small frame. Various prizes were arranged along the shelf below the painting; everything from stuffed animals to glow-in-the-dark stars attached to the ends of wands, to boxes of candied popcorn with a surprise prize inside. Randy latched onto the popcorn as I suspected he would, given he'd already chosen a toy animal. For just a second, I thought I saw the painting of the monster shift a little, as if aware of Randy's presence. Ridiculous notion. As ugly as it was, it was just an acrylic paint image on a piece of sanded plywood. I stared at it and didn't see anything amiss beyond its visual grotesqueness.

"An excellent choice," the carny man laid a hand on one of Randy's shoulders and leaned down to grin at him. I saw that the man's teeth were yellowed and broken in places, probably due to years of neglected dental work and fistfights.

"Come along, Randy," I said too forcefully. The carny man stood up and when he turned to regard me, his smile froze like egg white on his face, the teeth aligned in their deformity, the smile as frozen as a winter landscape. His eyes went dark, then light again. Then the moment broke, as quickly as it had occurred.

"You enjoy the fairgrounds, son," the strange man in the frock coat told him. "It's a magic place. Do you believe in magic?"

Randy peered up at him, his gorilla tucked under one arm, his free hand grasping the pink, blue, and white box of carnival popcorn. "Like Santa Clause?"

"Something like that."

"Yes."

"Good for you," the carny man smiled wider, so wide that I thought the corners of his mouth might wrap around the sides of his face. "Something needs you to believe in order to exist." He leaned down and whispered something in Randy's ear. Randy went quiet for a few seconds, then nodded and smiled back at the man.

"Randy, now!" I hurried towards the two of them.

"Your boy's coming along," the carny man told me, his tone low and serious. "Allow the child to enjoy the wonder of the place."

"He's enjoying himself just fine," I barked and caught Randy's hand in mine, hurrying him away from the stand. "Don't talk to strangers. What did he say to you?"

When we'd hurried away for a number of seconds, dipping in and out of the crowd, I paused and looked back. I could still see the ugly monstrous sign of the beanbag toss and the carny man looking directly at us, still watching us as other people moved about us. I shuddered and cast him a withering glance.

"Randy, tell me what he said to you."

Randy looked a little perplexed. "He said to believe in autumn. It's a magic time."

I scowled, then shook my head. "He didn't say anything else?"

"No." Randy shook his head.

"Let's go over to the Ferris wheel. Do you want to see our town from the top of the wheel?"

"Yes, Daddy."

I felt relief when the rest of the crowd swallowed us up and the strange man with his ugly booth was no longer in immediate sight. I thought about what the creep had said to Randy. He said to believe in autumn. It's a magic time. Okay, fine. I had to agree that autumn was the time of year that these carnivals often came around; that or late summer, and that autumn could elicit a kind of melancholy, almost a spooky feel in the fading of its colors and the casting away of its leaves for the stark, encroaching winter. Still, it seemed like an odd thing for an adult to say to a child.

"Trying to sound worldly and mystical," I mumbled.

"What, Daddy?"

"Nothing, Randy. Daddy's just thinking out loud. Here we go," I took his hand as our Ferris chair came to a stop for us to alight, and within moments we were swept skyward, Randy laughing with glee, the metal bar of the chair holding us in firmly. Me with my arm, protective around my son, as a panoramic view of our town ascended into view.

"Look...there's our street way over there!" I pointed out for him. "And there's our house...the one with the bright green roof. See?"

Randy leaned forward a little, and for one terrible, heart-stopping moment I felt the Ferris chair dip too steeply. I lunged to grab him, knocking his pink gorilla from his one hand in my attempt to ensure that he didn't slip forward in the seat.

"Daddy! My toy..."

We watched the gorilla, its brown cowboy hat and thick, stubby arms and legs pinwheel down until it fell from sight.

"I'm sorry, Randy. I didn't mean to make you drop your toy, but I'd rather it be that toy than you. These stupid chairs shouldn't swing this easily." I held him closer until the wheel began its descent again, a few inches at a time. Halfway to the ground, the fair came into closer view again. I glanced around randomly, thinking we might do one more ride before calling it a night, and saw the beanbag toss stand again in the distance, its monster mouth looking wide and open for something, and its eccentric man leaning against the frame of the painting...

...watching us.

"What the hell?" I muttered, and then the chair was down and the monster stand and its worker fell from view.

"I think we should go home now," I said to Randy.

"But Daddy, we just got here a little while ago."

"I know, but we've had a few rides and it's starting to get colder out. Daddy has to work tomorrow."

"Can I find my gorilla?"

"We can look for it, although it could have fallen anywhere around here," I said.

When we disembarked from the ride, we searched around the immediate vicinity of the base of the Ferris wheel, to no avail. I asked the wheel operator, a kid of about eighteen whose face sported enough acne that I felt immediate pity for him, if he'd seen a pink gorilla on the ground.

"Nope, sorry mister. Maybe somebody else picked it up."

"That's probably what happened," I said. "But thanks."

Randy began to cry. I heaved him up into my arms. "It's okay, sport. You still have your popcorn. I can get you another stuffed animal at the mall this weekend. We can look for another gorilla or anything else that you'd like, okay?" He nodded his head and did his best not to cry. The truth was, I didn't want him to eat the popcorn that he'd picked up from that eerie stand. I didn't want him to have anything to do with any object that the weird carny man had given to him, or that had touched the base of the wood where that painting waited like some terrible thing with its open mouth. However, if I took the popcorn away from him, he'd become inconsolable.

We'd have to walk past that stand again in order to leave the fairground, given all the stands were set up on both sides of a dirt track which led to the entrance and exit points. As we edged closer to the beanbag stand, I made a point of keeping my eyes straight in an attempt to ignore the carny man that I could see peripherally, leaning against the side of his booth as other people stepped up with their tickets.

"Put your head on my shoulder, Randy," I told my boy.

We went to move past, quickly.

"Daddy! He has my gorilla! Look!"

I felt myself freeze, even as I continued to move. My legs tingled and a feeling of dreamlike surrealism took me over. I felt myself drawn to turn around with almost magnetic force, to regard the carny man and his beanbag stand. There, propped on the edge of the stand and coated in smears of black mechanical grease (for it must have hit parts of the Ferris wheel frame on the way down) was Randy's gorilla.

Believe in autumn. It's a magic time.

"Someone found your boy's gorilla and dropped it off here," the carny man said to me, his voice low but clear. "Here it is." A low, almost bacterial smell came to me.

"We don't want it, thank you," I said, curt. "It's filthy now."

The carny man smiled his shark-like smile again. "Suit yourself," he said and tossed the pink gorilla into the monster's mouth where it disappeared somewhere on the other side. Three bags a prize does be...one for you and one for me.

"So you got his gorilla, you turd," I whispered, lifting Randy up into my arms and hurrying from the fairgrounds.

"What's a turd, Daddy?" Randy asked.

"That man," I hissed, knowing that what I said wasn't a nice comment, but unable to help myself. "Never mind, Randy."

* * *

We reached the car, one of about two hundred parked in two rows along the dirt road leading to the fairground and I got Randy hooked up behind the seat belt in the front passenger seat. Then I got in and started the car, flipping the heater on as the night had grown cold enough to elicit some sporadic snow flurries. Given it was early October, it wasn't surprising. I reached over and zipped up Randy's fleece jacket.

"I'm c-cold, Daddy."

"The car will warm up in a couple of minutes," I assured him. He opened the top of the popcorn box and I saw what looked to be normal pink sugarcoated popcorn on the inside. I relaxed a little. Yeah, the carny man was an oddball, and no doubt took great pride in depicting an aura of almost gruesome mysteriousness for adult and child alike. I'd hated his stand, the painting almost 3-D of something that almost looked animated, but enough already. Randy had chosen a box of candy popcorn with a prize inside. Let him enjoy that during the drive home. My wife and Randy's mother, Leonora, would ensure he brushed his teeth before going to bed.

"Good?" I asked him as he unloaded one handful after another of popcorn into his mouth.

"Yup."

"Can Daddy try a piece?"

"Yup, okay." He poured a generous helping into my extended hand and we laughed together. "That's very nice of you." I tossed the kernels into my mouth and began to crunch them down. They weren't completely fresh. The popcorn was a little spongy, probably from humidity. I bit into something hard that made me recoil from its bitterness.

"What the heck?" I said. I stopped the car near the end of the road and spat the contents out into my hand, examining the wet, desiccated pieces of popcorn. An object small and dark sat amid the rosy hue. I stared, reaching with my other hand to flip on the car's overhead light. I retched. The crushed remains of what looked to be some kind of a beetle sat amid the partly chewed food.

"Gross!" I yelled, hurling it through the open window. "Randy, don't eat any more of that." I pulled the box from his hands. He'd already dumped another handful into one small fist, and amid the handful was a tiny paper box, no doubt the prize.

"It's stale and an insect got into it," I babbled, feeling nausea threatening to well up in me. "It's not clean to eat."

"Mine was fine." His voice broke a little.

"Randy, you can't eat any more of it. Give me the rest of it."

Reluctant, his lower lip trembling, he handed over the popcorn, but kept the small, pale white paper box.

"Okay, you can keep the prize, as long as it isn't something else to eat." I tossed the rest of his popcorn through the car window, along with the box. "Ridiculous."

I entertained the thought of driving back there and directing a verbal volley at the creep carny man—that an innocent little boy should end up with a filthy box of popcorn harboring some kind of possibly toxic or bacteria-causing insect. I thought of the oily feel of the beanbags, likely filthy from years of use by hundreds of pairs of hands, and shuddered. Everything about the guy and his stand felt wrong.

I alternated my gaze between the road, turning off the dirt lane and back onto a proper causeway into town, and whatever might fall from the box that Randy shook in order to extract the hidden prize.

What fell into his hand was an acorn; an ordinary, brown, dull acorn.

"An acorn," I said, perplexed. Now I felt more irate. What if a kid attempted to eat the acorn, possibly breaking a tooth on the hard shell, or worse, choking on a solid object? What kind of joke was this? The evening adopted a veneer of the absurd—whatever fun we'd set out to obtain having long fallen away.

I thought of my wife's feelings about circuses and carnivals and how she refused to attend one. She's terrified of carnival types. She'd had a guy in a skeleton suit scare her at a fair when she'd been a little girl around the same age as Randy, what she remembered as 'this towering freak with bloodshot eyes and whose breath reeked of stale booze.' No doubt, it had been some carny worker who'd stayed up too late to party and had performed his shift trailing entrails of the previous evening's indulgence. But she'd never gotten over it. She said he'd 'looked at me too long,' like he'd wanted something.

"Pervert?" I'd asked, thinking it probably wasn't uncommon. Some of these guys were ex-cons taking work wherever they could find it.

"Maybe," she'd said. "Or something worse."

"Like what? A perv is bad enough."

She'd shrugged and a little shiver danced along her spine. "Almost like he wanted a part of me, like he could look right into me. I'd rather not think about it."

I scratched it up to her having been just a kid and overreacting, but even I had to admit that I'd often wondered what these carnival types did once the crowds went home. What went on in those tents and trailers in the off-hours, in the murk of the silent ten-in-one's lined up like a row of black, curtained boxes with their jars of pickled dead things, their anatomical freaks, their tricks and dark enchantment. They lived on the edge of society; flaunting themselves for a few hours, then retracting behind canvas tarps and dark trailers. Maybe they made love. They probably drank too much. They cooked meals over propane burners and kept their hands warm by lighting fires inside oil drums. But I always had this creeping feeling that they did other things while a town slept.

"Throw it out the window, bud," I told him. "I'll bring a nice treat home for you tomorrow." I shook my head, wondering what other dark things hid in the prizes along the shelf of the carny man and his monster. Now both my wife and my son had experienced something dreadful at a carnival. I felt like any man would when he feels his family has been slighted; I felt pissed off enough to want to do something about it.

* * *

We arrived home a few minutes later. I cut the engine and looked over at Randy who sat silent in his seat, his young face solemn.

"I'm sorry that your prize turned out to be such an awful thing, and that you lost your gorilla. I didn't want to take it back from that man."

Randy turned his head to look at me. "Do you think he's a bad man, Daddy?"

I felt a little start at the words. I didn't want to set up some future paranoia in my son like my wife suffers from, so I chose my response with care. "I don't know if he's bad, Randy. Odd, maybe. Carnivals can attract unusual people to work for them, people that don't always fit in well with the rest of society. Maybe he just tries to put on this creepy act to make you feel like you got your money's worth by going in there. "Don't worry about it, champ. Like I said, I'll bring something home for you tomorrow, and this weekend we can go to the mall and you can pick out a new pair of ice skates for the winter. What do you think about that?"

He grinned at me. "That would be okay."

"Let's get you inside and ready for bed. It's getting late."

In fact, it was a little before 8 PM. Randy's only in second grade and his usual bedtime was 8:30 PM.

Randy got out of the car and ran ahead to the house where Leonora waited in the doorway to greet us.

"How was it?" she asked Randy.

"I got two prizes and I lost one," Randy told her.

"Oh...how did you do that?" she asked. I wondered what Randy might say to her and if Leonora would question me afterwards. That's why I don't like those things, Dean. There's something not right about them.

I shut the car door and went to pocket my keys when I was overcome with a feeling of unsubstantiated dread. I paused, my breath held tight in my chest and stared around me. Something didn't feel right. I had a crawling sensation that something had followed Randy and I home, some residual essence that clung to our car like a sticky mist. I got down on one knee and peered beneath the car. I'm not sure what I'd expected to find hiding under there, perhaps clinging to the exhaust pipes or undercarriage. Some flattened out and moist thing, its eyes exaggerated disks, its fingers almost human, fingers that would flash out and grab my throat, squeezing the esophageal tube until I couldn't breathe, strangling me in my own driveway.

"Stop it," I said. Nothing was there. I was letting my imagination get the best of me. Yet, I felt chilled. I turned towards our house and, in the process, happened to glance towards the area where the carnival sat in the field. My eyes picked up the skeletal shape of the Ferris wheel towering above the town, its frame still lit up by ground lights.

And I swore I saw someone sitting in the chair at its top.

Yes. There was a figure there, whereas the other seats were empty.

"What the fuck?" I felt myself freeze. I kept a pair of small binoculars in the trunk of the car, along with a map book and other items for whenever we'd take a drive. Nature watching was one of my and Leonora's favorite pastimes. I unlocked the trunk and took the binoculars out of their case, bringing them up to focus on the top of the Ferris wheel.

I almost dropped the binoculars.

The carny man from the monster beanbag toss sat alone in the top seat, his long silver hair shining like polished nickel in the moonlight, his dusty black coat forming a sooty silhouette against the seat. And he was looking right back at me, his eyes caught within the twin disks of the binocular glass. I felt winter grip each of my ankles, sending frost lines racing up each leg.

"What do you want with me?" I whispered. At my words, he smiled. He looked right at me and he grinned that wraparound grin, the corners of his lips stretching back towards each cheek, his teeth yellowed and broken like...

(like old snapped bones) my mind shot up.

"You stay away from my family, you deceitful son of a bitch."

Leonora stepped out onto the porch again. "Dean? What are you doing?"

I shuddered and returned the binoculars to their case. "Just looking at the carnival skyline from here," I said. It wasn't a lie. Without the binoculars, the carny man became a small human shadow in the seat again, but the wheel held him in place, high above the town. And I knew he still watched me as I went inside the house. I had a feeling that he sat up there for quite a while, observing my place of abode. The stink of smoke and damp leaves followed me inside. I lit a fire, throwing several logs onto the grill to ward off the chill damp that pressed against the windows and walls of the house.

With Randy put to bed, Leonora joined me and we sat by the fire, each of us clasping a glass of wine, watching the logs pop and glow.

"Hard day at work?" she asked me.

I glanced up at her, shaken from my reverie about the dark man. "Huh? Oh, no, not more than the usual."

"You seem lost in thought. Randy seemed to have enjoyed himself, other than he lost a toy gorilla and his popcorn was stale."

I shrugged. "Yeah, he did. He dropped his gorilla from the Ferris wheel. Somebody else picked it up." I forced a grin, not telling her about how the gorilla had been 'found' again at the monster stand. My grin faded when I saw that odd shadow cross her face. I thought of how Randy and I could see our house clearly from the top of the Ferris wheel and wondered if that creeper still sat up there, looking this way.

She sipped her wine. "I'll be glad when they move on. They always bring this strange kind of feel into the town, like ink floating through water." She shivered, her shoulders giving a little shake. She moved closer to the fire.

I shivered at the image her analogy created because that had been the kind of sensation I'd felt trailed us home. Only for me, it was more like something spreading through the damp of the streets, sneaking under hedges and through wet leaf piles, floating within the various autumnal scents and ribbons of wood smoke, hidden among everything out there that was cooling and dying with the season.

"You just had a bad scare when you were little and it's never left you," I said.

"I'm not little anymore and those things still terrify me." She gave an embarrassed laugh. "I know it sounds stupid, but it's true." She shook her long, dark hair over one shoulder and I saw that she really did feel uncomfortable just talking about it.

"What exactly scares you still?" I wanted to know. "You said that circus guy loomed over you, but you were a little kid. All adults seemed too tall and stern."

Her face grew more solemn. "I don't know; just this feeling that there's something out there whenever they're around. Something dangerous that travels with them. I don't want to go to a show because—" She stopped talking.

"What?" I implored.

"Because I'm afraid I'll see whatever it was that frightened me again and this time it'll get me," she finished.

"That guy would be dead by now."

"It wasn't just him. There was something about him, something with him, like this feel of a shadow lurking nearby. I remember feeling like he'd followed me and my parents' home, even though there was nothing there." Her words shook me.

"What?" she said. "You look horrified. All these years later, I've never seen him again, but then again, I don't go to those things."

"Nothing," I told her. "Just got a chill from the cold air tonight. Forget about that man, Lee. He's long gone. But I agree with you, these things are made to feel creepy. That's why people are attracted to them, to see the bizarre, to obtain a cheap thrill for their buck. It's why we go see horror movies."

She stood up, finishing the last bit of wine in her glass. "I'm going to take a shower. I'll see you in bed soon."

"Okay." I watched her move into the depths of the house and sat by the fire for another minute, moving closer to soak up its warmth. Her words had echoed the very sensation I still felt from tonight. I couldn't recall seeing this dark man there last year; he was new with this year's show. When I heard the hiss of the shower head turn on and knew she was occupied, I stepped back outside into the driveway and took a look around.

I noted the ground lights at the Ferris wheel had been turned off, setting the shape of the wheel into a black circle against an indigo sky. I had the same crawling sensation that the carny man was still up there, in the dark, watching me.

I peered inside the car. Everything looked normal. On impulse, I got down onto my knees again and looked underneath.

A pair of golden eyes, lit up in the dark, stared back at me.

"Oh!" I fell back on my ass at the same moment a dark grey cat shot out from beneath the car, and into the road where it disappeared through someone's backyard.

"Shit!" My heart pounded. I didn't know whether to laugh or cry. Somebody's cat out prowling. If a neighbor should ask what I was up to, I'd feign an innocent excuse. Oh, something's been rattling under there while I drove around today. Loose bolt or maybe the muffler needs some work. What else could I say? That I felt I'd brought some kind of a bogeyman home, something unseen that had noticed me and my little boy there this evening and had hitched a ride home with us somehow? Unable to help myself, I got the binoculars out again and trained them on the distant Ferris wheel. I didn't see him up there, but I felt him close by. The night smelled almost fungal in its encroaching frost. A wind picked up and sent a pile of loose leaves into a twirling dervish in the road, their dryness making soft scraping sounds as they danced. Wood smoke from many fireplaces hung heavy in the air, and underneath it all that cloying, dying scent of a season going to sleep.

I walked back to our porch to go inside. There, in the center of our step sat a solitary brown acorn, just like the one Randy had found inside the little white cardboard prize box in his insect-infested popcorn. It couldn't be the same one; I'd watched him toss it through the window back at the fairground. I kicked the acorn off the porch and into the damp grass of our lawn. My mind reasoned: maybe he'd hung onto it anyway, only pretending to throw it out, and had dropped it on the way inside. Somehow, I'd missed it. Well, what the heck; it was only a stupid acorn.

Annoyed with the night, I got into bed beside Leonora and held her until she fell asleep. I lay in bed, listening to the night, listening to the wind tick and tap at the windows, smelling that miasmic perfume of smoke, leaves, damp, an undertone of rot and felt winter coming, the dead season that would shut us all down for months. When Leonora was asleep, I got up and walked across our dark hallway to check in on Randy whose room sat directly across from ours. He was fast asleep, his blankets tucked under one arm, his favorite teddy bear nearby. A small night lamp provided a soft glow to the entrance of his room so that he could see where he was going if he needed to get up to pee at night.

"He can't touch you," I whispered. "He won't."

Why did I feel then that the carny was after my boy, my family?

"Because he's a jerk, and jerks have that effect on people." I got back into bed. I took a long time to fall asleep, and my sleep was riddled with dream pieces about candlelit lamps, greasy black beanbag sacks, quiet carnival stands, the last one being the monster, its mouth wide and eager, and its painted lips quivering with anticipation in the void of night. What did it want? I wasn't sure and I didn't want to speculate.

* * *

My job at a local newspaper office often has me working late shifts. This evening I was slated to start at 5 p.m. until midnight. On the way there I had to drive past the carnival ground, its rides lit up against the waning evening, its cloying stench of oil drum fires, popcorn grease, spun sugar and cigarette smoke creating a formidable perfume that infiltrated the car's shut windows. I slowed a little, staring at the place. At the top of the Ferris wheel, which now held innocent riders who'd paid their ticket prices just like I had the evening before. The road twisted around the natural circumference of the farm field, with a second narrow lane where they'd lined up their trucks and sleeping tents at one end. I watched it for a while, then prepared to change lanes as my exit came up shortly.

He stood in the center of the lane, just beyond the end of the last eighteen wheeler truck parked there; his frock coat tails blowing in the wind, his hair looking like alabaster entrails that looped and curled over his shoulders, his smirk as wide and toothy as ever. He held an ebony walking stick in one hand, its head adorned with a ruby set into silver, and on the other end, speared to it like a crab caught at sea, was the pink gorilla, its fake fur still smeared with grease. The carny man held the stick up for me to see, watching me brake hard, the car sliding all over the road and almost going into the ditch as I brought it to a halt on the soft shoulder. Something hard ticked off my windshield and bounced before coming to a rest against a windshield wiper. It was an acorn.

No, the acorn. I knew it. The one that Randy had tossed from the window here last night, but that had somehow managed to end up on my front porch over an hour later; the one that I'd kicked from the porch and onto our lawn…was here, resting at the base of my windshield. I felt fear as old as tectonic plates shift in me, shoving me a little in my seat. I saw the carny man laugh, heard his laughter coming through the air,

(like dark ink looping through water)

this sound like ice cubes impacting against glass. He spun about, the pink gorilla still spiked on the end of his walking stick as he slipped back behind the truck and disappeared somewhere into the fairgrounds where the crowd ate him up. I wanted to get out of the car and run after him, haul him back by those slimy locks of his, and punch his face repeatedly until his grin would become a broken, bleeding thing, like a piece of raw liver spread over his face. He wanted something from me. He was taunting me, watching me…teasing me with some kind of malevolence. But if I went after him, I'd be late for work—and I couldn't be late. The printing machines had to be set up, the papers produced for the morning newsstands, where the skeleton crew would take over from my midnight shift.

"If you ever come near my family, I'll kill you," I yelled through the open window at the fairground. I had the feeling he heard me, and that he continued to cackle as he took his place in front of his monster frame, his dusty, ancient beanbags lined up for a toss. I flipped the wipers on to hurl the acorn from the car. It landed on the soft shoulder and rolled to the edge of the ditch. On impulse, I got out of the car and, using the heel of one shoe, I proceeded to stomp and crush the acorn down into so many small bits of shell and flattened nut meat. I danced on it, oblivious to how I might appear to other drivers who slowed to regard me, until the acorn was nothing more than fine shards and moist dust in the ground.

"See if you can come back again after that!" I told it. I got into the car, chilled from the cooling night air and from having seen the carnival freak watching me. I pulled out into traffic and drove to work, but before heading into the newspaper building, I walked across the street to a small gift shop and purchased a new stuffed teddy bear and a box of fancy jelly beans for Randy, as I'd promised him I'd do. I used my cell phone and called home, getting Leonora on the other end.

"How's things?"

"Fine, hon. What's up?"

"Oh, just thought I'd touch base with you before another late evening. What's Randy doing?"

Leonora laughed gently. "He's outside, playing with his friend Kevin. They're raking leaves into a huge pile in our front yard and jumping into them. We'll have to get those things bagged for pickup soon."

For some reason, the image of him in those leaves bothered me. I thought of my kicking the acorn into them the evening before, yet I knew I'd destroyed the acorn out on the soft shoulder of the highway barely twenty minutes earlier.

"Don't let him play in those things," I said. "They're wet and decaying." They smell of autumn, and autumn is about rotting and dying things, isn't it, Dean? Isn't it? It's the time when the circus always comes to town.

"Oh, they're fine." I could hear her doing things while she no doubt had the phone squeezed between her cheek and shoulder; the sound of a pot being placed on a stove. Good, normal, household sounds. I wanted to be home with my family right now. I didn't want to be here, away from them. I was letting that creep get to me, scaring me in a way I didn't understand and wouldn't be able to explain to anyone. I couldn't even call the police because he hadn't directly threatened me. I couldn't tell them I felt threatened because I happened to see him sitting on the top of a Ferris wheel five blocks away, or that my kid had picked a stale box of popcorn that contained a dead beetle, or because he'd taken a fancy to pushing a greasy stuffed animal onto the end of his walking stick; odd, eccentric, mentally unbalanced in an uncanny kind of way, perhaps. Had he broken the law, per se? No. He just brought a shiver to my skin. I started to wonder who he was, who he'd been, where he came from. What had he been like as a kid?

He was never a kid. I stopped at the thought, my foot on the first step of the newspaper building. I needed some answers and I would get them tonight before going home, once my shift was over. I'd find whoever owned the carnival, their boss, and I'd talk to him about how one of his workers had made me feel distinctly uncomfortable, and that if he'd had that effect on me, he'd have it on others too. I'd tell him that it wasn't good for his business. I'd have the dark carny man brought before his boss to explain himself to me, and where I could tell him what I thought of him and that he'd better not ever come near my family for any reason. Then, somehow, I got through my shift, one of the paper's articles being none other than a photograph of the lurid fairgrounds from the entrance to the park, and a write-up about how carnivals bring a 'special magic' with them wherever they travel.

"Magic, my ass," I mumbled. It was more of a burlesque perversion, a fascination with the dark side of things that bordered somehow on dangerous, and it had to do with that man and his monster sign.

* * *

2:15 a.m. I idled on the road, knowing that the public had long gone home and were tucked into their beds, perhaps a few people still up to watch late night television or to read, this carnival on the edge of our town like shingles resting against skin. I had the distinct impression that he knew I was here, my headlamps off, my engine idling so that I could keep the heater going in the car to provide warmth against a night that had brought a thin layer of snow to the ground. I could smell the carnival ground trailing in through the heaters; the paper and chunks of wood that they burned in their heat-blackened oil drums, the stink of bags full of trash…discarded bits of hotdogs and fries, castaway soda pop cans, baby diapers, remnants of cotton candy clinging to sticky paper tubes. Their fires cast an orange glow against the backdrop of trucks, stands, and tents.

It struck me that this traveling show was the epitome of autumn, that season of sleep and dying where everything rots down and goes quiet. This carnival had managed to capture all of its aromas, its shadows, its lingering frosts, the symbolism of decline and fear caught within the folds of its heavy curtains and costumes, in the whirl of sparks amid the fire eaters, the serpentine menace of its snake charmers. Our ancestors had feared autumn's approach with the falling of its leaves and the shortening of its days as fields grew brown and bacterium set in; fires set and sacrifices made to appease the gods of fate. This show tempted fate; it played with images of death, teased it in its death-defying acts, invited it close enough so that you could smell it everywhere.

I couldn't make myself go there now. It would be me against them, all of the regular public gone, and only the carnival types huddled in circles around their luminescent cans, their features half-lit by the flames, watching me approach. No. I'd just go home and we'd wait for them to leave in the next few days. They'd move on and the field would freeze under another winter, killing any residual essence that they'd left behind.

I arrived home barely ten minutes later and parked the car in the driveway. That same sense of having been followed and being watched persisted, but I scratched it up to having seen the carny freak with the stabbed gorilla earlier. The Ferris wheel still looked black against the sky, flurries marring the image a little. I peered under the car, preparing myself for anything...but nothing met my gaze. No acorn on my front step, either. I let myself inside, grateful for the warmth of the wood stove and for the comforting embrace of my home and family. I carried the new teddy bear and jelly beans under one arm and stepped in to Randy's room to place the gifts at the foot of his bed, where he'd discover them in the morning. A pale band of yellow light from a nearby arc sodium lamp cast a glow in the room, as it always did.

His bed was empty. Panic tore at my legs, sinking nails into flesh. I spun about, dropping the box of jelly beans and the bear. Okay, he had to have crawled into bed with Leonora, something he often did when I worked late. Relax. Everything was okay, I reasoned. I pushed into my and Leonora's bedroom, darker in here because she always drew the drapes against the street light, and sought them in the dark. My hands landed on our bed, feeling, grappling for the warm, familiar shapes of my wife and son's sleeping forms. The bed was cold, empty, the sheet and blankets pushed back.

"Lee!" I yelled. I ran and slapped on the light switch, filling the room with brilliant yellow light. They weren't in here. I can't recall running from room to room through the house, checking the kitchen, the living room, the bathroom, the basement laundry room and furnace room, finding them nowhere. Frantic, I sought any rational explanation as to where my family might be at almost 3 a.m. on a cold

October morning, some note of clarification as to where they'd gone. My mind raced. Something must have happened. One of them was sick and at the hospital. It wasn't like Lee to not leave me some kind of a note or call me and leave a message on my cell phone.

"Where are you?" I screamed, desperate, hysterical. I stood in our kitchen again, the dark red digital numerals of the clock in our stove face reading 2:39 AM, looking at our refrigerator with its plethora of happy, colorful magnets, looking at a cutting board with crumbs from bread still sitting on it, looking at our table and chair set with its three bright orange placemats set out for meals.

And on the center of Randy's placemat sat a single acorn, brown, shiny, almost perfectly spherical in shape.

Suddenly, I knew where they were and that I'd have to go back if I ever hoped to see them again. I also knew that, if I should call the police to accompany me that we wouldn't find them. Somehow, like an optical illusion of magic, they'd be held outside of sight. It would have to be me and me alone.

* * *

I set out, racing, not caring about speed limits as I made my way back to the highway that would lead me to Barker's field and the huddled shadow of the traveling carnival show. I steered the car over potholes, hearing gravel fly up and tick at the undercarriage, until I got as close to the structures as possible. I got out of the car, leaving the doors unlocked and marched with determination towards the area where I saw the glow of their oil drums in front of their sleeping tents. I moved past the various stands, the single O's with their exaggerated depictions of deformities and freaks, of dark promises of things worse. Step up, step up and see the bloodied, riddled clothing from the Bonnie and Clyde death car that they wore on the day of their ambush, ladies and gentleman. The blood is real. See it and touch it for yourself…

I came upon a group of them huddled around a fire, two women and three men, some still sporting remnants of their face makeup, some sipping hot coffee that they brewed over a small butane stove.

"Where is he?" I demanded of them. "That freak who runs the beanbag toss over there!" I pointed at the sign, its monster face almost glowing in the radiance of the tin fire, its open mouth easily two feet wide and looking like the entrance to a sooty tunnel.

One of the women, a specimen with long, straggly red hair and equally red fingernails, cackled at me. "You looking for John Gore?"

"Is that his name? Gore? Yeah, I'm looking for the bastard. He's been taunting me and my family since we arrived here yesterday, and now I can't find my family. It's the middle of the fucking night and they aren't home, my wife and my little seven-year-old boy."

The carny workers didn't appear fazed by my emotional outburst, as if it was an ordinary occurrence for them to witness this kind of display.

"He's around somewhere," one of the men said. He still wore a clown suit, but he'd removed his face makeup and wig, an undergrowth of dark beard clouding his face." Maybe your family went to visit someone."

They tittered as if amused by my situation.

"Not at this time of the morning," I shot back.

"Well, maybe your boy got sick and your wife took him to the hospital," the redhead leveled back at me. "It might have been an emergency and she just went there."

I thought of the popcorn, of the potential for disease in it. I thought of the acorn that kept reappearing, and that I'd forgotten on Randy's placemat back home in my haste to come here to find them.

"Come one, come all and try your hand with the beanbag toss!" A voice as cold as January river water trickled through the night air. "Many prizes wait to be won! We have stars that glow, games and tricks, candied popcorn, and gorillas on sticks!"

I felt myself turn slowly, taffy-like, the feel of a bad dream where the feet stick to the ground, and saw him before his stand. A dull green spot lamp highlighted the face of the monster, the black cloud and shining eyes around its open maw, its curled fingers that threatened to reach beyond the edge of the plywood sign. The carny freak named John Gore stood before the stand, his two hands held out in my direction, bearing the three black oily beanbags.

"We have a woman and a boy, the most delectable toys, come win them back if you can get all three bags through this mouth, intact. Try your hand, dear man, if you believe that you can—may your aim be astute if you wish to see them again. One bag for her, one bag for him, and one bag for you, and one chance only to see this through."

A gust of wind picked up, a lonely note that gusted the stink of ash and fire around us. I felt myself pulled towards Gore. He hurled the three oily bags at me and I caught them, feeling repugnance at the sensation of them, but knowing that my boy had held these same bags just last evening. They weren't filled with beans. One of the bags tore a little as I caught them and what came out into my hand were several acorns. The others felt different; my fingers explored them a little and what I thought I felt in the other two were linear, sharp...the feel of bone fragments of different shapes and sizes.

"Drop one, you lose and they become mine, a small autumnal sacrifice carried through time."

"Fuck you and your carnival rhyme," I spat at him.

Gore, his ruby brooch glowing unnaturally beneath his throat elicited that same cold laugh that he'd done just hours ago. "Ah, the man has a poetic bent." His face went solemn, his features half lit, half shadow in the dancing fire behind us.

"I'm going to have you charged with kidnapping just as soon as I find my wife and son," I told him. "You tell me where they are or I swear I'm going to hurt you."

"Hurt me?" he hissed. "Impossible. You can't stop the season."

He made no sense. He pointed at the sign of the monster. "This is autumn, or what some of you call 'fall.' I bring fall to the carnival, the encroaching season of death and sleep. See the blackness of its storm clouds, see the orange glow of its fiery pits, your pitiful attempts to ward it off. You can't stop the arrival of the dark season, of sleep, of cold, Mr. Arthur."

"How the hell do you know my name?"

"Because they told me."

"Where are they?"

"They're in...there!" He pointed to the mouth of the sign he called fall. "Waiting for you to take perfect aim and win your prize."

Enraged, but puzzled, I walked around the stand and looked on the other side of the sign; it was flat, unpainted plywood on the other side. It bore no room, no chamber in which anyone could huddle. And then it occurred to me that, given this, how could beanbags sail through its open mouth if it had no chasm behind it for them to land within? The nonsensical absurdity of it made me feel like fainting.

I bore back at him, one fist clutching the dirty cloth bags, the other curled. I grabbed Gore by the collar of his coat and drew him to me, my own teeth clenched as I addressed him. "You tell me where my family is right now or I swear I'll kill you."

He felt like his bags; slippery, dust-encrusted, and smelling of yellowed, forgotten paper. When he laughed, I saw his teeth up close and bits of what looked to be raw meat wedged between the broken calcium husks. "You can't kill what's already dead, Mr. Arthur. Toss the bags, or toss your chance, I offer it once...take it, or I'll recant."

The night moved into me. Behind me I heard the rest of them gather, the carnival workers, circling to watch a show instead of presenting one, all of them unsympathetic towards me. A few lit cigarettes and sat up on small stools.

"What will it be?" Gore repeated.

"You miserable, diseased fuck," I said to him. I walked up to the edge of the stand, noting the hideous open mouth of the sign that led to nothing on the other side.

"Daddy?" I heard Randy's voice coming from somewhere inside that mouth and my mind bent, along with my heart. It had to be an illusion; although the sign was flat plywood, my family was somewhere nearby.

"I'm here, baby," I called out to him.

"The bags..." Gore growled.

I saw the collection of popcorn boxes lined up along the shelf, each one no doubt filled with an acorn and a dead insect, residual bits of autumn tucked inside each box. The collection of other shiny, lurid prizes, and Gore's walking stick leaned into a corner, Randy's dropped and filthy pink gorilla still speared to the bottom of it.

"Why do you hate me and my family so much?"

Gore raised his eyebrows. "But I don't. I consider you all rather...delectable."

I took aim with as much care as possible, given the shaking of my arm and tossed the first of the disgusting bags. It sailed through the monster's mouth and I heard it land somewhere inside. I shuddered.

"Very good, Mr. Arthur. Now do it twice again."

I steadied myself and, lips trembling, hurled the second bag. It, too, sailed through the mouth and landed inside an impossible place.

"One to go, create the show, win the prize, or your family dies."

I shut my eyes and prayed.

I let go of the third beanbag, feeling my arm swing up, my fist open, allowing the dark cloth with its innards of bone shard to soar forward, closer, closer to the monster's mouth–

Where it hit the edge of the bottom of the mouth and leaned inward, the majority of the bag still sliding, but slowing.

Someone behind me whistled, and the carny crowd tittered.

"Shall it slide or shall it stop? Tick-tock said the clock!" Gore taunted me.

I felt him stare at me as I watched the third beanbag begin to slow.

"Get in there, you bastard." My voice broke. What felt like forever slid past, dreamlike and stinking of rancid clams, of backed up sewer tunnels, of wet, dark places, of smoke and leaves, the stench of descending autumn somehow culminated in this man and his stand.

The bag teetered...and dropped in.

The night stopped. Even the carny workers behind me didn't issue so much as a chuckle or whisper.

"You did well, Mr. Arthur. You may go ahead, into the monster, and retrieve them."

"There's nothing on the other side of that platform," I clenched my teeth at him.

"Ah, but there's the magic. You come to the carnival because you want to see magic tricks, don't you? Well, we don't disappoint. Go ahead, and look for yourself."

I shoved through the small wooden gate that separated the bag throwers from the plywood and walked up to the mouth of the monster named fall. This close, I smelled the thing. A cold, residual air issued through the black hole of its mouth, smelling of rotting leaves and putrefaction and worse; smelling of rotting meat.

I stuck my hand through the mouth and felt damp, dark air in there.

"Randy? Leonora?"

"I'm here, Daddy," I heard my boy whimper somewhere in there, in the darkness of this invisible, darkly magical place; the innards of the monster that lay somewhere between reality and death on the other side of this plywood.

I hauled myself up and into the mouth, my foot stepping on one of the disgusting bags as I felt my way through the dark until I found Randy who clung to me, sobbing. Frantic, I gripped him to me, and tripped over the unconscious form of my wife on the wooden floor of this diseased bunker.

"I'm here, son. I'm going to lift Mommy over my shoulder, and you're going to take my other hand. We're going to go back out that open hole again, okay?

"There's no hole, Daddy."

I turned around and looked. Whatever dim light had been in the background from their wood fires had extinguished. We stood in darkness. Time went still.

I let go of Randy's hand and beat with both fists against the backdrop of the plywood.

"You let us out of here, you filthy son of a bitch!" I screamed. My voice broke and salty tears filled my throat.

"I'm cold, D-daddy," Randy whimpered, hanging on to my leg. "I want to go home."

"Somehow, I'll get us there," I promised him. No begging, screaming, thrashing availed us. We were locked in the dark someplace behind the sign. Hours passed and hunger and thirst set in. Leonora woke up and sobbed against me.

"It's him," she said. "And he hasn't changed a bit."

"Who?" And then I knew; the same carny worker that she'd seen as a little girl who had frightened her almost twenty-five years earlier. Impossible—much like a flat plywood stand that encompassed missing people.

During this timelessness I became aware of a small pinprick of florid crimson light that danced and floated in the dark above us, pulsating. It hovered just beyond reach and when I stood to try and touch it, I felt it emanate a cold heat, like dry ice; painful. It made me pull my hand away. No doubt another of Gore's tricks.

The fairgrounds went quiet. Then the sound of people arriving, and with it, John Gore's voice as he took his place in front of the stand.

"Step up, step up and win a prize, you there, young lady, dare you try?"

We listened as the first of the beanbags thudded against the outside of our prison. Another soared in through the dark and hit my shoulder. The third bag missed.

Over and over it went through the evening. We grew colder, stiller, and I knew that we were dying as the hours passed. We'd come looking for the ultimate thrill, the titillating magic act, and we'd found more than we could bear. We'd been an autumnal sacrifice, a gift to whatever dark powers granted them their magic, a time-long tradition upheld by the traveling carnival, a small appeasement to the gods.

During the quiet hours, when I knew that the public had long gone, we heard the footsteps of numerous people approach, and within that shuffle, the sliding growl of John Gore's voice.

"Let's get it onto the truck right away," Gore said, "and we can divide up the payment afterwards." I felt several people lift us up from the platform that the monster billboard had rested upon, and we were transported a short distance. The Monster sign was slid onto the flatbed of a truck, my unconscious boy rolling against me. I reached out for him and felt that his skin had gone cold.

"Randy?"

He didn't respond. I found Leonora in the dark and pulled her to me, realizing as I touched her that she'd already died. Her body contained no pulse.

"I hate you!" I screamed inside this void of darkness and heard Gore chuckle.

"It sucks to lose," he said to one of the other workers. "Try your hand with fate, mate?"

"Not me, thanks," the other voice said.

"He'll quiet soon enough, once we're fully engulfed by the night," Gore told him.

"I won't be quiet!" I shrieked. "I'll scream until someone notices."

Tears broke past my eyelids and burned my cheeks. That unusual light appeared to my left again. It grew closer, larger, and then I saw that there were two orbs of icy luminescence. Something large, heavy, and rancid with fetor rushed at me in the dark, those fiery circles baneful and hungry. Something opened in the dark, like a suck hole giving way and I felt teeth slice into my legs, hauling me towards it—all of this within the timeless void attached somehow to a traveling monster billboard. The essence of death had found us, its hunger an innate, formidable thing, and it was not merciful.

Then it began to swallow.

The End

WEATHER

SYSTEM

By
Carol Weekes

Weather System

The radio had been predicting a storm all day, and with the heat and humidity that had built up by noon, I was surprised that it hadn't happened sooner. Normally, I like storms and enjoy sitting out on our deck with the family, watching the clouds approach us across the bay. But I knew, as soon as this system started to move in, there was something different about it, and that it wasn't good. I couldn't have begun to fathom the true extent of it until after it was all over.

It was a little after two in the afternoon when the sky deepened to a hint of ash and the wind fell off, making the air sauna-thick. I was in the backyard of our cabin out on Random Lake, a string of lakes that makes up a chunk of cottage country just north of Kingston, trying to dig a trench for a drainage hose. Lenny, my six-year-old son, played in the sandbox not far from me, pushing a Tonka front-end loader through the sand, forming endless rows which he'd then flatten out again. Our golden lab, a nine-year-old female named Honey, lay beside Lenny, always protective and loyal to the kids. I paused for a moment to rub my lower back. Jennifer had gone into town with our nine-year-old daughter, Tia, to get stuff for supper and to get her hair trimmed. They were due home by 4 PM. I glanced up at the sky and noted that first, telltale band of grey peeking across the horizon of the southwest.

"Here it comes," I said more to myself than Lenny. Maybe we wouldn't be eating supper out on the deck this evening. I felt a moment of disappointment, followed by the familiar gut-thrill of knowing that storm cells were on their way.

"Here comes what, Daddy?" Lenny asked, not looking up. He used both fists to direct the front-loader through a mountain of sand, sending it spraying in all directions, including down the front of his shirt and through his longish, brown hair. Between the sand and the sticky remnants of a popsicle, the kid would need a bath before dinner.

"Thunderstorm," I said and the enthusiasm in my voice made him look up. Lenny didn't like thunder, but he'd tolerate it as long as he was cuddled in either my or Jennifer's arms.

"I don't like those, Daddy," he said. "Make it go away."

I laughed out loud at the faith system that children carried concerning their parents' abilities. Kiss the boo-boo and make it better; check under the bed before shutting off the lamp to ensure the monsters are gone; dispel the scary storm.

"I can't, son," I said. "Daddy has no control over the weather. No one does. It's just part of nature."

"I don't like them." He stopped playing and stared at the sky with me. The soft azure of a summer afternoon was, slowly but definitely, eaten up by the weather system moving in.

"Dad will be with you," I told him. "You don't have to be scared of storms."

I felt a little guilty telling him that, thinking of several incidents I'd heard of around here that directly contradicted that statement. Like last summer when a storm created a flash flood and washed out the little bridge that connects Random Lake to its mainland, Loon Bay. A tourist's car had gone into that watery rampage and the man had drowned. And then there was Mike Mitchell, a local mechanic who got struck by lightning a few years ago while trying to guide his wind surfer back to shore. He lived to tell the tale, but he has a scar as purple as a bruise and the size of an orange on his shoulder where the electricity entered, and on the bottom of his left heel where it exited, that he shows tourists and locals alike whenever we get to jawing about storms around here. Looks like comet impacts onto a planet, those scars do. They always make me shiver a little.

"God must have wanted you around for a while longer," I told him when he first showed them to me.

"Beats me," he said, shrugging. We both laughed, but entrails of unease had stayed with me for a good while afterwards.

By three o'clock thunderheads rolled in, their tops billowing white but their undersides a black menace. I finished packing gravel and dirt on top of the drainage hose and hurried to put my tools away in the shed. "Time to get ready to go inside, scout," I told Lenny. "It's going to start raining any time now." The air smelled strongly of lake water and faintly of ozone. I paused for a moment and noted sheet lightning flickering inside clouds, lighting them up the way a faulty bulb can illuminate a dark room. This followed by the first imminent murmur of thunder.

"When's Mommy coming home?"

I spoke over my shoulder to him as I reached the small board-and-batten tool shed and tossed the shovel and pickax inside. "They should be home in another hour, bud. Daddy's going to go get dinner started. I can still barbecue, but I think we'll be eating inside the screened porch tonight. From the look of those clouds, it's going to pour buckets. Leave your toys, Len. Come on."

He stood up, reluctant, but I saw his small face turn up to regard the sky. Cloud banks had already blocked out the sun, throwing his visage into shadow. A chill crossed my skin at that moment, a sense of dread so unnerving that I stopped moving. I looked at my son's face…noted the expression of unadulterated dread in his innocent features and realized the meaning of true fear in the mind of a six-year-old. In his world, the monster was coming, and it wouldn't be until later that day that I'd realize he was right.

I scooped Lenny up into my arms as the first fat raindrops began to fall, hitting our skin hard like directed bullets. Wind increased, hurling the clouds forward so that the former blue-green of the lake turned black, foamy white tops splashing against the shoreline.

"Time to run," I said and sprinted across our long backyard. Honey followed at our heels, her long pink tongue lolling as she raced ahead of us.

We were situated on our waterfront property that was abutted on either side by thick privacy forest that Jennifer and I had saved for, for the past five years. This place was our getaway from the city and our little condo there; our sanctuary of green and calm, our piece of earthly Nirvana when the day-to-day stressors became too much. We came up here almost every weekend, even during the winter. We held this cottage in our hearts, teaching our children how to swim, how to canoe, how to survive in the woods, and all the other skills that we, as parents, felt was pertinent to their long-term survival.

We pushed into the rustic parlor as the first of the downpours erupted, throwing the room into darkness. Trees bent over as wind picked up with a hard, sudden force that ripped leaves from branches. Lenny began to cry and pressed his face into my shoulder. Honey circled my legs, whining soft and low in her chest.

"It's okay, it's okay," I reassured them both. "We're inside. We're safe."

"What about Mommy and Tia?"

I felt that odd little shiver again at his words. "They're in town with many other people, Len. They're safe in a car. I'll give Mommy a call as soon as I get us set up here."

I went around the room and into the kitchen, turning on lamps, filling the rooms with the artificial warmth of electric light.

"You sit here at the table while I get a washcloth," I told Lenny. "I can't bathe you with a storm like this." I recalled my parents' words when I was young as we'd watch storms move past together. How you shouldn't talk on a telephone, lest the wire get struck by lightning, nor bathe, boat, swim, or be anywhere near water due to its conductivity. How standing under trees or being the tallest thing in a flat field could be dangerous...the sheer, daunting ubiquity of the threat. A storm seemed like a dark thing to me back then, something that penetrated walls with its thunder and reached around corners with its probing fingers of lightning. I knew exactly how Lenny felt. I hadn't forgotten, but I masked that sour-gut feeling over with adult logic that stated that, as adults, we could always makes things safe. I filled a bowl with warm water and a little mild soap and proceeded to wash Lenny's face, arms, and hands. It would do until we could get him into a bath. I noted the time. Three-thirty-one PM. Jennifer and Tia should be on the road, halfway back between Kingston and Loon Bay by now. They'd be following Highway 10 from Kingston, a narrow two-lane strip of blacktop that wound through lake country. They'd be hitting the storm, face-on.

"Just sit tight while I give Mommy a quick call." I gave Lenny a glass of chocolate milk and a cookie to occupy him. Honey stayed close to us, her big golden eyes wary as she, no doubt, picked up on our emotions. I plucked the receiver from the wall phone and punched in Jennifer's cell phone number. A crack of lightning filled the house with an unnatural brilliance, followed by an ear-splitting cough of thunder that shook the cabin. Lenny dropped his glass of milk. The glass shattered on the floor, sending liquid and bits of glass in all directions. Honey barked, frantic.

"Daddy!"

"It's okay, it's all right, Len. I'm here," I squeezed the receiver between my chin and shoulder as he ran to me. I scooped him up. "I'll clean it up. It's no big deal. It's just thunder, scout. It can't hurt you. It's just a big noise. It's just warm air and cool air coming together and—" I happened glance through our kitchen window at that moment, at a heavy bank of cloud rushing past. For a moment, just a terrifying moment, I'd swear I saw an unearthly face regarding me in the clouds, a part of the clouds themselves—this expression of intensity in the form of expanding cobalt eyes, a drawn out mouth of agony, a growing expression of horror. Then it was gone, as quickly as it had happened. The phone rang twice, three times, five times...

"Pick up, Jen," I mumbled. Len gripped me, his small arms too tight around my neck and throat. Then I heard her cell phone connect, followed by her voice and a flood of relief swept through me. My wife and daughter were okay.

"Where are you both now?" I asked.

"We left Kingston fifteen minutes ago. We'll hit Westport in another twenty. Quite the system that's blowing in."

"It's forceful," I said. "Be cautious driving with this wind and rain. Take your time. Stop somewhere, if you have to do it. Listen to the radio reports."

She laughed, her infectious laugh that, sadly, failed to relieve me right now. "Sweetie, you worry too much. I'm a big girl. I've driven in a lot of storms over the years, the winter ones much worse than this. We'll be fine. I'll take my time. We may not get home until four-thirty or closer to five."

"That's okay," I cut in. Our reception started to break up, turning her words into fragmented pieces that made little sense. "I'm losing reception!" I yelled into the phone and felt Lenny grip me tighter. "Len, you're choking Daddy. Jen?"

Our line went dead. This could happen in the city, or within loops of hills in the country where signals became weak or nonexistent. I held the receiver to my ear and heard the solemnity of silence from the other end. Lightning flared overhead as the day darkened to the point of midnight and wind screamed around the cabin, hurling torn leaves, branches, bits of dead grass, wayward paper past the windows. Then, a huge crack that shook me to my core so deeply that I felt a buzzing inside my teeth. The receiver hummed in my hand. I dropped it as if it were hot. Lenny and I watched the telephone receiver dangle, oscillating back and forth like a pendulum from its cord, counting off the seconds as day turned to night and calm to turmoil.

"She can't try to drive in this," I thought aloud, then shut my mouth as I realized that Lenny would internalize everything I said.

"Is Mommy okay?"

"They're fine, son. They're on their way home." They had thirty-five or more kilometers to travel, depending upon which route Jennifer chose to take. She could come up Highway 10 straight to Westport and cut through Sydenham, or she might go further west before heading north to Random Lake. All of it cottage country, all of it surrounded by water that would feed the storm, so much of it over bridges and through dips and hills. Then the power went out, shoving us into darkness, other than from lightening. Honey began to pace from room to room, moaning, frightened.

"Daddy," Lenny cried.

"I'll find our flashlights and lanterns," I said. "You come help me, bud."

We went through the cabin to the small storage closet in our bedroom where we kept emergency gear like candles, batteries, and such. I carried two glass candleholders with me into the kitchen, then went back to retrieve a flashlight and a small, battery-charged transistor radio. I plugged the radio in, lit the two candles, and Lenny and I sat down at the kitchen table, the room's sliding patio doors overlooking our verandah and the lake, to listen for updates to the weather report. One came on within minutes.

A series of strong storm cells is currently making its way across the Great Lakes region and into Eastern Ontario. A severe thunderstorm warning is being advised. Areas currently being hit are—

Another flash of lightning. I happened to glance out at the lake, my mind drifting a little as I listened to the report, Lenny nestled into my lap, when I saw an image of Jennifer superimposed in the glass of our patio doors. It was a strange kind of image, one that lasted mere seconds in the flash, but which continued to show itself as an aftereffect upon my retinas. She'd been smiling and walking towards me, her hands extended out, her hair blowing in the wind. The image of Jennifer blinked out. Wishful thinking on my part, I reasoned. I just wanted them home.

This was followed by a series of resounding crashes as thunder broke directly over us. Lightning illuminated the sky again, highlighting the boiling clouds and I watched with horror as it hit an ancient maple across the shore from us, splitting the trunk and sending a volley of sparks up into the air. A cacophony of splintering wood, followed by a resounding shudder as half the tree fell to the ground, shook the house. Lenny screamed and clung to me. I felt my heart crawl up into my throat and my mouth came open in stupefied awe at the fury of the storm. I thought of the face I'd imagined seeing in the clouds just minutes ago, a malevolent face that had swept past, the heart of the storm. Honey took her position beneath the kitchen table, whining and shaking at my feet. I reached down with a trembling hand and gave her a weak pat. At this moment, I didn't feel any more confident than my son or our dog, but I needed to be in control. The idea that Jennifer and Tia were out in this, fully into the lake region now, made me feel sick. On impulse, I found my cell phone on a nearby cabinet and tried her number again. It rang, endlessly.

"Come on...pick up," I begged. My mind imagined everything in the next few seconds. A car crash, a plunge into a lake, hydroplaning into an opposite lane, a thick tree limb crashing down at the wrong moment...

The line picked up at the other end and I heard Jennifer's voice. "Hello?"

"Hon? Are you both okay? Lenny and I just watched lightning ruin a large tree across from us. I'd rather you both pull over somewhere and wait this thing out."

The line sounded odd, almost tenuous, the way a telephone connection can sound when calling somewhere to the other side of the world.

"I'm just fine," she said, her voice light and airy. She didn't sound the least bit phased.

"How's Tia doing?"

A pause. I heard wind in the background then, a low, moaning wind that suggested they either had their windows open, or that the gale force was picking up around them. Then the wind screamed and through it, Tia's voice came to me. "Daddy...daddy!" I heard Jennifer begin to sing to her, the way she had when Tia and Lenny had been babies and needed comforting, a kind of crooning lullaby with vaporous tones. Hush little baby, don't you cry, Mama's gonna sing you a lullaby...

"Tia?" My voice, urgent. Lenny looked up at me, his big brown eyes stark and full of question. "Jennifer?" Nothing. The connection had simply evaporated again, like mist sucked out by a cross-breeze. Terror seized me. I knew, instinctively, that something was wrong. Perhaps they'd encountered some kind of trouble and Jennifer was doing her best to remain calm and keep Tia mollified, but it wasn't like her to make light of something with me. I'd been married to her for twelve years and I knew every nuance of this woman. I sensed a change in something for which I could not quite pinpoint, and this feeling bothered me more than the storm itself. I sensed she was riding it out, even though she knew she shouldn't, determined to get home and be with us. I tried her number again and this time the phone rang without response. Frustrated, I clapped the phone shut and hurled it onto the counter.

"Where's Mommy and Tia?" Lenny pressed.

"On their way home," I said. "They should be home soon." I glared at the clouds boiling past the window, the endless roiling of black condensation, the fury on the lake producing five-foot wave swells that moved docks around with the ease of a child slapping bath toys back and forth. Our stove clock read four-thirty PM. Soon it slipped into five PM, then five forty-six PM. I tried her number again, frantic, debating whether or not I should dial the local police and have a cruiser search for them. What might they find? What if they didn't find anything and my family still didn't come home? I wanted my wife and daughter here with me, safe, warm, dry, where we could sit and wait this thing out together. Desperate, I turned to the radio again, Lenny clinging to me like a young orangutan to its mother.

...tornado touched down just south of Westport. We're awaiting damage reports at this time, but key witnesses say they saw an unusual funnel cloud move over Lake Echo, sucking up water before crossing land through forest and distant roadways. Police are advising travelers to postpone all travel through the Leeds and Thousand Island Region...

"Oh my God," I whispered. "Oh my God, where are my girls?" I felt tears sting my eyes. I rationalized. I'd just spoken to them only minutes ago, and although I'd heard terror in Tia's voice, she'd been alive and, thus, all right. She and Jen had been fine, Jen singing to Tia, trying to keep her calm inside the car. I ran for the phone and dialed the local Ontario Provincial Police precinct to try and gain more details about exactly where the tornado had landed. I got a dispatcher who asked me if I had a personal emergency at that time. I couldn't think of a worse scenario than this.

"I don't know where my wife and daughter are!" I yelled into the phone. "I was just talking to them minutes ago and our line got cut off. My daughter sounded frightened. They're out on the roads, trying to come home. Where did the tornado touch down?"

"Calm down, sir. Your wife and daughter are most likely just fine and have probably pulled over to find shelter in a local business or otherwise. The tornado passed over Wolf Lake near Westport and into the northern section of Highway 10 before entering a section of woodlands. A few cars are off the highway, but our cruisers and other emergency personnel are just arriving now. We're awaiting word on whether or not there have been any casualties. In the meantime, sir, try to stay calm. I'm sure everything will be fine with your family."

"How can you be sure? How can I stay calm when I don't know where they are?" I bellowed. Lenny began to cry. For a second, just a fleeting second, I thought I heard Jennifer's voice singing again somewhere along the telephone wire...hush little baby, don't you cry... It faded as soon as it began.

"Sir, if you'd like to check in with us in the next little while, perhaps we'll have further details for you, but at this time, unless you're experiencing a direct emergency yourself at this time, there isn't much more I can do. I can assure you that we and other emergency crews are doing all we can."

I felt my head drop so that my chin rested against the top of Lenny's head. "I understand," I said, although my gut screamed 'No, you don't! Nothing makes sense!' I hung up and shut my eyes. "They'll be all right," I murmured. "They'll be home any time now." Honey began to moan beneath the table; she howled a melancholy note until I snapped at her to be quiet. Still, she growled, her nose tucked under her tail, her eyes alert to the room around her.

* * *

A knock on a front door during a time of duress has to be one of the most heartwarming and terrifying moments in a person's life. On the one hand, you hope it is your loved ones, a neighbor, a friend, a helpful Samaritan offering blankets or some other form of aid. You don't want to see a police officer at your door. The knock came at 6:01 PM. The worst of the storm had passed with pockets of blue sky beginning to show in the west. The lake had calmed down and the broken chunk of tree swelled softly up and down in diminished waves.

There were two of them standing on the step in their crisp, dark blue uniforms, their hats forming dark shadows over their faces, one young officer in his twenties, the other somewhat older like myself, in his mid-to-late thirties. From the expressions on their faces, I knew that things weren't going to be all right. Lenny had fallen asleep on the sofa in the parlor, his favorite blanket wrapped around his shoulders, his thumb in his mouth. His sandbox lay filled with water in the distance, its toy trucks and cars half submerged in filth.

"Mr. Stirling?"

I swallowed hard. My Adam's apple stuck in my throat like a lump of hard, dry bread.

"Yes?"

"Can we come in sir? We need to speak with you. Are you the husband of Jennifer Stirling of civic number 21117?"

"Where's my wife and daughter?" I felt weakness begin somewhere in the ankles and move up into my knees, rendering my ability to stand almost obsolete. Somehow, we floated into the house and up into the kitchen where I took a seat at the kitchen table where Lenny and I had spent the bulk of the late afternoon, watching the storm move through.

"Your daughter, Tia, is in a hospital," the older officer told me gently. Both had removed their hats and their faces were full of reserved empathy. I saw it in their eyes, the unspoken words that any spouse and father dreads to hear and which only come to him in his worst nightmares, or as the aftereffects of a particularly nasty storm front. I thought of the face in the clouds, the vehemence of the system, its mercilessness.

"She's in serious, but stable, condition and has been airlifted to hospital with a broken hip, a broken arm, and numerous lacerations. She's asking for you. She keeps saying your name. Their car...met the tornado almost head-on on Highway 10 and your wife tried to turn back. Witnesses, whose cabins were, miraculously, spared on the opposite side of the highway...who understands how these things work...said she did her best to outrun it, but it lifted them and hurled them over an embankment. Your wife died instantly upon impact. We are so sorry to have to bring you this terrible news. Mr. Stirling?"

I heard the words like distant wind chimes playing discordant notes in my ear. I felt inside myself, watching myself direct my gaze towards the sliding patio doors where I'd been planning on serving us supper this evening once Jennifer and Tia arrived home. I rehearsed, in my numbing mind, the scenario I'd imagined: how I'd have made a pitcher of Sangria for Jen and I after supper so that we could sit on the deck and watch the weather system move out past us over the lake, past our spot of Nirvana which she'd been frantically trying to reach when she'd met the monster head-on.

And in the glass, again just for seconds, I saw her walking towards me, her hands outstretched, her hair wet and flowing behind her in the wind, her smile sweet and timeless. As the clouds finally broke and a beam of sun ribboned out, I heard her sing her sweet song, and this time I saw both officers turn their heads, puzzled, to also listen. That's how I knew it was true; that she was really dead.

Hush little baby, don't you cry, Mama's gonna sing you a lullaby…

The hairs came up on Honey's back and I saw her staring at the glass. Then her tail began to wag.

The weather system blew out, and with it, the image of Jennifer walking towards me over the lake, the sliding doors of the patio framing her in the last remnants of the cloud banks dispersing in the distance. I knew we'd watched the storm pass through together, she and I like we'd done for years, and like the system, both were now gone. Honey let out a mournful wail as she ran towards the glass, sniffing along the floor. A thin trickle of water appeared out of nowhere on the tiles, in it a fragile wisp of lake grass.

And I knew that I'd be watching the clouds in every storm thereafter, for the rest of my life, while listening for her song. Traditions die hard.

The End

Cadaver Extremis

Night when rains prevail and winds
Pry fingers cold around head stone
Its flesh gone soft, its glistening entrails
Jaw swings pendulum from its chin
Held loose with cartilage
Pale as moon, phalanges scrape the landscape grim
Mission set in eyeless sockets
Dark as wings, the crow sets flight
There's no point in locking your windows
Cadaver's crawling, eyes alight

It smells your fear and feels you tremble
Drawn to terror with rising zeal
You wait with breath held, listening…out there
Imagination? Or truth revealed
Along still glass the wind does travel
Whistling low close to the ground
Or is it bone that lingers near by
Seeking, prying, horror-bound

You
Slide down beneath your covers
Eyes squeezed shut, hands set to prayer
On this windswept night it finds you
Glass shatters inward, moist cool air
You feel it enter, lingering nearby
Glides in with you, like a lover
Cold and warmth embrace together
Lipless teeth over yours, they hover

Bone enwraps you, circling, tightening
Femur, fibula, hard skull kisses
Teeth that sever, nails gone yellow
Cadaver embrace, carnal wishes
With mission set, it'll always find you
Your terror bittersweet perfume
On windswept nights, the bone-man rambles
To drag you back, a waiting tomb

BLACK

LIMOUSINE

By
Carol Weekes

Black Limousine

It rained on the day the limousine showed up. Before I begin this tale in earnest, you need to know something. Tayside isn't a big place. Everything here is as predictable as clockwork. The last census listed our population at 2,006. Anything different from the 'norm' stands out. The center of town consists of two blocks of stores, a garage, small businesses like a lawyer's office, a medical clinic, a hairdresser, an insurance company, and the local high and elementary schools that sit side by side in matching brown brick. If a stranger drives through in an ordinary vehicle, like a nondescript old Honda or pickup truck, that's enough to turn heads and jaws to gossip. *Who the hell is that?* Heads shake. *I dunno; tourist, maybe. Or somebody lost.* If it's a fancier vehicle with shiny rims, it's *drug dealer or pimp.* Then the stranger will move on and so will the conversation, back to the mundane and expected.

The limousine pulled into town on a Tuesday, out on R.R. #5. Weather had turned 'funny,' bringing heavy rains that knocked leaves from their branches and freezing puddles over in thin veils of crunchy ice. Jay Bening, who grows most of the town's corn, soy, and alfalfa saw it coming along the road under a watery morning sun.

"Moving like its wheels weren't even touching the ground," he told the rest of us. "Just floating like a big, fat shadow." We sat around a wood stove in Kenny's Sports Bar. Kenny Goodman wiped beer glasses dry and set them beneath the counter, his ear cocked to the conversation.

"Its windows (Jay pronounced this as 'winders') were as dark as smoke. Couldn't see the driver or any passengers. Never heard it coming, either. I looked up to scratch at a bug trying to land on my forehead and there it was…big ugly car…right in front of me. Gave me a chill. Smelled funny too, like its exhaust was made out of a big, old fart."

"Diesel fuel?" I queried.

Jay shrugged his shoulders. "Diesel's tend to have noisy engines and I ain't heard of a limo with one, but I never heard this bastard sneaking up on me." He groaned a little and rubbed at his belly for a minute.

Dewey Newman, one of the barmen, paused in his wiping potato chip crumbs from our table. "I saw it just before I came in today, over on Grant Street."

"What was it doing there?" I asked. I hadn't liked the mention of this car in town when Jay first saw it, although why, I couldn't say. A limousine's an odd thing. Any time the local high school has a graduation, the grade twelve kids will rent one or two of them from the city and get ferried to and fro half the night. But those ones were long, white stretch limos. Not like this one, dark as soot. And being October, I couldn't imagine a reason for it being here.

"Just sitting there, idling," Dewey said. "In front of Pickerings."

"Maybe some movie star is passing through." I grinned at the raised eyebrows.

"Through Tayside?" Dewey snorted.

"Well, we do keep good gas prices compared to the other towns around here. It was in front of Pickerings?"

Pickerings is one of two small grocers in town, the other being a franchise IGA in the south end. Pickerings catered to the more expensive and unusual items. If you wanted something different, like pickled catfish or fresh oysters or even some odd vegetable like arugula, you went to Pickerings for it. My wife once did a full order there and I had a word with her for it too. Cost me $250 in groceries that week instead of the usual $125 so that she could ferry a basket home full of things like some fancy bottle of pomegranate syrup and fresh figs. Figs. Sounds like a perfectly good cuss word to me. Fig. Fig on that, I told her. You don't shop there again. They're ripping people off for these big city items. Plain old pork chops and mashed potatoes will do. I don't want to be eating things on a cracker that look like they might fight back on their way into my mouth.

Old man Pickering didn't do without. He was one of the few in town to drive around in a spanking new vehicle every year, this year being a grey Lexus; him chewing on a Cuban cigar like he had a penchant for wet wanker. Roll down the window and knock ash from the end of the thing, he would, letting the sun catch and form a prism off his diamond ring.

Word had it Pickerings was a front for other kinds of business; underground enterprise and maybe why vehicles with shiny rims or with unidentified faces often cruised in and out of the town. Figs on the outside, illegal pharmaceuticals, and I even heard porn and snuff films on the inside. It was all talk, grant you, and talk in a small town often comes out of a bad mix of boredom and speculation. But I had to admit that Donny Pickering with his fat, pink fingers and heavy jowls left a bad taste in the mouth. He had what my wife called 'fish eyes' — opaque and cold. If he looked directly at you, you felt like you needed to wipe something from your face.

"Maybe someone's coming for payment," Kenny said. We nodded. Could be criminal, although the choice of car was conspicuous for something sneaky about to go down, unless they wanted to make their presence known and shake things up.

"Someone's gonna get killed one of these days. Don't think it can't happen in our town."

"Couldn't say I'd care if it did happen to him," I cut in, dry. "Fig."

"What?" Kenny asked. I ignored him.

"It kind of hovered there, like whoever was inside of it was studying me," Jay resumed his story. "Then it sped up and over the hill, leaving its stink in the air. Gives me goose bumps." He rubbed at both arms and took a long swallow of beer, then grimaced.

"Taste bad?" I asked him.

"Bad gut."

"Oh, go on," Dewey waved a hand at him. "Next thing you'll be saying you saw the grim reaper peering at you through the back window.

Jay's face was solemn. I felt a little chill move along the air just then, as if someone had cracked open the bar's front door and let a breeze in.

Jay scowled. "There's something not right about that thing."

No one said anything for a long moment. A knot of wood popped in the stove, making us jump.

Kenny resumed his glass-drying, cutting the moment in two and breaking the immediate tension. "You's imagining things."

Dewey laughed and walked back to the bar.

Jay looked pissed. "Never mind," he said. "I won't be mentioning it again." He ordered scotch in place of beer and slung it back, swallowing hard and squeezing his eyes shut to the burn. We changed the topic to football, and when everyone went home that evening, I can't say any of us thought of the limousine again.

The next morning I heard that old man Pickering had been found dead in the back office of his store, just before the lunch hour. According to his employees, who spread the gossip to customers, Pickering had been giving some instructions to an employee, Brett Hilstrom, about how he wanted imported jars of antipasto stacked near the dry goods, when Pickering's face went a little pale. He'd been talking and suddenly he stopped in mid-sentence, looking past Hilstrom's shoulder like he'd seen a mouse or something skitter across the floor. Hilstrom said Pickering's words just faded out and his mouth fell open. When Hilstrom turned to see what had caught Pickering's attention, he didn't note anything unusual—but he later admitted he smelled something a little "off," like "meat gone bad" for a few seconds.

"What's up, boss?" Hilstrom had asked, but Pickering didn't answer him. Instead, he'd walked past Hilstrom and stepped toward a shelf containing a wall of soda cracker boxes on sale. Pickering had been cautious when he peeked behind the display stand, his fists curled and his neck craning forward.

"Weird," Pickering had said.

"What's weird, sir?"

Pickering shook his head. "Never mind. I have some paperwork to finish in my office. Get those jars up before noon."

"Yes, sir," Hilstrom complied. He'd watched the big man saunter away. Then he'd taken a look for himself around the soda cracker stand, his curiosity eating at him. He hadn't seen anything amiss and whatever smell he'd detected moments earlier had dissipated. That was the last time anyone had seen Pickering alive. But as more gossip spread, it was learned that two of the employees who worked cashier positions at the front of the store had, just like Dewey

Newman, seen a black limousine idling in front of the store. It had been a little past nine-thirty in the morning. No one had seen anyone step out from the limousine, but then there'd been a lineup at both cash registers and everyone had been busy. It was only after someone went to knock on the boss's office door, had pushed the door open when they got no response, and that person had screamed when they found old man Pickering slumped over his desk with blood running from one nostril and his eyes wide and scared and already clouding over, that the one cashier saw the black car pull out and move into traffic. But before it did she swore she saw old man Pickering's face peering at her through the car's open rear passenger window. He'd mouthed the words 'help me.' Then a long thin hand had appeared over Pickering's left shoulder and hauled him back from the glass. The limo's window slid up and became a square of darkness again. Impossible, she'd later been told. Pickering was dead at his desk. He hadn't gotten into any car, never mind a limo. I know what I saw, the girl insisted, but she looked scared.

"What do you think she saw?" Kenny asked us that afternoon. We'd gathered again after work for a pint and a game of darts.

"I think she's looking for attention from the media is what," I said. "Everyone wants their moment of fame."

Kenny scratched his head. "Queer is what it is. I wonder where that car's gone. Anyone see it around lately?"

Dewey shook his head. "I ain't seen it at all, and I'll tell you another thing. I'm not worrying about it. This is just a bunch of hocus." We all let out a titter. Jay nailed a dart smack center of the board. We howled, impressed. The moment of unease and the limousine were forgotten.

A few minutes later nature called and I walked into the men's washroom at the back of the bar. It's a small room with a single toilet inside a private stall, a urinal on the opposite side, and a cracked porcelain sink with a yellow stain where the hot water tap continuously leaks. Jay keeps a couple of those blue disinfectant pucks in the urinal to cut back on the smell of piss. Jay pushed through the door as I stood at the urinal, relieving myself.

"You think the Wildcats are gonna..." I began and noted his face. He looked like he was going to up-chuck his cookies. I finished and hurried over to where he stood in the toilet stall, one hand balancing himself against a wall.

"You have too much to drink, man?" I asked him. As far as I knew, he'd only had a couple of beers so far, but maybe he'd gotten into a hard shot or two while my back had been turned.

"I don't feel so good," Jay told me. He took a deep breath, then clutched at his stomach and heaved. "Haven't for a few weeks now."

"Well, why haven't you gone to see a doctor?"

He shrugged. "Just the flu, maybe. It'll pass."

"Maybe not with the kind of bugs going around these days."

A stream of puke came out of him, splashing into the toilet and over the edge of the seat. At the same time, I felt this cold breeze squirrel past the back of my neck, and with it came a smell that was different from the stink of hops and stomach acid filling the room. It made me think of wet leaves and old wood, the aroma of things gone soft with rot. It was the odor of still, quiet places: basements, closed attics...

"Hey man," I stepped forward to help him up. That's when I saw the blood in the toilet water; ropy strings of fresh, red blood mixed in with chunks of food and beer.

"You're bleeding," I said, feeling stupid stating the obvious. It came to me that the flu doesn't cause you to hemorrhage. Time stopped, these moments that dangle in front of your face like a spider on a filament of web. I saw Jay heave again and more blood came out of him. The water in the toilet bowl turned a deep crimson.

"I've had some s-stomach pains for a while," he began. He gripped both sides of the toilet seat with his hands. I saw his skin had gone pale.

"Jay, let me help you up. I'll drive you to the doctor." I glanced through the small window above the toilet tank. It faces the parking lot behind the bar. It's a small window, no curtain, grimy with dust. Caught within the window frame like a nightmarish work of art was the black limousine. Its headlamps faced me. They blinked on and the light that came out of them was as red as the blood in the toilet. A trickle of exhaust formed a bluish cloud behind it.

"Jay, stand up," I said. "Gimme your arm, man." I recognized what the limousine wanted. I didn't know what condition Jay might have had, but I knew it was serious. I had to get him out of there, away from the vehicle that waited for him in the back of the bar. There was that smell again, the stink of worms on a rainy day and something more rank—the door to the washroom blew wide open on a gust of it and I retched. I felt Jay go limp against me.

"Jay, no!" I screamed. I dug my fingers around his wrist, gripping him. His pulse was barely discernible, as soft as an insect under fabric. I felt my head crick up on my neck, against my will, so that I stared at the limousine. Although I still gripped Jay's arm, I watched him walk across the parking lot towards the limo. He looked as real out there as he did in here.

"Don't get in that car!" The limo's rear left door opened and Jay hesitated for a moment. He looked dubious as he bent to peer into the car's interior.

"Jay!" I screamed. Then, he seemed intrigued by something in the limo. I watched him lean toward it, until he was inside. The limo's door shut behind him and the car pulled forward, coming at me with its fiery lamps. It swerved at the last second, barely missing the bathroom wall, then it was gone.

I struggled for breath and glanced down at the man whose wrist I still held, and whom I'd just witnessed, impossibly, getting into that rancid vehicle. His wrist was limp and I could not detect a pulse.

* * *

Autopsy results confirmed what I'd suspected: Jay's innards had been riddled with cancer. But that's not what bothered me the most. When I'd been asked by the others in the bar, and the police who followed up, what had happened in the bathroom, all I could bring myself to say was that I'd found him up-chucking blood into the toilet, and that he'd died while I'd tried to help him to his feet. I couldn't admit the part about looking through that window and seeing that ghastly car waiting out there for him; waiting like a hungry dog with its eyes on a close bone.

Everywhere I went, I kept an eye out for that limousine. I didn't see it directly again, but gossip spread that it had made a couple more visits over the week after Jay had died. It had idled in front of the retirement home over on Addison Street; an old woman had been wheeled out into an ambulance a short while later, DOA at the hospital. It had appeared again in front of the house of a suicidal teenager who'd left a note with melancholy song lyrics that recited a message about burning bridges. No one could ever make out the face of the driver. And why would they. I suspected it would be faceless.

Angry, I sat in Kenny's this afternoon, a glass of ale in my hand, my thoughts scattered. The bar was filled. Kenny, Dewey, and a co-worker of mine, Tommy Miller sat around the wood stove. Kenny had stoked it with good rock maple. Despite the full heat that thing gave out, I felt chilled. Everyone was talking about that damned limo.

"We have to find that thing and run them out of town," Kenny said, irate. Despite the 'No Smoking' ban, he lit a cigarette and took a long, shaky drag before expelling the smoke toward the ceiling.

"Who do you think they are?" Dewey challenged them. "Pickering likely had debts. You want to mess with people like that?"

Kenny guffawed. "Well, are we all just going to sit here feeling scared like a bunch of schoolgirls?"

I couldn't bring myself to admit what I saw in the bar's bathroom last week—how that car waited for Jay out in the parking lot and how I watched his double-step into it just before his pulse left his body. I didn't think anyone would believe me, but worse, they might challenge me as to why I hadn't run out to that limo when it had happened. I knew why: because I was scared. Scared of what I'd find if I looked inside that thing, and more frightened of being swept up into it. I knew what the limousine was. It had arrived to collect and it was leaving its calling card in different places around the town, just like it and others like it did in every town and city around the world, every second of every day.

"I don't know if you can run this thing out of anywhere," I said, morose. "You can't halt the inevitable."

Kenny eyed me. "I have me an F150 with a mounted shovel hitch, deer lights, and a shotgun between the seats. That sneaky mother wants to try anything else, he's gonna face my music."

"And what, exactly, do you propose to do when you find it and whoever's driving it?" Tommy asked. He looked about as calm as the rest of us. We all just sat there, some of us tapping our fingers on the tabletop, others smoking quietly, and still others just watching everyone else. We'd all become edgy. Outside, a tailpipe popped, making us all jump.

"Threaten them with death or some serious pain," Kenny said, serious.

I almost laughed. Almost.

"You have any better plans, sunshine?" Kenny squared his gaze at me.

I sat for a moment, thinking. I felt a trickle of condensation slide down my glass and ease its way into the edge of my sleeve, turning my wrist cold. Its headlamps as red as Jay's blood in the toilet bowl.

"I wouldn't go looking for trouble, if I were you."

"Chickenshit," Kenny said.

"Maybe," said I. We stared hard at each other. Finally, he looked away.

* * *

The limousine showed up again that evening, this time in front of Kenny's house. I know because I got the call from him shortly after 7 pm. I'd just finished eating supper and had settled down to watch a television show when my wife, Cara, motioned for me to take the phone.

"It's Kenny Goodman," she said. "He sounds upset."

I sat forward and my stomach curled around itself in a little knot. I took the phone.

"What's up, man?"

"It's here."

"What's…" I began, then stopped, understanding.

"In front of my house—just sitting there," Kenny's voice broke off. He lived alone, divorced for years, his only son grown and gone.

"Is anyone else with you?" I asked.

"No."

I heard him swallow, this dry click that echoed into the telephone receiver, and I knew he was scared.

"Call the police, Kenny. It'll take me twenty minutes to get there."

Silence.

"Its windows are tinted and all I can see in them is the reflection from the streetlamp," he continued. "I want to kill the bastard driving it."

I wanted to tell him that I didn't think that was possible; that it would work the other way around.

"Do you have anything wrong with you, Kenny?" I asked him. "Any illness or something?" He didn't answer me for a long moment.

"No. Why?"

"Just wondering," I mumbled. I felt scared for him. My hands shook.

"I'm on my way. Don't go out there."

I went to put the receiver down when I heard him say the words, "Its door's opening."

"What?" I barked into the phone, but the line went dead. When I called him back, the line just rang. I grabbed my truck keys, and on second thought, went for the hunting rifle I kept locked in a cupboard upstairs.

"What are you doing?" Cara followed me from room to room. "What's going on with Kenny?"

"I don't know," I grabbed a box of shells and stuffed them into my jacket pocket. "But I want you to promise me something—if you're about the town and see a black limousine anywhere...you get away from it as quickly as possible. You understand?"

"I've heard other people talking about it," she said, her eyes wide with fright. "What is that car?"

"Stay in the house and keep the doors locked. You hear?"

"I hear," she whispered. "What's wrong?"

Death is what's wrong, I thought, *and it seems hungry for the flavor of Tayside lately.* If we'd never noticed the limousine before it was because it hadn't come around for anyone we knew intimately before this.

* * *

I reached Kenny's street. The whole time I drove, I kept asking myself what the heck I thought I was doing. What did I propose to do once I got there? Shove a shotgun into the face of Fate and cock it? Blow the headless head off of something I couldn't see? For that matter, what might I see if I got a look inside that car?

Kenny lived on an unpaved road. It contained two street lamps that burned like watery yellow eyes against the night. His house was the last one on the road before it ended in an abrupt shock of field grass, woods, and cow fencing.

I didn't see the limousine anywhere. My gaze shifted over to Kenny's place. Only his front parlor was lit. The rest of the house was dark. His truck sat silent in the driveway. It struck me that maybe I should have called one or two of the boys to come out here with me; create a little posse of sorts to deal with this. I would have loved some company. I became aware of how still and cold the night was. Mist turned to ice pellets, ticking off the windshield and melting from the truck's heater. I had to get it done. I had to find him. Kenny was a good friend and part of the community's business backbone.

"Damn," I muttered. I killed the truck's engine and gripped the loaded rifle. I mounted his porch and rapped hard on the door.

"Kenny? It's me." No answer. I tried the door knob and the door opened. I stuck my head inside and yelled his name again. Still nothing. I crept into the landing and peered around the living room. A lamp provided soft illumination. A newspaper lay open on the coffee table. The house settled around me; a clock somewhere in the background ticked off seconds. The furnace popped on with a soft hum. I could sense him nearby, somewhere, in or around the house.

"Kenny! Answer me if you hear me."

A footstep made a floorboard squeak in a room off to my left. I felt my hair prickle along my scalp. I cocked the rifle and, swallowing hard, moved towards the room in question. In a darkened house, my eyes needed time to adjust. I approached what I knew was his kitchen. It was in the back of the house, the windows along one wall facing the yard and fields behind him. I came around the corner, both hands on the rifle and raising it into firing position when I saw his outline in the window. Kenny stood on the other side of the glass...stood on the back porch, his face looking in at me through the window. His form was dark with shadow, but his eyes were wide and scared. Then he was bathed in dark red light, like a spotlight coming on behind him, and I knew. Kenny began to turn around.

"Don't go near it!" I screamed. I ran towards the kitchen door, my hands frozen to the rifle, watching him walk away from me—and tripped over something on the floor. I went reeling, dropping the weapon, which clattered away from me and slid along the smooth kitchen floor. I landed hard against a wall and took a moment to right my balance and stare at what I'd just tripped over.

Kenny's body lay on the floor, his head and torso under the shadow of the kitchen table, his legs extended out.

"Oh, my God no..." I mumbled. I slapped along walls, searching for a light switch; found one, and the room flooded with natural light. Blood trickled from his mouth and nose, and a large, purple welt adorned the left side of his head just above his temple. Clearly, he'd fallen in the dark, fallen trying to run from something.

I spun about and saw the blood-red headlamps pull back from the yard and spin around the corner of the house towards the street again. I felt, more than saw the shape of the limousine sweep past the house, but as it did I saw Kenny's face framed in the ruby square of its open rear window. We looked at each other: me, one of his best buddies, standing in his kitchen with his body behind me, and whatever remained of the man I'd known and drank with for years now sitting inside the car. He looked resigned. I saw others sitting in the car with him. Someone pulled him back from the window and the opaque glass slid shut, shutting the view of his face.

"Why?" I screamed at him. I flew out onto the porch and gripped the rail in time to hear the limousine's tires crunch over gravel and then the sound stopped entirely. I caught a whiff of a foul odor that made me gag; it smelled of death. I rushed back through the house and into the street again, in time to see the car lifting off the road and soaring into the air where it became highlighted for a few seconds in a flurry of ice crystals, its fiery headlamps creating a ribbon of crimson ahead of it, and then the crystals thickened into snow and the shape disappeared. The street fell silent again; just me, my idling truck, and Kenny's empty house behind me...

I walked around to the side of his house and inspected the dusting of ice and snow that had gathered there. No tire tracks anywhere to indicate the presence of the limousine that had arrived to cart him away. Only after a few more minutes could I force myself to walk back inside his house and call the police, but not before I tucked the rifle under the seat of the truck. All I said was that I'd responded to a call from him that he'd needed help…he wasn't feeling well, I lied…and I'd arrived to find him already gone. It wasn't a full lie; the second half of that statement was true. His death was chalked up to an accident; internal hemorrhaging from a fall in the dark and slamming his forehead against the edge of his kitchen table. I knew he'd been running through the dark house when his front door blew open, then shut again, and that something darker had been on his heels.

* * *

We haven't seen the limousine again since Kenny's death.

When I lay in bed at night, with my wife's warmth beside me, I still feel chilled. It isn't the cold October air. It isn't the snow crystals or the north-westerly wind that pries at and rattles the eaves trough. It's the knowledge that the limousine is out there, gathering passengers with its preordained itinerary all over the world, operating at all hours of the day or night. And that it could come back any time.

"I won't go," I say into the dark. But still, I watch, fearful for the tiptoe of crimson light along my walls and the hum of a distant engine growing closer.

The End

THE
WISHING
WELL

By
Carol Weekes

The Wishing Well

They were into their new property a week when their ten year old son, Cory, discovered the well. It sat a good one hundred yards away from the house, a 110-year-old farmhouse that Jan had fallen in love with, but which had pushed them to their limits in affordability. And now that they were here, she'd lost her job. Money was tight, but she loved the place and Terry was determined to make her happy. The well was mostly covered over with planks of silver plywood that had gone rank in spots, making the surface a little spongy and sending a chill up Terry's back, seeing his son run up to the thing yelling, "Here it is, Dad!"

"Get off that platform," Terry yelled. Terror seized him. He'd vaguely remembered hearing the real estate agent mention something about an old cistern that had once been used to water the property. But the house had gone on to town water just a few years prior, one of its selling features while still maintaining a quiet, rural location on the edge of town. He hurried and caught up to his son who was busy trying to pump the iron handle of the cistern in an attempt to bring water to the surface.

"I don't think it's supposed to work anymore," Terry said. He reached out and lifted Cory from the platform that sat two feet higher than the soil around a circular concrete pipe that formed the aboveground basis of the well. "These things are dangerous. They can plunge fifty feet or more into the earth and can still contain a lot of ground water. You fall through that wood, you're a goner. Hear me? You're not to play on this thing or go near it."

Cory shrunk back a little over this. "Can you make it pump water, Daddy?"

Terry shrugged and stepped up to the handle. It had once been painted a cherry red, but time and weather had removed most of the paint, leaving only chips of faded red against dark steel. "Well, we can give it a try. But only this time, understand? I'm going to come back out here and cover this thing up more securely than this. It's a liability, is what it is."

"What's a liability, Daddy?"

Terry felt mild amusement override his initial fear. "It's a problem, where something could happen to someone and they'll turn around and sue you for it. I don't like these things. They're outdated technology." He grabbed the long, slender handle and began pumping it, again and again, fifty times or more. They heard something inside the well, a soft splash of sorts and the sound of something like air running along a pipe.

"I think we might have a little success, although I expect the water will be rank," Terry said. Within the next minute a gush of darkness flew out of the cistern spout, spraying the boards with a vibrant red-brown liquid. At the same time, the air around them turned rancid. Terry dropped the handle and stepped back, aghast. He used one hand to hold his son back.

"What in God's name is it?" He leaned closer to take a better look. Initially, he'd suspected foul water mixed with soil and perhaps the slime of algae, but this stuff was redder than black or green slime. Indeed, standing water had sprayed out from the tap, but bits of raw, meaty stuff floated in it, and upon inspection, Terry saw chunks of what looked like matted hair or fur. Maybe some animal that had fallen through the platform's gap lay rotting in the water.

"I think some animal fell in while sniffing around for water," Terry said. "You head back to the house. I'm going to find something to cover this hole. This is dangerous. Go on now."

He watched Cory trudge home, his face disappointed and his running shoes kicking up dust along the ground. When the boy rounded the bend in the path, Terry turned his attention back to the cistern. Raccoon maybe, or even a fox or coyote might have taken the plunge. No matter; he didn't want Cory sneaking back out here to peek into this thing. He went to retreat. When he heard a sound issue from inside the well. Terry froze. He knew animal noise well enough.

But this echo that he'd just heard…it wasn't animal. He was sure he'd heard words uttered, and that the words, echoed and distorted, had been something like 'chickenshit.' Couldn't be. Even if a person had fallen in there and survived, why would they insult him? Call for help, maybe. The pump handle sat still and silent, a tenuous spider web undulating in the breeze. Fetor on the board dried in the sun. Insects crawled over it.

Terry returned to the well and, using a forearm to steady himself, leapt onto the edge of the frame. He strained to listen, wrinkling his nose. Air issuing from the cistern reeked of mud, standing water, and of rot and feces, none of it earthy or pleasant.

"Hello?" he called down the hole. He heard his voice die out. He touched a fingertip to one of the dark, coagulating globs, smudging it between thumb and forefinger. It was softened flesh. A bit of dark hair stuck to it and the smell on his hands was that of road kill in high heat. Gross. He wiped his finger off on his jeans. He heard only a distant drip of liquid. He'd come back with a powerful flashlight. Take a good look before sealing the thing up. Whatever had fallen in and died down there didn't matter—they weren't planning on using or improving the condition of the well. As for the words he'd thought he'd heard, it must have been the way the wind can sometimes play tricks on you when it whistles through hollow places. Still, the thing spooked him, and as he walked away, he looked over his shoulder twice, as if expecting to see someone standing back there, watching him go.

* * *

Jan asked him what he was doing when she came out of the house, after stacking the supper dishes, to observe him loading six-foot lengths of galvanized lumber into the back of the pickup.

"Covering up a well Cory found out in the field." He didn't lie. "Don't want him playing around something that isn't sealed properly. You know how he can be. You tell him 'no' and he takes it as three times a 'yes.'"

"Must have been what Jake Dean told us about," she said, referring to the agent who'd sold them the property.

"Yup. It still works, but the water's rancid and not even good for watering plants. No point in not covering it."

He waited until she returned to the house, then grabbed a powerful laser flashlight, a 100-foot length of nylon rope with a grappling hook, and his hunting rifle and ammunition. He didn't know what was down there, but he'd take a look and he wanted some protection, just in case. He drove the pickup out to the field. It was going on eight o'clock at night and the sky had deepened to a rose hue along the cloud line. The well's silhouette looked dark and barren in the fading light, its handle hunched like a giant praying mantis. Terry stopped the truck and cut the engine. He sat for a moment, listening to the night. A few crickets, a heat cicada, the sound of his own breath. He lit a cigarette and inhaled softly, blowing the smoke out into the breeze while his eyes never left the well and his ears remained alert. He decided to watch for a few minutes. Let the landscape go still. A small groundhog waddled along the barren part of the track near the well where the grasses thinned out. It paused, unaware of Terry sitting in the truck watching it, then with curiosity it leapt onto the surface of the well cover. It sniffed at the refuse coating the wood. It went very still.

Stinks, doesn't it, Terry thought. Terry ground the filter into the truck's ashtray and went to open the cab door, unconcerned with the groundhog, when something dark bore its way through the well's broken boards where Cory had played only hours before. With incredible speed and impact, it seized the groundhog. The groundhog shrieked in pain and terror. Blood dark as ink shot into the air, coating the boards and surrounding grasses. Something large shook the groundhog repeatedly until its body went limp.

Terry felt his lower jaw fall open. So taken by surprise was he that he could only stare, still gripping the steering wheel. He watched as whatever had snagged the gopher emerged with shoulders that were hunched together in order to fit through the hole. A dark arm spread out against the backdrop of the sunset, followed by the second arm. A man's shape hoisted itself through the well cover. It held its catch between its teeth. The man's hair was long and matted. A fresh stench floated through the air. The man was naked, but covered in slime and filth.

"Oh shit…" Terry blurted. His voice caught the man's attention.

The man's head swiveled and Terry was met by the most malevolent pair of luminescent golden eyes he'd ever seen. What looked like a cross between a human face and something beyond simian regarded him. Its upper lip quivered, dark and livery skin that trembled in the way a dog's mouth will when menaced. It was ageless in the ripple of its muscles set against the sheen of its colorless hair. It squatted on the rotting boards of the cistern, and when it saw Terry looking at it, it dropped its now-dead meal and leaned forward on its haunches, its gonads oscillating beneath its buttocks, its broken nails gripping the boards, its toes wide and splayed. It lost interest in the groundhog as it concentrated on the man sitting rigid in the truck's cab. If it had once been a man, it had mutated for reasons Terry couldn't understand. His mind raced. Chemicals or toxins in the soil, a birth defect…

"What in God's name are you?" Terry felt horror looking at it, thinking that while Cory had played down here alone earlier today, this thing had slept below him. It could have been his son that had been grabbed like the now-mutilated groundhog. He couldn't fathom how or why, but Terry understood one thing—he had the choice of running for the rifle, or stepping on the gas and reversing. If he ran, the thing would pursue him; he felt certain of it. He threw open the driver's door and rushed to the rear of the pickup, grappling for the rifle. He got the weapon and flipped the safety at the same moment he heard it coming for him, its feet tearing up stones and bits of grass in its wake. Terry whirled in time to see the beast-man leap at him…and over him, knocking Terry backwards onto his ass. It still held the groundhog in its mouth. The rifle fired a shot into the sky. In the time it took Terry to catch his breath, roll over, and to bring himself back up onto his feet, he saw the beast disappearing into low scrub to his left. A rustling noise, then everything went quiet.

"Damn it!" he exploded. His pulse pounded in his veins. Now the thing was out there. Had it been coming and going like this regularly, and would it return to the well, he wondered? Terry ran in the beast man's direction, the rifle ready. He found himself standing in waist-high grass and alder. The creature could be anywhere, huddled in the tall grasses, watching him search for it. Night went silent around him again with the exception of a distant train rattling along tracks.

"Terry?"

Terry screamed and spun about, the rifle coming up to his shoulder.

Jan faced him, her face drawn, her eyes wide with concern. "It's me...what are you doing with a gun? What's wrong?"

His mind raced. What could he tell her? Would she even believe him?

"I...I thought I saw a cougar in the field. Something big—I'm concerned about Cory playing out here."

He saw her relax a little; cougars could be a concern, but they were natural, a part of the landscape here.

"Oh hon, you're a good dad. Still...do you really think it was a cougar?"

He felt his shoulders sag as he brought the rifle down to his hips. "I don't know," he said, ashamed to lie to her but knowing her reaction if he'd said a thing that looked part human, part gargoyle had just crawled out of their abandoned well.

"I'm not sure what it was." At least that much was truth. He saw her move past him to regard the well.

"What's all over the wood?" She edged closer.

"Don't go near it!" he exploded.

"Terry, take a pill, for God's sake. I'm an adult here, too. I can make decisions for myself. This is fresh blood! Did you wound something?"

"I—" he began, not sure what to tell her. "I might have. I took a shot, but I thought I'd missed."

"Where was it hiding?" she wanted to know. "Was it in the grass?"

He shut his eyes, then opened them again. The evening, a pale indigo now, urged him to get her home. Given the stress they were already under, they didn't need this.

"It came from the vicinity of the well," he snapped. "Stop asking me questions. It all happened so fast. We need to go home. I'm not sure where it is, but it might still be close. It had a smaller animal in its mouth. That's where the blood comes from." He took her hand and pulled her towards the truck. "Get in and lock your door."

She shook her head, got in, but didn't lock the door. "What's gotten into you? I know whatever it was frightened you, but since when can cougars open truck doors?"

"Lock the door, Janet," he insisted. When he used her formal name, he meant business and she knew it. She locked the door without taking her eyes off him. He did the same, then started the truck, the rifle behind their seats.

"You're not telling me something," she said, pressing him. "I know you well enough after twelve years of marriage to know when you're keeping something back. What is it? Hon, I know we're both under pressure, but we'll make do until I can find work again. Honest. I think you're being a little jumpy."

"Trust me, I'm not." He flipped on the high beams and drove slowly as he observed the dark landscape, the headlamps cutting a yellow path ahead of the truck. Other than a jackrabbit sprinting across the track, they saw nothing else. Yet he felt it close by, watching them. He lit another cigarette, his hands shaking. "You wouldn't believe me," he said. He saw from her face that she felt both guilty and incredulous. He shook his head. "Never mind," he said. "We'll work it all out."

* * *

He contacted Jake Dean the next morning by phone, and caught the real estate agent in his office just before he stepped out the door to meet a client.

"What do you know about the well on the property?" Terry asked him.

Dean paused for a moment. "Only what I told you about already; that it hasn't been used in years. It's original to the house, almost ninety years old. It was upgraded a couple of times, and then the water began to turn rank after a while. Too much copper apparently, a problem in these parts. At least, that's what the owner told me when she put the place up for sale. Something in the pump had finally broken, but the water that was coming up wasn't useable.

She had someone board the thing up after an inspector deemed it too toxic to drink. She didn't want to spend the money to drill a new well. Then when the town brought the water line out this way two years ago, she opted to go onto municipal water. She'd been purchasing bottled water prior to that. I'm not sure how she managed or did laundry or bathed. Why do you ask?"

Terry weighed his next words with care. "Did she ever mention anything odd happening with the well? Any strange smells or anything unusual?"

He could almost see Jake Dean shaking his head. "Nooo," Dean enunciated. "Have you had something occur with it?"

"I thought I saw something large hanging around it yesterday; something that took down a small groundhog. I didn't catch full sight of whatever it was because it was getting dark," he lied, "but I was wondering if she'd ever seen a large...animal...lurking around."

"Well, we do get the occasional black bear out here," Dean told him, chuckling a little. "And the county just reintroduced some cougars a few years back to keep the fisher and even the deer population at bay. Too many farmers complaining about fishers attacking and killing chickens and young livestock like lambs and such. As for the deer, the highway accidents are the reason to introduce a natural predator."

"Hmm," Terry said. "Nothing else?"

"Nope. I know the cover of the thing was going rotten. Getting someone to seal it permanently with a concrete slab would be a good idea, but I'm not following why you're concerned about the well in conjunction with local animals of prey. I don't believe the well water would attract them for any reason."

Terry felt desperation.

He'd told Jan the only logical thing he could think of saying: that he'd thought he'd seen a deranged person with an animal...maybe a hare or a groundhog.

"Could be a street person that trapped something," she'd said. He'd let it go at that, but even she hadn't liked the idea of a stranger loitering nearby and he couldn't bring himself to tell her what he'd really seen and that it hadn't been completely human. He could imagine her reaction: you're as stressed as I am, Terry. Money's tight, but we'll work it out. There are no monsters out there. It was just a deranged person wandering through the neighborhood.

* * *

The night passed, uneventful. Cory was strictly instructed not to wander out into the fields. Terry felt afraid to let the boy out of the house, but knew that, should he try to restrict him too much, Cory would revolt. Terror ripped at his imagination…his son being late from school…his son not coming home for lunch when called…

He considered placing the house back up for sale again and bringing his family back into the safer confines of the big city where crowds kept you safe, but he knew that Jan would protest, as afraid as she was of the bills coming in. She hadn't given any more thought to Terry's sighting of 'an odd person' on their property, leaving him alone with his concerns to the point where it interfered with his ability to concentrate on much else.

He grabbed the rifle and drove back to the well that afternoon, determined to take some kind of action. He spent two hours hammering new boards over the old and securing them with dozens of nails. He also set out a chunk of fresh beef on the ramp and moved the truck back, to watch. He kept his doors locked and his window rolled down a few inches to allow a breeze to circulate. Half an hour passed and nothing occurred. He remained patient, his gaze focused on the cistern, convinced the beast would try to return to its den. The well had been its safe spot.

Something banged on the driver's window, making him scream. He lashed at the rifle, twisting about in his seat to peer through the glass. An old woman with long, thin hair that pooled over her shoulders regarded him. She must have been in her eighties, her face thin and lined, her pale eyes and skin giving her a drained appearance. She wore a baggy, ill-fitting blue sweater over a faded house dress.

"You Mr. Terrence Cobb?" she asked.

He had to swallow hard before he could catch his breath. He almost wept, convinced he'd see the face of the beast, its lips glossy with blood, its eyes lit like twin lanterns, waiting for him on the other side of the window before its fist would smash through the glass.

"Yes, I am? Who are you?"

"My name is Emily Gerhard. I sold this house to the person before you. They didn't stay long. I didn't think they would. I had a call from your agent, Mr. Jake Dean earlier today, asking me if I'd ever had anything unusual happen around the old well. Apparently, he didn't get anything out of the previous owner, who just hung up on him. I'm not surprised. I hear you have a young boy lives here with you. Your son?"

"That's correct," Terry said, terse. "I just sealed that well today. I didn't want him playing over it with its rotten wood." He decided he'd let her lead the conversation. "What's wrong with that well?"

"Covering it won't do you much good. Tried that already m'self. What have you seen?" she asked, and her eyes held a kind of acknowledgement, as if she could read his face.

"What do you know about it?" he countered.

"You willing to roll down your window and talk directly to me? I'm a harmless old woman. It isn't me you have to be afraid of, Mr. Cobb. It's my husband and who he cavorts with. I'm only here to talk to you because I'm old, I'm dying with the cancer, and I've lived with this secret for the last number of years. I even called the police about it at first, but they didn't believe me. Told me I should think about seeing a doctor." She tapped one temple with an index finger. "They think it's all in my head. Animals going missing all the time, including people's pets. Street people disappearing. Soon enough, it'll be someone's family taken."

Terry debated. "Okay, you can get in the truck." He unlocked the passenger door and let Emily Gerhard step inside. "Now, you tell me what's going on. What about your husband?"

Emily sighed and clasped her hands in her lap. "I'm only here because I heard you have trouble, and I know what that trouble is. Twenty years ago Duane...that's my husband, and I got the well serviced. We'd been having problems with the water. A lot of iron in the rock around here; it tainted everything. Called in a local well driller to fix the problem. They came out and drilled and for a while everything seemed fine. Then, the water started tasting bad again. Real bad. I stopped drinking it when I started to get an itch on my skin, but Duane brushed me off and said I was being too fussy. He kept on drinking it, but I only used it for watering the plants around the garden and such.

One day, three years ago, I went to get garden water and when I pumped, it was blood that came out of that spout, Mr. Cobb. Not water, and not mud. Blood. I know blood when I see it. I grew up on a farm, and my daddy used to slaughter our cows, pigs, and chickens. What came out of that spout was pure, fresh blood. I dropped my watering can and went screaming all the way back to the house for Duane to come see. He did. He told me to go back to the house to get cleaned up. He got some tools and took the cover off the well so that he could shine a light down there to see what might be up. Told me some animal must have gotten into the well and was breaking apart. He said he'd get it taken care of.

"Well, he didn't come back to the house for two hours. Finally, when the supper hour came around, I walked back down there to see what he was up to. The sun was setting. It was late summer, August, and everything had this sheen of gold about it. I came around the corner of the field and saw Duane standing in front of the well. Its cover was clean off and his tools were scattered around him. He was standing with his back to me, and his hands were in a praying position, held up in front of his chest. He was mumbling something. I got closer and I heard a few of his words here and there. He was speaking in some language I'd never heard before. Something old. Then I saw him walk around the other side of the well and pick something up from the ground. I saw he had a dead rabbit in his hands. He drops the rabbit into the well. I said 'Duane, what are you up to?' Well, he looks up at the sound of my voice, but his eyes were different. His eyes caught the glare of the sun and for that moment, it looked like his insides were on fire, the way a candle reflects at night. He didn't seem to know me. We stood there, man and woman who'd been married for over forty years, and he's staring at me the way a mean dog will look at a squirrel or cat it wants to take down."

Terry shifted in his seat. He tapped a cigarette out of its package. "Mind if I smoke?"

"Go ahead," Emily said, her voice soft. "I used to do it too. That's what got me. Better than him getting me."

"Go on," Terry urged her on. "I'm listening."

Emily picked up. "I shouted 'Duane! What's wrong with you? That's when I saw something come out of the well behind him, this shadow that rose like thick smoke. The dead rabbit came up with the smoke and it was shredded like something had torn it apart with its teeth. Duane dropped his head back and opened his mouth. That smoke started going into him, Mr. Cobb. It entered him, like some kind of reverse tornado that pushed instead of sucked. Next thing I know, Duane goes for the remains of the rabbit. He starts chewing on it, tearing at the bones and hair with his teeth, blood running down his chin and neck. He's looking at me the entire time he's doing this until there was nothing left of that rabbit. Then, he came for me, feral as a rabid dog."

"My God..." Terry began, horrified. "What did you do?"

"I ran, Mr. Cobb. I ran back to the house as fast as these old legs could carry me. I got there just seconds ahead of him and slammed the door in his face, locking it. I went through the place, slamming windows shut and locking them too, him following me from one to the other, hurling himself at the glass to get in. His eyes were still electric, with blood smearing glass wherever he hit with his fists. I called the police and told them to get out here—that my husband had lost his mind and was after me. By the time they arrived, some twenty minutes later, he was gone. I told them what happened; Duane in front of the well and about this cloud that came out of the thing. They didn't believe that part at all. In fact, I think they figured I must have been mad and that my husband had finally snapped on me for it. They looked around for him and couldn't find him. They left without doing anything."

Her hands shook. "Maybe I'll take your offer of a smoke, Mr. Cobb."

"S-sure," Terry handed her the pack and his lighter.

"What you saw, Mr. Cobb, was either my husband...what's left of him...or the power that got into him in the first place and changed him. It's old, it's bad."

"What is this power?" Terry asked.

Emily lit her cigarette and took a long drag like a woman familiar with the pleasure of a smoke. She explained what she'd learned about the history of the land around their home. "Seems that the original owners of the house, a Zachary and Bernadette Waters, had been involved in some unsavory practices back at the turn of the century. He'd been a prosecutor for local trials. Back then, petty criminals were often condemned to death, sometimes for crimes they didn't do. I dug deep for this information, Mr. Cobb. I started talking to townsfolk who, at first, wouldn't divulge a thing. Finally, I found one woman in town who put me on to a great-nephew of the Waters. He wasn't going to talk until I came out and told him what was going on with my husband and that, if he didn't help me, I'd send my husband after him. I said to this younger Waters 'You can call me crazy all you want, but you can come out here and I'll show you what happens at that well. You'll see the blood for yourself.'"

"So what did he do?" Terry prodded her. "I'm afraid for my family. I've seen it...this thing. Is it your husband?"

"It could be him. It could be Waters or his wife. Waters and his wife had taken on the practice of drinking blood. They were part of a club, a secret club in town who'd gather to do this sort of thing. They'd capture wild animals or steal local pets. But, as Waters' nephew finally admitted to me, they loved nothing better than human blood. It supposedly brought a special kind of power to them—that whatever they took from, they possessed its best attributes, be it good or evil. Seems they found a particular succulence drinking the blood of other men and women. That's where some of the local prisoners came in, those sentenced to death. All of them terrified; all of them pleading for their lives...all of them vowing revenge as they died. They weren't executed in traditional style, Mr. Cobb. They were taken out into the woods and slaughtered, used, and their bodies hurled into that same well that sat fresh and new on the Waters' land. Convenient it was; a hundred feet down it drops if it drops a foot and no one questioning a figure of authority back then. People were told these prisoners were buried in an unmarked grave deserving of murderers. Think of it. Killers calling the kettle black. It went on for years."

"Unbelievable," Terry muttered. "No, not your story!" he exclaimed when he saw Emily's face. "Just the facts of what happened."

Emily nodded, grim. "Duane came back a few days later. Quiet, moody, changed from what he was. He started going down to the well all the time with animals he'd caught in traps, offering them to the darkness in the well. He wished for things with his tokens; for money, for longevity. We came into money in odd ways for a while...an inheritance from an aunt of his who just up and died without good medical cause; insurance from an automobile accident when some car, without reason, suddenly swerved and slammed into Duane, killing the driver but Duane walking away without injury. Blood money, I called it. That's when things between him and I got really ugly. He laughed at me when I threatened to expose him. He said, 'go ahead; see who believes you. You bring them down here and all they'll find is rank well water with too much iron in it. Guess where the iron comes from?' He came home less and less. One day I found his body half in, half out of the well...torn to shreds like some big animal had gotten him. Maybe he wanted to die. He'd become completely devoted to them, getting fresh meat for them—whenever they wanted. He'd become one of them.

"You sell this house, Mr. Cobb. Put it back on the market and get your family out of here. I tried destroying that well. I poured poison into it. I used holy water. I even tried setting off dynamite in it...Duane kept the stuff around to get rid of boulders out in the fields...nothing worked. Every time I took a stand against it, it took a stand against me. They got into the house, into the pipes, into the foundation, into the core of my home. Accidents, mishaps, and now the sickness. So, I left while I could. But I can't sit here and watch this happening to another family."

Terry's fingers shook as he finished his cigarette. He looked at Emily. "So what am I supposed to do? You're telling me dead people are in my well, and that they still move about. My wife wanted this house. She loves it."

"You love your wife and boy? You leave with them. You go now while you're all still safe. The Waters, Duane, and the others they associated with...they're in the ground, in the ground water, in the soil, in the property. You can't get rid of them. They're in every cell, every ounce of soil, every rain drop here, Mr. Cobb. I have nothing else to tell you, except leave with your family while you still can. All I've ever told is the truth. I hope you'll believe me instead of just thinking me another senile old woman who's lost her mind. You can take my advice any way you like. Thank you for the smoke. I bid you good day."

Emily got out of the truck and shut the door. Terry watched her walk away in the reflection of his rearview mirror. He smoked another two cigarettes once she disappeared around the bend, and he mused over what Emily had told him. He wanted to scoff, but the gooseflesh along his arms told him otherwise.

*   *   *

Twilight, the sky clear and freckled with stars. Terry made his way down to the well with the body of a young mourning dove that he'd hit by accident in the road while driving into town after Emily had left. He'd gone to the beer store to get a six-pack; he needed to quell himself. Jan had taken Cory into the village to get Cory a new pair of running shoes. She'd come home with two more bills; more than they had the money to pay that month. He felt desperate.

He stood in front of the well he'd just boarded over, and using a pry bar, removed one of the boards. He tossed it aside to the ground and stood before the dark, foul hole, containing the toxic ground waters and the remnants of killers.

"I don't want to become one of you," he said, making his wish. "I just want some extra money so that I can take care of my family. Okay? So, I'm offering a small thing. A little favor for a little extra money. If you want more meat, I'll get you meat. I'll get you blood."

He left the dove's body on the boards and stepped away from the well. Within a minute something approached through tall grass opposite him, and when it stepped out into the moonlight, Terry knew that it was the entity that had been Emily Gerhard's husband. He was naked, his skin as slimy as his soul, his eyes filled with the light of greed, pestilence, and…admiration.

"So...you aren't so chickenshit, after all," Gerhard told him, its teeth shining like pearly needles behind its blackened, wet lips. "The bigger the gift, the bigger the prize. Bring something larger if you want to keep your home." Its breath stank of decay.

Two days later Terry discovered he'd won several hundred dollars on a chance lottery ticket he'd purchased on a whim earlier that week. He returned to the wishing well that evening, this time with a young buck he'd shot in the woods that morning.

"It's bigger," he told the things in the well. "How big do you need for me to be able to pay off my house? I need three hundred thousand dollars just for that. Okay? Just that. I'll be able to afford the rest." He left the deer on the wood and watched as its body was dragged over the edge, followed by a splash of fresh blood as they dug into it.

His bank account read an extra ten thousand dollars a day later. Better, but not good enough. Terry sat and thought about what he might be able to offer next that would bring about the kind of money they needed to pay off the house. Cougar perhaps? Bear? Jan came into the room behind him and lovingly stroked his head.

"You seem so lost in thought these days," she murmured and kissed his cheek. "Where'd we get the several extra thousand from?"

"Old business contact I'd forgotten about," he lied. "Extra money came through."

In fact, his business had declined over the last little while, given all that was going on.

"I've got to go into town to pick up some groceries," she said. "I'll be back in an hour."

"Okay." He kissed her on the lips and thought it better she be away from this place anyway. He had to find something bigger to offer them while she was out. She couldn't discover what he was up to. She'd never forgive him.

An hour later, as he prepared to hunt for bear or moose, the doorbell rang. Terry answered it, to discover two police officers standing in his doorway, their faces grim.

"Are you Mr. Cobb?"

"Yes," he paled. Had someone witnessed his offerings at the ᵛwondered?

"You might want to sit down, sir. We have terrible news," one of the officers said.

* * *

Jan was gone. Car accident; weird accident. She'd swerved, on a dry road in clear daylight, their car hurling through the covered bridge and into the river below it. She was killed instantly. Cory survived with only some bruising. As Terry sat, his hand shaking with his cigarette later that evening, Cory sobbing in his grandmother's lap, it occurred to him that Jan had taken life insurance out on herself while she'd worked...two hundred fifty thousand dollars, enough to bury her and to take care of her husband and son, should anything ever happen to her. He knew, before the funeral parlor called with more terrible news, that her body would go missing. He knew where it would be and that she'd be one of them by now; the price enough to pay for this house. He couldn't say a word if he hoped to save Cory. He placed the house up for sale the next day, stating they couldn't stay there, given their pain.

He didn't bother to cover the well again before they moved. It would make no difference. He couldn't say a word to the new buyers. He took the insurance money and he and Cory drove back into the city, but he never stopped checking his rearview the entire time.

The End

THE UMBRELLA MAN

By
Carol Weekes

The Umbrella Man

It had rained all week and the weather report was pessimistic about when the downpours would end. Water churned past sidewalks, miniature rapids overfilling gutters, flooding basements and turning everything into a soppy mess. Drew listened to the radio for another few minutes, but when two songs in a row sucked, he shut it off. He'd left the village perimeters behind, the pickup truck's wipers barely swashing a clear view of the path ahead, and moved onto the back roads towards home. It was going on a little past four in the afternoon, the clouds as black as coal dust as another storm front moved in on the tail of the last. Crazy weather. Things had been a little odd around town lately. Folks complaining of bad dreams and restless nights. Animals acting strange. A freak twister had torn the roofs off two houses and a barn just last weekend. A lightning strike had started a massive fire in an animal feed processing plant. And someone from the town had gone missing—old man, likely dementia, Drew figured, who'd just 'up and disappeared' a few days ago according to his grieving relatives. Local police and rescue workers were still out there, combing woods, fields, and nearby rivers and creeks in hopes of finding him.

His cell phone rang. He flipped it open. "Yeah?"

"It's just me," Bonnie, his wife said. "Are you on your way?"

"Just left the dump. What's for supper?"

"Potatoes, burgers, corn."

"Got beer?"

"Picked you up a case of twenty-four earlier today."

"Good girl," he said. "I'm looking forward to just sitting down with one after supper." His back was killing him. He hauled junk for a living, some of it salvageable, some of it worth a bit of money at local dumps. People were always looking for someone with a truck to get rid of stuff. He sidelined in grass cutting and snow removal to help make ends meet. He knew almost everyone in town. When he saw the dark figure walking along the road, hunched forward under a wet, black umbrella, he slowed a little, not wanting to splash the man with the puddles that had formed in deep potholes. He didn't recognize the figure. The man wore a long, black coat that appeared to be drenched, and the umbrella was the wide variety with many silvery spindles that held each section tightly apart, like webbed fingers. Drew debated whether to offer the guy a lift. Where he might be headed on a back road like this, moving away from town rather than towards it and with another five or more miles before he'd reach anything else like it, was anyone's question. It was early September and the nights had already begun to cool. Still, Drew wasn't fussed for picking up strangers.

He tapped the brakes as he eased up on the figure, moving out into the opposite lane so as not to over-drench the fellow. The guy was stick-figured and held both of his hands high to chest, the fingers intertwined and as pale as his coat and umbrella were dark. He wore a somber fedora-style hat pulled over his brow so that only the lower portion of his face showed. The blackness of the umbrella spread behind his head like a geometrical awning. Drew noted a long chin and a pair of thin, dark lips that were pressed tightly together. Linear shadows spiked each cheek bone. He stared at the man as the truck eased by the figure, wondering if the fellow might summon him for a lift. He rolled down the passenger-side window.

"Where you heading, buddy?" Drew called.

The man's head twisted towards the truck and Drew saw a pair of eyes burning a brilliant vermillion beneath the brim of the hat. The eyes had no whites, just a lurid lamp glow that lit the underside of the hat in the way of coals reflecting inside a hearth. A stab of horror made Drew step hard on the brake pedal, forcing the truck into a fishtail that hurled a wall of water at the man, coating the black umbrella and soaking the coat even further than the rain had already done. The dark lips spread apart as his mouth came open in a hiss, revealing two rows of broken tooth shards, the ends black with decay, as obsidian as the clothing and the formidable bumbershoot. Then a long black tongue, skeletal like a withered licorice whip, shot out of the man's mouth, several feet long, and bore in through the open passenger window — its tip split into two ends, each bearing what looked like jagged tarantula fangs. The fangs caught the fabric of the seat and hooked on, pulling themselves towards Drew. Drew shrieked. He got control of the truck, planted a hard foot onto the gas and tore forward. He heard the thing scream as the tongue got stretched beyond capacity, then let go with a snap.

Drew felt his stomach seize as vomit tried to reach his throat. He raced, almost blind to the torrential rain, hitting potholes blindly until he felt he'd gained a safe enough distance from the thing that he'd thought was a man, before he finally slowed the truck and pulled over to the side of the road. He went to roll the window back up when he saw that one of the tongue claws was still attached to the seat and inching its way towards him, as if aware of his presence. A ragged piece of dark, leathery flesh trailed behind the ebony claw that pulsated as it moved with a life of its own.

"What in the hell?" Drew opened the glove compartment and found what he sought: a heavy duty flashlight that he kept in the truck for emergency purposes. He used it as a baton and smashed the claw, repeatedly, watching the thing gyrate, then fall, trembling to the seat beside him. He raised the flashlight to hit it again, but saw it finally go still. Drew let his breath out. His heart pounded through the veins in his neck and temples and he broke out in a sweat despite the cooling weather. He didn't want the thing in the truck with him, but it was the only proof he had. He'd take it to the police.

He rummaged through the glove compartment until he found a small, metal matchstick holder. He emptied the wooden matches into a plastic bag, then used lid of the holder to push the now defunct claw with its ribbon of horrific DNA into the container. He sealed it and left the container in the ashtray where he could keep an eye on it until he could get home. As he drove, he kept his gaze rotating, from one side of the road to the other, convinced he'd see the umbrella man with his reptilian mouth hunched in a ditch, waiting to leap at the windshield. He pondered about telling Bonnie. At least he'd have the tongue-claw as evidence to back himself up. He wanted to get home and lock their doors and windows. Because now he thought he knew what had happened to the missing man in town. Somehow, this creature had blown in with the rain and landed here, like a mutated insect caught on a foul cross-breeze, and it wanted flesh. He'd go to the police later. Right now, he needed to get home and secure his house.

* * *

He got the truck into the garage and hurried to shut the door. He carried the silver matchstick case inside, a little nauseous at the idea of bringing a part of the thing into the sanctity of his home.

"That you, hon?" Bonnie called.

He debated showing her and decided not to do it. He shoved the capsule into his shirt pocket as she entered the room, her soft perfume and long brown hair always a comforting entity for him. She gave him a quick kiss on the lips.

"How was your day? You're soaked."

"Had the cab window open for a minute," he said.

"Why?"

He paused. He thought he felt a tickle of movement in his shirt pocket, and a shiver like a diseased nail slid along the trail of his spine. "Trying to let some air in to cut the condensation on the windshield," he lied.

"Ah. Well, go get changed and come down for supper. I've made a spectacular berry crumble for dessert."

He'd lost his appetite, but he couldn't bear to tell her. He kept thinking of the way the tongue had lashed out and connected with the seat, its dual clawed heads pulling themselves forward...if they'd penetrated him instead of material...he couldn't finish the thought. What had the creature been? His mind toyed with the idea of some adolescent in an early Halloween costume out playing tricks, but the glowing eyes had been part of an actual head, and the rotted teeth...the tongue-claw still gyrating on the seat afterwards...it had been no costume.

"Lock the doors and windows," he told her. "Storm's getting strong."

"Oh, the breeze is kind of nice," she said, amused.

"Bonnie—do it!"

She winced a little and stared at him. "What's gotten into you? You're acting a little odd."

Something's blown in with this rain. Don't know what, don't know why, but I've got a part of it here in my pocket and I can feel it moving again. It's tickling around inside this canister like a stinging insect trying to find a way out.

"Old man's still missing from town."

"Oh, Drew. It's a shame, but it's nothing for anyone else to be afraid of, other than his poor family. The old fellow probably tried to go out for a walk and wandered off before anyone could stop him. It's not like he'd be any kind of a threat."

No, but there's a dark man walking our way and he wears a darker coat and hat that's shadowed beneath a sinister umbrella. He has a fanged snake for a tongue.

"Just do it, for me," he said.

"Fine," she said. He could see that she was perplexed. He could only imagine her facial expression if he tried to explain what he'd seen on his way home. He hurried upstairs, eager to examine the claw that had, clearly, not been destroyed. He found dry clothing, got into it, and locked the bathroom door. He put the plug into the tub, then opened the matchstick canister and shook the ragged bit of claw out against the white porcelain. It immediately began to circle as it tried to find traction against the smooth surface, dragging its tail of now hardening flesh behind it. Then, it began to tap its way across the tub—tick-tick-tick-tick-tick—the noise of a hard-shelled insect hitting against the inside of a jar. The ticking became frenzied. Tickticktickticktickticktick! Tickticktickticktickticktick! It bore back and forth in the tub, its bizarre dark claw capable of gripping. It tried to lunge up the concave sides, to fall back in again. It was determined, to what end he wasn't sure, but he didn't want to allow it any further freedom in order to find out. It dribbled a faint pink liquid behind it now, seepage from its biting tip.

"Shit!" he exclaimed. He used a wad of toilet paper to shove the claw back inside the metal container. It tapped madly, creating a faint staccato, the canister rolling lightly back and forth on the counter. What to do with it?

"You coming down for supper?" Bonnie called.

"Almost done," he yelled back. "Just give me a couple more minutes."

"Supper's getting cool!"

Frantic, he opened cupboards and drawers, seeking a place to store it. He noticed that Bonnie had placed a big canning jar with a seal-lock lid under the sink. It held an inch of bath salts. He unlatched the jar and hurled the matchstick canister inside, then sealed the jar. Not knowing what else to do, he put the jar back under the counter and shut the door. It would hold the cursed claw until he ate and could return upstairs. Not that he had any appetite at all. He felt sick. Worse, he felt petrified. Even as he made his way downstairs, he thought he heard it moving about in its prison, the faint tapping like seconds passing audibly as the storm increased outside.

* * *

As Drew made himself eat enough of what Bonnie had cooked for him in order to satisfy her, the Umbrella Man paused to sniff the night air a few miles away. He'd followed the road as far as it went, eager to catch up to the man who had been stupid enough to sneak up on him, startle him, soak him, then witness and injure him, and who would likely report him to this world's authorities before he had a chance to find an escape route. The road forked to the west and to the north.

He needed to obtain the piece of himself that had gone missing and which would draw all the wrong attention in this sphere. In his world, to recklessly lose a piece of oneself in defeat rather than victory, especially in the waking zone of humans, meant retribution of the worst kind. His tongue ached. Fear burned stronger in him. He'd gone for the jugular and lost. No matter. A new, finer fang had already begun to grow in its place and the regeneration would be complete within the hour.

Lightening cut the sky, highlighting him between air and soil, ozone and oxygen, life and death, killer and demon, invigorating him with renewed force and filling his eyes with deeper fury for this place. He'd blown in on this system by accident during the dreaming hours, caught along the astral jet stream and hurtled into a sea of black cumulus cloud when the cosmological lines that, on rare occasions intersected his world and that of this planet called Earth had somehow, magically, connected during a vicious storm that had opened an unexpected pathway between the two parallel realms.

He bore dark wings over his head, the wings conical and connecting at each tip above the hat, the bones of each wing a line of mechanical cartilage that formed a bas-relief of a geometric grid that shone in the dark. Whereas these humans of this place were mortal, he was not; whereas they were good, neutral, and evil, his evil was paramount. Whereas their hunger could become satiated, his could not. Whereas they were mostly omnivores, he knew only flesh and blood and the sweet marrow taste of bone which he required almost continuously to recoup energy and remain alive.

He killed, he ate, and he eviscerated souls as tokens for home. It was expected. He delighted in the quivering of freshly killed flesh and in the essence of terror that permeated that flesh like a fine, exotic spice. Human flesh was the best. He was a human's worst nightmare, the kind that crept in during the longest night hours when minds and dreamscapes kissed most often, and where he slunk within the folds and crevices of lucid dreams. He was nightscape, the dark shadow that lingered in far corners, that clung to early morning hours like the chill of wet spider web that followed these humans through their days and into their nights like pestilent déjà vu, waiting to jump out at them with the vengeance of a torn and bleeding Jack-in-the-box. He hid within dreams in the way a tick can nestle deep into skin. And now, through some metaphysical fluke, he found himself actually here in their physical plane, walking the earth and clad in their garb, rather than enjoying the clandestine security of a dreamscape, his wings emulating an umbrella in an attempt to shadow his face and keep himself dry and protected until he could find a portal back home.

He needed to find darkness and he needed to concentrate. But before he went, he had to eliminate the one who had taken a part of him with the intention of showing it to the authorities. They would seek him. And if they caught him before he could escape; if those in his realm discovered this, he'd be barred from returning home, and worse. They'd find him in his dreams; they'd leave his body, but they'd take his essence and they'd do things to him. Bad things, horrific things, the stuff of nightmares from which he came. Beneath the clothing his body was the color of ash, his muscles hard ropes of intention. When he reached the fork in the road, he studied the ground for signs of tire tracks but the rain and wind had washed it away. He inhaled deeply and smelled the air for a track of the man's fear, his body trembling, his eyes floating like coals in the dark, his tongue probing for direction.

There. To his left, the west, a sourness that lingered like old, forgotten wine. Needing to make time, the Umbrella Man released his wing tips and took flight, the wingspan scoring eight feet across, their flapping the sound of tropical leaves bending against a heaving rain, dark dreams cutting the night.

* * *

"You're picking at your food," Bonnie said. She seemed a little annoyed.

Drew placed his fork on the table. "I don't have much appetite tonight. I'm sorry, babe. Maybe I'm coming down with something."

She got up and placed her hand on his forehead with maternal warmth. "You don't seem to have a temperature. We can finish the rest of this tomorrow."

Something upstairs fell over with a soft bang.

"I wonder what that was?" Bonnie asked.

"Wind probably blew the window open." He scraped his chair back and went to head back up to the bathroom.

"Can you help me with the dishes?" she asked him.

He paused. "I'll come right back down. I forgot something upstairs. I'll check the window too."

He hurried back up to the bathroom and, locking the door, opened the cupboard to look for the jar. It was on its side, the metal and glass lid having rolled away from the jar. Bath salts had sprinkled out into the open, but the claw and its trail of flesh were gone.

"Unbelievable!" Drew bit his lower lip in fear. He did a quick search of the cupboard and didn't see it anywhere. He scanned the floor and noted a little line of cerise fluid closer to the door. If the thing had gotten loose into the house, he'd have to find it and soon.

"Drew? You coming down?"

"One minute!" he yelled. "There's some water on the floor. I'm cleaning it up." He had to buy a bit of time. "You go ahead and do them. I'll help with something else in a few minutes. I promise." He heard her sigh, but also heard the customary sound of the tap turning on, followed by the soft clink of dishes.

"Where are you, where are you, where are you?" He scanned the bathroom, found nothing, and moved into the upper corridor. They had three bedrooms up here, his and Bonnie's at the end of the hall, their son Dennis' room across from him, and a guest bedroom at the other end. Dennis would be home soon from a part-time job. The idea of this thing hurting his wife or kid was more than he could bear. He had no idea what kind of substance was contained within the claw, but he knew from the force of the lingual attack that its impact and penetration would be lethal.

He hurled the light on in Dennis's room, his shoulders slumping at the realization that this fang could be anywhere: amid a closet full of shoes, clothing, odds and ends, beneath a rug, inside the fold of a curtain, under a mattress...

Panic set in. All he could do was keep an eye and ear open for it. The thing tapped. If he heard the slightest sound, he'd check it out, something not easy to do with a storm raging outside and hurling rain in torrents against the windows. He returned downstairs, debating what he could say to Bonnie to make her alert without frightening her.

"There's a large wasp loose in the house," he lied. "I thought I'd gotten it but it's disappeared somewhere. I don't want us getting stung. If you hear it or see something small and dark move, let me know. I'll get rid of it."

Bonnie finished drying the last glass. "Oh, I'm not concerned about a little insect. So, you said you'd give me a hand with something else. That laundry needs doing."

"Yup." He got it into the washer and set the cycle, hating the noise in the house, hating the storm outside, wondering where the creature with the smoldering eyes and serpentine tongue might be now.

"Bleeding to death from its injury, hopefully," he mumbled.

"What was that?" Bonnie asked from the parlor where she'd gone to read a magazine.

"Just thinking aloud," he said, sour. He shook each piece of laundry out, examining both sides before folding it. Nothing in the house was safe now. And considering what walked around town out there, nor was any other area here.

*   *   *

The Umbrella Man soared above low shrubbery and trees, his eyes capable of detecting infrared pockets of living creatures everywhere, from squirrels wrapped tightly in their nests, birds huddled in bushes, a lone traveler in a car below, a group of deer huddling, terrified beneath a swatch of tangled vinery. He cast his tongue out into the night and rain, tasting the air, searching for that distinct tang of fright that arrived in dispersing bits every now and then. His original and newly grown fang connected in a rapid series of taps, firing out a plethora of sonar signals to the lost portion, then listening for its response.

Nothing yet. But it would come. It had to come. Fright urged the Umbrella Man on and fright also heightened his sense of outrage. Then a gust of wind brought a succulent aroma of the terror of the one who had taken a part of him, and the umbrella man swooned for a moment. Then he opened his blackened mouth and elicited a low, wet snarl, the sound of a moldy door sliding open in the rain. He turned his wings more westward and followed the scent which became stronger until it solidified into an easy trail.

In the distance, the Umbrella Man saw a dark dwelling, its rooftop forming a murky flap against the waning sky. Heavy rain and gusts of wind bent trees in half and tore grasses from their root beds, but the house contained several lit windows and through its walls the Umbrella Man detected two large infrared shapes and one small one, each in different parts of the dwelling. With a hiss of jubilance, he pushed both wing tips forward into the shape of a guiding spear and bore towards the house. Soon enough, he heard the sonar tap of what he sought...his fang was in there, moving about, seeking its host, the smallest infrared hurrying through the upstairs portion of the human's dwelling.

The Umbrella Man felt an electrical rush move through him. Lightening cut the sky in a fury of sparks and within those sparks he saw the faces of his superiors, cast in a temporary portal, watching his progress, warning him that he'd best be successful. His diseased heart sank. He was being tracked. So, they knew. Then the portal snapped shut; not that it would have done him any good to attempt re-entry without the missing DNA. He had one chance to retrieve it, soon, or he would run out of time.

* * *

Drew carried the laundry upstairs, glad that Bonnie had decided to cut him some slack and let him do his own thing. He flipped on the light switches in every room and the corridor. He strained, listening. The damned thing could be anywhere. He wouldn't be able to sleep. It had to be found, otherwise chaos would begin in so many different ways. What might attract it, he wondered. Then, an idea came to him. Meat. It sought blood and meat. He stole downstairs and quietly opened the refrigerator, seeking until he found what he sought: Bonnie had taken out chops for tomorrow night, but now they had leftovers. He took one of the chops and carried it back upstairs, then laid the raw meat on a piece of paper towel in the center of the corridor. He'd have to scoop it up if Bonnie started upstairs. He wouldn't be able to explain how this somehow correlated to a wasp inside the house.

He stepped back inside the edge of his bedroom, not seeing the fang bit anywhere, and watched, moving his gaze from around him to the corridor on a regular basis. Five minutes passed. Ten minutes. Twelve. He sighed, frustrated. He'd been wrong to bring it home, but he couldn't have just cast it out into the night where it could anywhere, possibly reproduce.

Then he saw it. It darted, quick as a mouse across the carpet, moving out of the guest bedroom, tearing along the hall, its single projectile tugging, frantic, like a one-legged man in a hopping contest. It aimed for Dennis's bedroom. Then it stopped short and wavered, trembling a little. He noted its fang rise up, the tip glistening as a drop of tinted fluid fell from the fang. It was still somehow generating poison. If it lit into skin, it would hurt, if not kill. But now it edged in jagged increments towards the chop lying like a sacrificial lamb in the center of the carpet. Drew held his breath.

"Drew? What are you doing?" Bonnie called from downstairs.

The fang stopped its movement and dropped, as if debating what to do next. Drew bit into his lip, angered. Perfect timing. He'd almost had the thing. He debated. Answer her or stay silent?

"Drew?"

"Oh for God's sake, I hear you!" he yelled, unable to contain his irritation.

"What the hell are you doing up there?"

He saw it shoot into Dennis's room, the chop now a moot point.

"Fuck!"

"What's wrong with you tonight?" she continued. He heard the springs in the chair cushion squeak as she got up. "You've been weird since you got home."

He went to tell her to stay downstairs when something solid slammed into the side of their house behind him, rocking it. Drew fell back into his bedroom. Bonnie screamed. The waylaid fang tore into the corridor again, going for Drew's feet. Drew shrieked and leapt up onto the bed just as the fang reached the doorway. It came at him, moving up the bed cover and across the duvet. Drew went to slap at it when the fang passed by him and fell to the other side of the carpet, tapping madly as if directing some skewed form of Morse code. Drew twisted around and understood why. He saw the Umbrella Man, dark coat spread out along the glass of the bedroom window like a crushed moth, dark face pressed into the cracked glass, its eyes burning like coals. It opened its mouth and its tongue, the same strip of leathery death that had almost gotten him in the truck's cab earlier, slid along the glass, undulating back and forth like a snake moving through water. Glass from the ruined window fell in an explosion of jagged shards and the Umbrella Man, its dark umbrella held above its head spread the fabric of its umbrella wide...and Drew knew that this was no town lunatic with a broken black umbrella. These were wings. He saw pale bone move under the translucent dark flesh as the thing stretched dark lips back from darker gums and hissed at him, revealing its broken lines of teeth around its probing tongue.

"You have something of mine," it told him.

"You can have it back. It's right there."

"Who did you tell about me?"

"I didn't tell anyone a thing."

"You lie."

The orphaned fang leapt into its father's hands and Drew watched as the Umbrella Man aligned the tongue tips with the stray fang, absorbing it into him. The tongue retracted, the dark man swallowed, and when the tongue tip lashed out again, it held three tips now, rejuvenated, each pulsating and eager, each glistening with death fluid.

"Drew, I think a tree fell against the house..." Bonnie making her way up the stairs. "Why are all the lights on? Drew? Why is there a piece of raw meat in the center of the hallway?"

She entered the room. Rain gusted about them, drawing in leaves, torn grasses, stray bits of paper, and the ink of the night beyond.

"You almost won," the Umbrella Man told them. "But I got it first. I win."

Bonnie screamed. She screamed and ran for Drew.

"What is it? Drew, what is it?"

"I don't know," Drew pulled her to him. He addressed the Umbrella Man. "You have your fang back. Let us go. All we want is our lives."

"And so do I," it told them. "And your souls." It stretched its wings out and shook off water, then retracted and folded the wings neatly behind its back. Its clothing hung in shards, its hat was gone, revealing a high, thin forehead of ashen flesh that ended in a point from which long strands of moving flesh circled its head, caressing it. "So do I."

* * *

In nightmares, the work involved removing the soul from the body, encouraging it to wander in dreams, dare, seek until it entered the vulnerable landscape of astral travel—and then they would shut the return entrance to the flesh, severing the life cord once the essence was caught, then transported back to their world for myriad purposes. But this was a prize; he had two within the flesh and if he could just find a portal at the right electrical moment in this mega-storm, he would bring them both; flesh and soul, nutmeat and shell, meat and sauce, back as offerings for those he knew watched everything through the night. He would be applauded and rewarded.

And then it came; a flash of lightening so formidable that it opened the sky and tore into the parallel realms once more. A burst of wind so foul that it stunk of minions that feast on decaying flesh came to them, and he knew—here was his chance. Grab them and go now, while the night and those beyond waited.

Bonnie went to run and the thing's tongue lashed out like a whip, one of the fangs catching her squarely beneath her jaw and hauling her back like a fish on a taut line.

"You son of a—" Drew began then saw the second of the three fangs unravel itself from the host tongue and come for him. Footsteps behind him in the corridor. His heart sank.

"Dad? What's going on?"

"Run Dennis!" Drew screamed, desperate. He'd brought this thing here because he'd brought a part of it into his home. He saw Bonnie collapse and turn pale as the first of the three probosces began to drink, drawing her life force from her. The fang tip penetrated her flesh, the texture of the tongue creating a scratching noise as it slid further into her like a finger probing an orifice.

But his son didn't run. Drew saw eighteen-year-old Dennis walk into the room, his face blank and curious, then curl in instant horror. And before he could speak, the second proboscis lashed out on a lengthening finger of tongue and hooked into Dennis's forearm where it hauled him forward, his skin tearing in the process. Dennis screamed as Drew leapt at the Umbrella Man, his fists pummeling, to no avail.

Drew did the only thing he could think of doing. He stepped into a puddle of water on the floor where the Umbrella Man stood drinking from his wife and son. He ripped an electrical cord from the end of a live bedside lamp, sending electricity through him, his unconscious family, and into the Umbrella Man. In the last seconds of his life, Drew realized that he'd saved his family at the final second: they would all die, yes, but they'd be safely removed from their bodies before they could be confiscated by this walking nightmare.

"You should have stayed home on a rainy night," he said to the Umbrella Man as fire burst through them all in a buzzing charge of fury. He had a microsecond to see the Umbrella Man's eyes burst in a bubbling mess, but before, he had the satisfaction of seeing that the creature had understood: it was going to perish, its goals unattained, and it was going to go back to where its kind came from without them. They'd crossed the gate of freedom at the final, teetering second. Then Drew blacked out completely.

The house fell silent. Smoke filled its rooms. The lone chop in the hallway turned black and curled in on itself. Somewhere, out in the stormy sky, three pinpoints of light traveled higher than the clouds, moving together, coalescing colors of calm against the storm. And beyond those clouds, bits of the Umbrella Man's body rained down in frenzied pieces into the Earth's realm as he was torn apart for failing. Echoes of his screams were heard as shrieks of wind as branches cracked and rivers overflowed their banks. Some school kids would find bits of him the next day, charred pieces of unidentifiable, hardened substance that would later be claimed as 'perhaps part of a passing meteor storm' for they consisted of a geology not yet identifiable on this planet.

And the world would sleep a little easier…for a while.

The End

AFTERWORD

Dear Readers:

Yes, this afterword is for you. Firstly, to say that I appreciate your having purchased a copy of this book is an understatement. I am greatly indebted to your generosity and reading interest. Now, on to the creepier things because that is what those of us who read (and write) horror are truly interested in, isn't it?

You may wonder what inspired my novel *Dead Reflections*.

I have a twisted sense of humor, dark and about as bent and misshapen as a weather vane caught within the vortex of an F5 tornado. People have always told me that I see things 'differently.' It's a condition called 'being a writer' and I can't tell you if it's a result of having fallen on my head several times while learning to ride a bicycle at the age of seven (and back then our road consisted of dirt and cruel nuggets of gravel that salivated at the thought of bare skin making a connection) or if it was just the way I was born. Regardless, it is what it is and it has made for some interesting stories.

I wanted to write a haunted house story, but also wanted to incorporate my basic fear of mirrors into the tale. My family and I lived in an actual haunted house for almost thirteen years and the mirrors in that house portrayed the movement of ghosts far too many times; sometimes it would be a hint of a transparent profile sliding along the glass. At other times the face of someone long dead would look back at us, the eyes dark globes and full of malice. Some of the ghosts were benevolent, but this particular one was not and the incidents we encountered in that house over the years removed any lingering residual doubts about the existence of ghosts.

Objects placed on countertops or furniture would disappear, only to reappear in the exact spot sometimes moments later. Taps would turn on and off on their own accord. Footsteps would stop halfway down the stairwell at night. Pets would growl and stare at 'nothing.'

Haunted houses have a reputation for being placed back on the selling market far too often with turnaround times often a year or less.

The house in *Dead Reflections* is no exception, ensuring its continued success in acquiring more unsuspecting victims for years to come.

I hope the stories have given you chills, thrills, and at least a few nights of tossing and turning, if not downright sleeplessness. After all, that's why you buy horror, isn't it? You want to be scared. You want that trickle of a shiver that feels like a cool, dead fingernail traipsing down your back. You want to meet the monster face-to-face, its smile quivering, wet, and full of sharp, decayed teeth. You want to travel on that road that goes nowhere and everywhere all at once, safe within the confines of your fictional vehicle…or so you think.

I'll leave you now, to ponder these concepts that begin like dark little nuggets of suggestion which eventually bloom into stories. When night beckons and you leave your hands to rest upon your bedcovers, don't be too surprised if something tenuous and slightly damp tickles your fingers, wanting to play during the wee hours. It will be waiting, in the mirror, at the edge of your driveway, or in the fold of sheets near the foot of your bed. Always. Sleep well, dear readers.

Carol Weekes
December 27, 2012